Fit for Murder

A *Murder, She Wrote* Mystery

A NOVEL BY JESSICA FLETCHER & TERRIE FARLEY MORAN

Based on the Universal television series created by
Peter S. Fischer, Richard Levinson & William Link

BERKLEY PRIME CRIME
New York

BERKLEY PRIME CRIME
Published by Berkley
An imprint of Penguin Random House LLC
penguinrandomhouse.com

Library of Congress Cataloging-in-Publication Data

Names: Fletcher, Jessica, author. | Moran, Terrie Farley, author.
Title: Fit for murder : a novel / by Jessica Fletcher & Terrie Farley Moran.
Description: New York : Berkley Prime Crime, 2024. |
Series: A Murder, She Wrote mystery
Identifiers: LCCN 2023026251 (print) | LCCN 2023026252 (ebook) |
ISBN 9780593640692 (hardcover) | ISBN 9780593640715 (ebook)
Subjects: LCSH: Fletcher, Jessica--Fiction. |
Murder--Investigation--Fiction. | LCGFT: Detective and mystery fiction. | Novels.
Classification: LCC PS3552.A376 F58 2024 (print) |
LCC PS3552.A376 (ebook) | DDC 813/.54--dc23/eng/20230616
LC record available at https://lccn.loc.gov/2023026251
LC ebook record available at https://lccn.loc.gov/2023026252

Printed in the United States of America
1st Printing

Robert Adam Moran,
best son ever

Fit for Murder

A *Murder, She Wrote* Mystery

Chapter One

I pedaled my bicycle along the streets of my hometown, heading for the wharf that edged the inlet of the Gulf of Maine that gave Cabot Cove its name. I marveled at how bright and warm the sunshine was for this early in the spring. Here we were, barely past April Fools' Day, and it felt as though we were moving rapidly from sherpa-lined-jacket weather to sweatshirt weather. Of course, we Mainers knew better than to expect a soft and easy slide from winter to spring. I'd be keeping my coats, jackets, scarves, hats, and gloves handy for some weeks to come.

I parked my bicycle in the rack at the north end of the row of storefronts that lined the street above the wharf. I stood for a moment, watching a sight I never tired of—all the activity that went along with boating and fishing. People carrying fishing poles and nets were scurrying about waving and joking with one another. I knew that the fishermen and lobstermen who worked these waters for a living had cast off hours ago, so those who remained on the dock this late in the morning were more relaxed. Their goal was a day of fishing that, if they were lucky, would result in some bragging rights along with a nice dinner of crispy fried flounder.

I looked at my watch, murmured, "Oh dear," and strode quickly toward Mara's Luncheonette, where, undoubtedly, my good friend and everyone's favorite town doctor, Seth Hazlitt, was sitting, tapping his fingers impatiently on the Formica table-top, because, according to my watch, I was nearly ten minutes late.

Two fishermen, sporting colorful fishing lures pinned to their bucket hats, were coming out of Mara's, and the smells of fresh coffee and sizzling bacon wafted through the doorway. I thanked the man who held the door for me and wished them both "good fishing." They smiled in reply.

I spotted Seth at a table toward the middle of the room. I was surprised to see he was sitting with Walter Hendon, our harbor-master, and Pierce Collymore, newly appointed chief of the Cabot Cove Fire Department. When the department's longtime chief Angus Billingsworth had announced he was retiring due to ill health, Collymore was among several out-of-town fire officials who applied for the job. Much to the chagrin of some of the locals who felt the job should go to a Cabot Cove resident, Collymore was selected by our mayor, Jim Shevlin, and the town council. He'd recently moved here from a village in northern Vermont.

I slid into a vacant chair and apologized to Seth for being late. "But I am glad to see that Walter and the chief have been keeping you company."

"Aye, Jessica." Walter's blue eyes crinkled as he laughed. "Doc here looked so forlorn; I couldn't walk by and leave him sitting by himself."

"Hogwash," Seth blustered.

"Not hogwash at all," the fire chief chimed in. "Never see you at a table that you don't have a crowd of your friends laughing and talking."

I could see by the look on Seth's face that he was ready to argue over this simple truth, so I quickly changed the topic. "When I was parking my bicycle I couldn't help but notice that the harbor is really bustling for so early in the season. I'm guessing it's this springlike weather we are having."

"Ayuh. You're right about that. Winter will be back right around Wednesday and the less hardy fishermen will be in rockers near the fireplace. 'Course those whose livelihood depends on the waters will be out there every day that doesn't feature cat-four hurricanes or severe winter blizzards." Pleased that he had defended the way of life that had been at the core of our town for centuries, Walter leaned back in his chair, crossed his arms, and gave me a satisfied smile.

I hadn't seen Mara come up behind me, coffeepot in her hand, until I heard her cheery greeting. "Morning, Jessica. Here's your coffee. I'm just about to serve blueberry pancakes to these fellows. Will you be having the same?"

"Not today, I'm afraid." I shook my head and patted my midriff. "I've been spending too many hours sitting in the library researching my latest book, so I haven't been getting enough exercise. I decided just this morning that I have to spend more time on my bicycle and watch what I eat for the next few weeks."

Mara scribbled on her order pad while saying, "One boiled egg and one mini blueberry muffin coming up."

"You know me too well," I said to her back as she hustled to the kitchen. She returned in a flash with three plates, each with a short stack of her piping hot award-winning blueberry pancakes. Try as I might, I could never figure out the special something that made her hotcakes so delicious. Whenever I asked, she declared it was a secret she would take to her grave. I'd begun to believe her.

After slathering butter on his pancakes, Seth reached for a tin container that sat midtable. "Nothing like true maple syrup. Comes from hearty New England maple trees. Mara gets this local, you know. Farmer up by Bangor." He passed the syrup to Walt.

"What do you think I am? A flatlander? Maine born and raised, and don't you forget it. I know real maple syrup when I taste it. It's the chief here that is new to our state and our ways. Tell him about your maple syrup."

The look on Pierce Collymore's face said he wasn't sure whether Walter was joking. "Walter, you do know that Vermont produces more maple syrup than any other state . . ."

But Walter had become too distracted to hear so much as one word that Pierce said.

"Oh, will you lookee there? Speaking of flatlanders . . ." Walt pushed back his chair and pulled his dark blue harbormaster cap off his head; a jolt of static electricity caused a few strands of hair to rise with the cap. He waved the cap to get someone's attention and then began signaling for them to join us.

Seth and I turned toward the door and I could barely believe my eyes. Evelyn Phillips, former editor of the *Cabot Cove Gazette*, who'd left to travel the country, catching up with family and friends, was walking through Mara's like a rock star, stopping to shake hands and even accepting a kiss on the cheek from

Cabot Cove town historian Tim Purdy, who was perched on one of the round stools that lined Mara's counter.

"Well, I'll be . . ." Seth said. "Of all mornings for Dan Andrews to be among the missing. Gregory Leung told me Dan's doing interviews at the hospital today."

Spontaneously, we all stood as she approached our table. After Evelyn shook hands all around, Walt introduced her to Pierce Collymore and then indicated an empty chair. As she settled in, I realized that in the time she'd been away from Cabot Cove very little about her had changed. Her tousled gray hair appeared a bit longer than I remembered but still didn't reach her earlobes. Her black quilted jacket was unzipped, revealing what I'd come to think of as Evelyn's usual uniform of jeans and a plaid shirt. This one was black and green.

Mara placed my breakfast on the table and filled a clean cup with steaming coffee for Evelyn, who dropped on the floor her massively oversized tote, which landed with a thud that nearly shook the room. Then she looked at us expectantly. "What is going on in this town? I checked into the Hill House last night, and just as I was leaving reception and heading to my room, I ran into your good mayor and his wife, Jim and Susan Shevlin. They'd had dinner at the hotel and were heading home. We exchanged greetings, and I assumed they would spread the word and ruin my surprise arrival for sure. But no one seems to have heard that I'm in town. What has happened to the Cabot Cove gossip mill?"

"Nothing at all wrong with the gossip mill," Seth said with an evil grin. "I suspect all it means is you're not as popular in these parts as you thought you were."

"Oh, Seth, don't tease Evelyn like that." I gave his hand a light slap. "Evelyn, we are all delighted to see you. I, for one, can't wait to hear of your adventurous travels."

"Actually, Jessica, that's not what brings me—"

Walter interrupted. "Much as I'd love to hang on your every word, Evelyn, I have to get back to work. Stop by the wharf later and fill me in." He stuffed a fork overloaded with pancake into his mouth, stood, and walked to the cash register without waiting for a reply. And I suppose Pierce felt out of place, because he dropped a piece of bacon on top of a pancake and wrapped it in a paper napkin. He picked it up, said a quick round of good-byes to us, and followed along behind Walter.

Evelyn dismissed them with a backhand wave. "It's really you two I came looking for this morning. I think there is a bit of a problem here in town that you might be able to help me solve."

I was content to let Evelyn give us more information, but Seth cut right in.

"Didn't you say you arrived last night? How in the dickens did you find out about this so-called *problem* so quickly?" he asked.

"Because I had my suspicions before I ever got on the plane in Chicago." Evelyn gave him a triumphant grin. Always a scrapper, she skipped a beat or two to wait for Seth's response, but when there wasn't any, a mildly disappointed Evelyn began her tale.

"You know I have a good many friends in Cabot Cove," she began, and I immediately gave Seth a warning look. Evelyn continued. "I keep in touch as much as I can, and I am always happy to hear back. But lately . . ."

She seemed to change her tack. "You both know Bertha Mae Cormier. Her great-great-grandfather was one of the first settlers of this part of coastal Maine and she's lived here all her life.

Naturally, when I took over the *Gazette* she was one of the people I sought out for background information, and as time went by, we became friends."

"Of course you did." I smiled and nodded toward the counter where our town historian was finishing his breakfast. "Just as you did with Tim Purdy and a number of other history buffs, as I recall. Smart move for a newspaper gal."

Pleased by the compliment, Evelyn's cheeks turned a pale shade of pink, and then she switched to all business once again. "Bertha Mae and I have been keeping in touch—letters, email, even the occasional text, although texting is not Bertha Mae's strong suit. But lately . . ."

"Has she cut off contact?" I asked, knowing how often in my book-tour travels I would meet someone in the business—another writer, an editor, or, oddly enough, even a bookshop owner—and we would strike up a great friendship and keep in touch for a while, be it long or short, and then somehow, the day would come when we were no longer in touch. "That often happens with time and distance."

"Believe me—that is not the problem. That I would have understood, but if anything, Bertha Mae has increased writing to me, and her messages are . . . well, the best way I can describe them is *weird*."

Seth had begun shifting in his chair, clearly bored with this conversation and anxious to get on with his day. But Evelyn had aroused my curiosity. Everyone in town had long known that Bertha Mae was flighty. What could her messages possibly contain that would cause Evelyn to be concerned enough to fly halfway across the country to check on her? She could have called any one of us—particularly her friend Dan Andrews, who had taken over as editor of the *Cabot Cove Gazette*—and asked that we check in on Bertha Mae.

"Weird in what way? Are her language skills slipping? We all know that happens as we get older," I said, since, as a writer, that was one of my biggest fears.

Evelyn shook her head. "I only wish that was it. No, it is her choice of topics. In one email she described how she is doing a new exercise program that will ensure she will outlive most of Cabot Cove. In another she talks about marrying a younger man and what a scandal that would cause. I am not sure if she is making this up or if her brain is going to la-la land. Seth, without violating doctor–patient confidentiality, how do you think Bertha Mae is?"

Seth stood and pushed his chair under the table. "Sorry to disappoint you, Evelyn, but Bertha Mae is not my patient. Even if she was I wouldn't give you so much as a hint. Now, if you ladies will excuse me, the patients I do have are waiting for me. Jess, I'll take care of your breakfast."

Evelyn smiled ruefully. "Doctors! They are as bad as lawyers."

"Evelyn, every profession has ethical constraints. I know Seth would respect yours, and you should respect his."

"I respect his ethics. I just wish he didn't follow them so tightly." Evelyn clapped her hands. "Say, I'm going to stop by Sassi's Bakery, and then I am going to surprise Bertha Mae with her favorite pastries—chocolate croissants. Why don't you come along?"

"I'd love to, but I can't. I have a hair appointment at Loretta's." I glanced at my watch. "Oh dear. I am nearly late." I crumpled my napkin, tossed it on my plate, and picked up my purse. "But, please, let's get together a few times while you're in town. I'll arrange a dinner party."

"Sounds good to me. And you can do me a favor while you are at the gossip shop. Drop Bertha Mae's name once or twice and let me know what chatter you pick up."

I nodded absently and ran for the door, grateful that Seth had settled our check.

Chapter Two

I dropped my bicycle's kickstand and left it parked under the short barber's pole attached to the wall between the large pink-trimmed window and the wide corner door that was the entrance to Loretta's Beauty Parlor. As soon as I opened the door I could hear the hair dryers and the patrons' chatter going full blast.

Pert young Coreen Wilson, Loretta's longtime assistant and manicurist, was on the telephone. She hung up, jotted a note in the appointment book, and came to greet me. "Hi, Mrs. Fletcher. Loretta is in the back, but she will be right with you. Please sit in her chair and I'll drape you."

Lavinia Wahl was under the nearest dryer. I asked how the leg she'd broken months ago was feeling, and was happy to hear her physical therapy was doing her a world of good. She stretched out her leg as if I could see through the black denim fabric that covered it and she issued her standard complaint.

"Of course your friend Seth Hazlitt doesn't want me sailing by myself anymore. Says I'm too old. Humph. What does he know? He's no spring chicken himself."

I thought it diplomatic not to respond.

Coreen settled me in Loretta's worn leather chair in front of the wide mirror in which I could see not only my reflection but that of the ladies under the dryers behind me. Ideal Molloy looked up from her magazine and gave me a friendly wave. Loretta came out from the back room carrying a box of beauty supplies, which she asked Coreen to put away. Then she pushed a few dark curls off her forehead and turned to me.

"Jessica, I was so surprised to see you on my calendar this morning. Seems like we just did a trim not that long ago. Perhaps you're looking for something else? Maybe a little change-up?"

"Oh, now, Loretta, please. You know I like my hair just as it is. Attractive and easy to care for." And then to end the discussion, I raised my voice so everyone could hear. "I had breakfast in Mara's this morning, and guess who I saw. Evelyn Phillips is back in town."

"The reporter gal?" Lavinia sounded mildly alarmed. "I thought she got run out of town a while back. You ask me, that Dan guy who does the *Gazette* now is much nicer. He's an even-handed sort of fellow."

I noticed Coreen open her mouth as if to answer but then change her mind and clamp it firmly shut. But I wasn't going to let Lavinia's comment be the last word about Evelyn. True, she was gruff and often more pushy than I liked, but she was honest and that counted for a lot. "People approach jobs differently. I believe ferreting out the truth is an important job, no matter the style of the reporter who does it." Then I changed course. "Evelyn mentioned that while she's in town she wants to visit Bertha Mae Cormier. I haven't seen her in ages. Have any of you seen Bertha Mae lately?"

Loretta said, "Bertha Mae stopped coming to me for haircuts about a year ago. Last time I bumped into her, we were both shopping in Charles Department Store. She had her hair rolled in a big old bun with a colorful scarf tied around it, nineteen fifties–style. Not at all becoming, but I expect she likes it." Loretta shrugged. "Maybe it makes her feel young."

Ideal shook her head, which caused her curlers to bang against the side of the hair dryer. "Haven't seen her lately, no, but when I do drop by to say hello, I am always hoping to see her dishy neighbor. Anyone else here know him? Martin Terranova? He is an exercise freak and, wow, does his body show it. Yummy. Speaking of yummy, Coreen, are there any more Boston cream doughnuts left?"

Terranova. Now, that name did ring a bell. My friend Maureen Metzger, wife of Cabot Cove sheriff Mort Metzger, had been raving about a yoga-and-meditation class she was taking. I believe her teacher's name was Terranova. I hadn't realized he was Bertha Mae's neighbor. I had to wonder if he had any connection to Bertha Mae's "weird" messages to Evelyn.

Coreen came around carrying a plate with an assortment of doughnuts and stopped in front of each client. When she got to me, I quickly declined. But she paused for a moment and said, "You know my friend Lena, don't you, Mrs. Fletcher? She works in that lawyer Joe Turco's office." She waved her hand in the general direction of Main Street.

"Certainly, I do. She's a nice young woman and quite competent."

Coreen lowered her voice. "Lena's aunt Greta works as a part-time housekeeper for Mrs. Cormier, so she'd be one to ask if Mrs. Cormier is doing okay."

"Thank you, Coreen. It's kind of you to let me know. I think it's quite important that Bertha Mae not be alone all of the time." Then I added, "She is getting on in years."

"Aren't we all?" Lavinia said. "Here I am, wasting time under this dryer when I could be sailing on such a gorgeous day."

Loretta took the hint and asked Coreen to turn off the dryer and bring Lavinia to a chair for her comb-out. And for the next few minutes Ideal read us all a recipe for double chocolate chip cookies she found in a magazine. When I got back on my bicycle, I was determined to pedal extra hard in the hope of eliminating a major chocolate craving.

The following morning was both cloudy and chilly. I threw on a heavy sweater and covered it with my bright yellow fisherman's slicker in case the rain the television weather forecaster predicted for later in the day arrived earlier than expected. I rode around local streets as the sky grew darker. For the past day or so I'd been stumped by a plot point in the mystery I was currently working on. I pedaled along, convinced that the combination of fresh air and exercise would nudge the solution I was sure was stored in the back of my brain and make it appear in usable form. I was so focused on my plotting that I didn't see the taxi that stopped next to me until the driver honked his horn.

I skidded to a stop and waved to the driver, Demetri, who, along with his cousin Nick, owned our town car service. Before I could so much as say good morning, Evelyn Phillips opened the rear door and demanded I get into the cab. Demetri turned off the engine, popped the trunk, and said, "We can take your bicycle. No problem."

I suppose my face showed how puzzled I was. "Evelyn, what on earth . . . ?"

"Jessica, you need to see this for yourself. When I went to visit Bertha Mae yesterday, she was really addled. I don't know how this town allows her to live out there with no help—no supervision."

Remembering what Coreen had told me yesterday, I said, "Well, I can't speak to supervision and I am not sure she would need it, but she certainly has help. I understand there is a part-time housekeeper."

"Yesterday I spent several hours at Bertha Mae's and I didn't see hide or hair of any household help. Come along, and see for yourself how befuddled she is."

I was beginning to realize that it was easier to give in and join Evelyn in a quick visit to Bertha Mae than to stand in the street arguing for the rest of the morning. I surrendered my bicycle to Demetri, who carefully placed it in his trunk, and I joined Evelyn in the back seat.

When Demetri pulled up in front of an ancient white clapboard saltbox house with its signature gable roof sloping deep in the rear, Evelyn asked if he could wait, and he agreed. "I have two airport runs later today, but for now I am happy to sit here, read the latest edition of the *Cabot Cove Gazette*, and wait for you two ladies. Do not hurry on my account."

As we walked along the pathway to Bertha Mae's front door, Evelyn was swift to point out the disarray that had overtaken what I recalled was once the pristine landscaping of Bertha Mae's front yard.

She kicked at some twigs that had fallen from a nearby tree. "Look at this mess. Branches, leaves that fell last autumn, pieces of paper that blew in from who knows where. When did you ever see Bertha Mae's yard look like this?"

I replied that we were barely at the beginning of spring and many yards here in the Northeast needed work to bring us to the lush glory we always experienced in late spring and summer. As I rang the doorbell, the Pollyanna inside me hoped we would spend a few minutes with Bertha Mae and then I could sign off on Evelyn's mission and go about my day.

Always impatient, Evelyn reached toward the bell herself, but I stopped her. "For goodness' sake, give Bertha Mae a few minutes to get to the door. It's a good bet that she's well over eighty. Another ring might startle her. If she begins to hurry and winds up stumbling or falling, well, it could be tragic."

Evelyn looked somewhat abashed, and we waited another minute before we heard the lock turn in the door. Loretta was right about Bertha Mae's white hair, which she had piled on top of her head in an untidy bun. A silk scarf sprinkled with green and pink flowers held it precariously in place. Odder still was the fact that she was wearing a dark green tracksuit and white jogging shoes. In all the years I'd known her, Bertha Mae's wardrobe had been given to tailored slacks and dark pumps with one-inch heels.

"Jessica! And Evelyn! How nice to see you both. Evelyn, didn't you once bring me chocolate croissants? I seem to remember they were delicious."

Evelyn and I exchanged a glance, each wondering how Bertha Mae had forgotten that Evelyn had brought the croissants less than twenty-four hours ago.

"Come in, come in. I'll make some tea." Bertha Mae led us to her living room, which had high, wide windows overlooking her gray slate terrace and extensive backyard. There was a jarring note I couldn't help but notice. The timbered fence that had always stood along the property line between Bertha Mae and her next-door neighbor was gone. When we sat on the couch Evelyn and I were directly facing the neighbor's yard, which contained not only an outdoor swimming pool still covered for the winter, and a large pool house, but now what looked like an outdoor exercise area, with a couple of treadmills and an elliptical occupying prime space.

Evelyn was wide-eyed. She leaned over and whispered, "I had no idea. Yesterday we sat at the kitchen table."

Bertha Mae clearly overheard, because she said, "I thought this would be nicer, roomier for the three of us, and besides, the show will be starting in a few minutes. I will be right back."

As soon as Bertha Mae went off to the kitchen, Evelyn looked at me with one eyebrow raised and said, "Do you see what I mean? What 'show' is she talking about? That's a window, not a movie screen."

"Oh, I suspect Bertha Mae is talking about a live show, not a movie," I said. Why else would the fence be gone?

Right on cue, a dark-haired man came out of the pool house and walked toward the treadmills. He was carrying a water bottle and wore a dark green tracksuit similar to the one Bertha Mae had on. Before stepping on a treadmill, he turned toward Bertha

Mae's house and, as if he knew we were watching, saluted us with the water bottle.

Bertha Mae came into the room with a tray of tea and, surprisingly, croissants. "Look at this! Croissants! It turns out I had them after all. I guess Charlene Sassi sent them over with that delivery boy this morning. Oh, look—the show has started. The view is so much better since I got rid of that old fence."

"Er, that's the show you were talking about? A man on a treadmill in the yard next door?" Evelyn said.

"Not just *any* man. That is Martin Terranova, the owner of Perfection." Bertha Mae pointed to a spot on her jacket just below her collarbone. When I leaned close I could just make out the word PERFECTION embroidered in tiny light green letters on her tracksuit.

"Really? I haven't heard of Perfection. What kind of company is it?" I asked, while placing my hand gently on Evelyn's arm because she appeared to be so keyed up that I was afraid she would pounce on Bertha Mae any moment shouting, "Get ahold of yourself, can't you?"

"Haven't you met Martin, Jessica? He is quite charming and extremely health conscious. He teaches yoga and meditation in his pool house. Why, I am a new woman. Instead of sitting around here waiting to die, I have mental goals and physical ambitions."

"I see. Well, it certainly sounds like you are on a healthy path," I said.

"Oh, Jessica, I am. With all the bike riding and jogging and such that you do, you certainly must meet Martin. He is an excellent teacher. And when you see his body close-up . . . well, let me tell you, his muscle structure is not to be believed. Those biceps! And his glutes!"

As Bertha Mae said those last words, Evelyn guffawed. I was grateful she didn't have a mouthful of tea, because it absolutely would have landed on Bertha Mae's Persian carpet.

"So, Bertha Mae," Evelyn began cautiously. "You are taking classes from this Mr. Terranova? Is that it?"

"That's it exactly. And since you are in town, you should come along to my class tomorrow morning as my guest. You too, Jessica. Martin won't mind one bit. He always says the more the merrier."

Evelyn hastily accepted, and poked me with her elbow until I did the same. Bertha Mae was pleased to no end. As we sipped our tea she told us to arrive fifteen minutes early because the class started promptly at eight and it might take us a few minutes to find a spot on the floor that "spoke" to us.

This time I heard Evelyn barely stifle a giggle, but she stayed silent. Within a few minutes she suddenly thanked Bertha Mae for her hospitality and was hustling me out the door.

As soon as we were well out of Bertha Mae's earshot I complimented Evelyn. "You showed remarkable restraint in there. I feared you might grill Bertha Mae relentlessly, but you were practically cordial."

Evelyn laughed. "Jessica, there is no need to 'grill' someone who is willingly telling us all we need to know. I am positive that the gymnast next door is the cause of Bertha Mae's mind being more of a muddle than usual. And tomorrow we will find out for sure."

Demetri folded his newspaper and jumped out of the car to hold the rear doors open for us. "So, tell me, ladies, what is your verdict? Did Mrs. Cormier pass your tests with flying colors or is it off to the nursing home for her?"

I didn't think he was the least bit funny but Evelyn chortled and said, "There's nothing wrong with Bertha Mae that a few good friends keeping an eye on her can't solve. Now do me a favor. Let's take a nice, slow ride past the house next door and see what we can see."

Chapter Three

So, are we now spies?" Demetri pretended to twirl his nonexistent mustache. "Or are you considering exercise classes, or perhaps some meditation? I can tell you there is nothing unusual going on at Perfection. Nick and his oldest son have been attending weight-lifting sessions there for some weeks now. They both like having something to do together and Nick says he feels ten years younger. I would begin the classes myself but I am already ten years younger than Nick." Demetri laughed at his own joke.

"I just want to get a look at the place and maybe even get a closer look at this Martin Terranova person," Evelyn said.

Then she squealed. "There he is on the front porch. Can you see him, Jess? He's taking a delivery from the Fruit and Veg. If the driver had parked the truck a few inches farther up the driveway we could get a better look. I need to be sure that Bertha Mae is not living next to a troublemaker."

"If you are looking for trouble, here it comes." Demetri pointed to an elderly man wearing overalls and a brown leather cap who was walking along the roadside.

Evelyn waved away Demetri's comment. "I grant you that Hillard Davis is a bit eccentric, but serious trouble? I doubt that."

But Demetri was insistent. "Old Hilly is getting crazier by the day. He has been running all over town accusing the new neighbor, that Terranova fella, of moving fences in the middle of the night to steal Hilly's land. Claims he is taking it inch by inch."

Even I had to question such a rumor. "That sounds quite far-fetched, don't you think, Demetri?"

"Jessica, I am surprised you haven't heard about it before now. It was the talk of Mara's Luncheonette a week or so ago. I suspect that everyone in Loretta's Beauty Parlor has been gossiping about it. Maybe you ladies should make an appointment to have Coreen give you a manicure. Catch up on the local news."

Demetri laughed and didn't stop even when I told him I'd been in Loretta's yesterday and the only gossip was about how "dishy" Martin Terranova was.

When we got to my house, I invited Evelyn to come back for dinner in the evening and she accepted. Demetri took my bike from the trunk, and as he parked it by my gate he said, "I warn you again, Jessica. Watch out for Hilly. I assure you, he is getting crazier by the day."

I waved as Demetri and Evelyn drove away, and then I went into the house to plan a dinner party. I made quick phone calls to invite Seth, Mort and Maureen Metzger, and Evelyn's friend, New York City expat Dan Andrews, who had replaced her as the editor of the *Gazette*, to join Evelyn and me that evening.

I checked my kitchen supplies; then I hopped on my bike and

rode over to the Fruit and Veg to buy fresh veggies for dinner. The delivery truck was parked by the store's entrance, and a nice-looking young man, a clean-cut blond who I would guess was in his early twenties, was loading boxes into the rear of the truck. I was settling my bicycle in the bike rack when he said, "That is a fine, sturdy basket on your bike. Basket like that could put me out of business." His smile was quite friendly.

"It was a present from my nephew's family. It's a Nantucket and you are correct; it's super sturdy. I'm Jessica Fletcher." I put out my hand and we shook.

"Peter Whitlock. So you are the famous writer. I have heard in Mara's that you are Cabot Cove's favorite celebrity," he said.

I could feel my cheeks tinge with a blush. "I am hardly a celebrity and I definitely won't be putting you out of business. Terrific as my basket is, I can assure you that I use the delivery service quite often. So, tell me, how do you like Cabot Cove?"

"I am beginning to really enjoy living here. People are nice to newcomers and that isn't true everywhere. I have even registered for some courses at the community college, where I am bound to meet some folks more my own . . ."

He hesitated, so I said it for him. "Your own age."

He nodded. "I didn't mean to imply . . ."

"Of course not. Anyway, I'd better get my shopping done. My dinner guests will be knocking on my door before I know it. It was nice to meet you, Peter."

As he tended to do, Seth arrived first, to "help out in the kitchen." He removed his snazzy gray and blue bow tie, unbuttoned the top button of his gray-striped shirt, and rolled up his sleeves before washing his hands at the kitchen sink. I was well aware that his idea of helping would be to examine every bit of food in my refrigerator and pantry until he decided what he would have as his predinner snack. Eventually he sat at the table and munched on a few wedges he'd sliced off a block of cheddar cheese while I stood at the counter and prepared a salad.

"This cheddar is mighty tasty, Jessica. Have you considered adding a few slices to that salad you're tossing?" This was Seth in "helping" mode.

"That's not a bad idea. Why don't you cut some pieces? And I will set them on a plate next to the salad bowl. Anyone who wants to can"—the timer on my stove signaled and I hurried to stir my clam chowder—"add cheese to their salad."

"When I stopped into Mara's for lunch I heard that you were kidnapped this morning, forcibly removed from your bicycle and pushed into a car. Gossip has it around town that we are lucky you are alive." Seth smirked. "I expect Evelyn dragged you off to see Bertha Mae Cormier."

"That she did. As it turns out, I can't exactly say Evelyn has no reason to worry about Bertha Mae. After all, as we age we do need to be more careful about, well, things. But I am not sure that Bertha Mae's being more lively than she was a year or two ago and having a—I guess you'd call it a schoolgirl crush on her gym teacher is reason for concern."

Seth said, "Ayuh, I'd be a tad more worried if Bertha Mae was exhibiting anxiety or depression. At her age there's no harm in feeling lively, provided she's not deciding to go off sailing all by herself like some people I could name."

"Ah, yes. Lavinia Wahl did mention you while I was getting my hair trimmed at Loretta's yesterday. As I recall she remarked that you were no spring chicken yourself, so who were you to advise her as to what she could or could not do?" I couldn't quite suppress a giggle.

"Woman, you know as well as I do that Lavinia Wahl is a stubborn, cranky—" Seth was interrupted by a knock on the kitchen door, and at the same time the front doorbell rang.

I waved Mort and Maureen Metzger in the back door and hurried to the front, where I wasn't surprised to find Evelyn Phillips talking a mile a minute. She was insisting that Dan Andrews visit the printing museum in Haverhill, Massachusetts.

Evelyn turned to me. "Jessica, can you believe a newsman with Dan's storied career has never been to Haverhill?"

Dan's cheeks turned ruddy, as they often did when he felt he was the center of attention. I was quite sure that he chose a career as a newsman because he preferred reporting the news and not being in the center of it. While Evelyn's style was aggressive and sometimes contentious, Dan was always polite and soft-spoken, but his dedication was reflected by a sign in his office that said DO NOT MISTAKE MY KINDNESS FOR WEAKNESS. In the time he'd been here I'd come to know him as a crackerjack reporter and editor of the *Cabot Cove Gazette*. We'd become quite good friends.

Evelyn took off her quilted vest and hung it on the coat tree in my foyer. Then she slung her huge tote over her shoulder, marched down the steps into my living room, and headed for the kitchen, shouting as she went, "Watch what you say, everyone! The press is in the house."

I had to laugh when Dan said, "She never changes."

*   *   *

"Jess, you make the best fish chowdah in all of Cabot Cove," Seth said as he slid his bowl toward the tureen in the middle of the table and reached for the ladle, but I got to it first. I filled his bowl with what I considered a generous second helping but he clearly disagreed.

"Woman, don't be so stingy."

I brought the level of his chowder nearly to the rim of his bowl and offered refills to everyone else. Dan and Maureen held out their bowls in a manner I thought was reminiscent of the "Please, sir, I want some more" scene in *Oliver Twist*.

I'd refilled the bread basket and was offering more wine when Evelyn said, "Jessica and I visited Bertha Mae Cormier this morning. Mort, as the sheriff, you should know—what is the connection between Bertha Mae and her new next-door neighbor?"

Mort took a fresh slice of bread and began slathering it with butter as he answered. "Don't know about that, Evelyn, but I can tell you that I had to send a deputy—you remember Floyd McCallum, don't you? Anyway, we got a call from Bertha Mae and she was all in a tizzy and Floyd took a run over to see what was what. If you can believe it, Bertha Mae thought someone stole all her medicines."

"After what I've seen of her these past two days, I'd believe anything. So, what happened to the medicines?" Evelyn pressed him to give us the whole story.

"Well, Floyd drove out to Bertha Mae's. By the time he got there she had convinced herself that the theft of the medicines was an attempt to kill her. Floyd spent a long while calming her down. Once he was sure he wouldn't need to call an ambulance, him and that lady who helps out from time to time . . ." Mort looked pensive, then snapped his fingers. "Greta Pacyna—that's it! Floyd and Greta carefully searched the house, with Bertha Mae trailing in their wake. They found a medicine bottle hidden in the guest room, under the seat of a rocking chair. When they moved downstairs, Floyd suggested that he search the garage while the ladies had a cup of tea in the kitchen, and then they could all search the main floor together."

"That sounds exactly the way I would expect Floyd to handle it. I have often noticed that he is particularly thoughtful when it comes to older folks," I said.

"Anyways, out in the garage Floyd was digging in an old metal box filled with rusty tools and found a recently dated prescription bottle of liquid medicine made out to Bertha Mae. Quite happy with himself, he brought it to the kitchen, but when Bertha Mae grabbed it from his hand and pushed it down—I guess I'd say down the front of her dress, he got worried, afraid she was overreacting.

"He told the ladies to relax with their tea and he would search the kitchen. When he discovered two more pill bottles in the pantry, tucked behind the canned goods, Bertha Mae completely lost it. She became hysterical, crying and moaning, saying over and over again that she didn't want to die."

Maureen reached out and covered her husband's hand with her own. "Oh, that is so dreadful. Poor Bertha Mae. And poor Floyd. Why was she upset? Was an important medicine still missing?"

"It turned out it wasn't about the medicines. Bertha Mae abruptly jumped out of her chair, ran to hide behind Floyd, and began yelling that Greta was trying to kill her by stealing her medicines, and she fired the girl on the spot."

The table shook when Evelyn slammed her hand down between her plate and Dan's. "So, that's why I never saw any sign of a housekeeper either time I was visiting Bertha Mae. There is no housekeeper anymore." Evelyn sounded as proud as if she'd just solved the most difficult part of the Sunday crossword puzzle. When she was still editor of the *Gazette*, I often heard her say that once she found enough pieces of information, they would fit together and she could write a news story. Clearly she was quite pleased to learn this piece of the story.

My take on Bertha Mae's health differed substantially from Evelyn's. I decided to ask the expert. "Seth, with someone of Bertha Mae's age, couldn't all these wild emotional swings be a sign of dementia?"

"How many times do I have to say it? Bertha Mae is not my patient. But even so, I am not going to speculate about her health." He folded his arms and pressed his lips tightly closed as if to settle the matter.

"I meant, just in general," I persisted.

"Woman, I won't say a word on the issue. Not a word." Seth was adamant.

Rather than continue arguing I began to clear the table for dessert and coffee.

Maureen stood and started to gather the dirty dishes. While I was loading the dishwasher, she said, "Do you think I should tell everyone that I know Bertha Mae? We met in Martin Terranova's meditation-and-yoga class at Perfection."

I handed her a lemon meringue pie already cut into wedges, gave her a gentle push toward the dining room, and said, "I can't think of anything they would rather hear."

Chapter Four

Maureen carefully put a slice of pie on each person's dessert plate while I poured coffee for everyone except Dan, who preferred tea. As she slid into her seat, Maureen said, "I know Bertha Mae fairly well. We became friends in our meditation-and-yoga class."

"Let me guess." Evelyn leaned across the table. "You both take the class at Perfection and Martin Terranova is your teacher."

"Yes. And our floor spots, where we place our yoga mats, are right next to each other, so we have a . . . a connection." Maureen ran a hand through her curly red hair, a sure sign that she was a little apprehensive, and said, "Martin is really a very nice man and an excellent teacher. He is especially kind to the older clients. He seems to know exactly what type of encouragement they need."

Evelyn arched an eyebrow. "I'm sure he does."

"Oh, don't say it like that, Evelyn. Once you get to know him you may feel differently. Say, why don't you and Jessica come to class with me tomorrow morning?" Maureen said.

Evelyn gave a vigorous nod. "Oh, we intend to go. Bertha Mae invited us."

Maureen clapped her hands. "That's great. How about I pick you up at seven thirty? You are at the Hill House, right? Then we will swing by for Jessica and we three will have a glorious morning of peace and serenity."

Even as I was thanking Maureen for the offer, I thought to myself that peace and serenity weren't exactly what Evelyn had in mind.

The Perfection studio had a fairly tranquil feel, considering that three walls were floor-to-ceiling mirrors and all sorts of exercise machines and weight benches were scattered around the perimeter of the room. But the shades were drawn on the window in the fourth wall, the lights were dim, and peaceful music punctuated by chimes enveloped us as soon as we walked inside. As if by agreement everyone spoke in hushed voices, at least until Evelyn boomed, "So, this is Perfection? Looks like every other gym in the world to me."

Maureen cringed but said nothing.

An extremely handsome man, perhaps in his mid-thirties, wearing the same green tracksuit that Maureen and nearly everyone else in the room had on, hurried over to us. Dressed in sweat suits, Evelyn and I were obvious newcomers.

"Namaste, Maureen. I see you have brought some friends." He turned to us. "I am Martin Terranova. I will be leading this morning's meditation and yoga. I am so glad you ladies decided to join us."

He took Evelyn by the arm and led her across the room explaining what the program would be. Maureen and I followed. The look we exchanged clearly said that neither of us could believe that Evelyn was so docile. She certainly gave the appearance of listening sincerely to Martin's explanation of the program to come.

He left the three of us next to a pile of yoga mats. He suggested we each pick a mat of our favorite color. Then he told us to find a spot on the floor that seemed homelike to us. That wouldn't be a problem. The only spot we were interested in was one as near as possible to Bertha Mae. We chose mats and Maureen led us to the area where she and Bertha Mae usually set up.

At that very moment Bertha Mae came into the room and was positively gleeful to see us. "You came! I am so glad! I promise this will change your life. Oh, and your floor spots are right near mine. Do you know Maureen? Of course you do. Just let me get my mat. I will be right back."

As soon as Bertha Mae was out of earshot, Evelyn said, "She sounds like she's on amphetamines." She immediately asked Maureen if Martin provided any pills or gummies or even juice to his clients.

Maureen pointed to a watercooler. "Only water. Martin believes water is the only liquid pure enough to drink."

The room was rapidly filling up with women who unrolled their mats and sat, some speaking quietly, more sitting in silence with their heads bowed as if in prayer. While Bertha Mae straightened her mat in the space between Maureen and Evelyn, she proceeded to explain that we would start with a guided meditation led by Martin (and I could swear she colored a bit when she mentioned his name), and then we would do a number of yoga poses, ending with a two-minute meditation.

Martin Terranova moved to the front of the room and stood facing us with his palms together, and in less than thirty seconds the room went perfectly still.

"Namaste and welcome," Martin said. "Now please turn off your phones, and as you do so, let go of your worldly cares."

There was a general rustling while those of us who had cell phones in our pockets took them out, turned them off, and set them on the floor next to our mats.

"Thank you. Now, if you are comfortable doing so, please lie down on your back. Make sure the position is restful for you," Martin said.

As we did so, I remembered that the minute we accepted Bertha Mae's invitation I had decided to go along with doing whatever the morning's session required, but now that we were actually in the class I was genuinely surprised that Evelyn followed Martin's directions without the slightest grumble.

He gave us a few moments to make ourselves as comfortable as we could; then he led us into controlled breathing, followed by releasing tension from our bodies, starting with our foreheads. I was familiar with guided meditation and Martin Terranova was an expert leader, so, all in all, I enjoyed the experience. He ended by asking us to rest quietly within ourselves until we felt our bodies were ready to sit up.

As the room came back to life, Evelyn leaned over and said, "Well, that was a new one for me. This may sound odd, but it made me feel . . . I don't know—I guess I would say super confident that coming back to Cabot Cove was the right thing to do."

Bertha Mae leaned in and said, "Wasn't that something? Every time I finish a meditation with Martin I feel a few days younger. I am already back in my sixties, gliding toward fifty-nine." She chuckled and then sat cross-legged on her mat waiting for Martin to begin the yoga portion of our class.

Martin's voice remained soft and gentle. "Ladies, today we are going to start with *Parsva Sukhasana*, the seated side bend. Now, remember to plant your sit bones firmly on your mat and elongate your body. Cross your shins on the mat directly in front of you, and when you are comfortable, rest your left hand on the floor. Take a breath and reach your right arm straight up, and exhale as you lean your arm over your head."

We held the position for about thirty seconds, and then he began giving directions for us to switch sides. Throughout the yoga session he walked around the room, stopping here and there to assist a client who needed guidance. As the hour passed it seemed to me that Terranova was particularly "helpful," in what appeared to be a touchy-feely, flirtatious way, with several of his more elderly clients. It was especially evident with Bertha Mae.

During each pose, he would find a reason to touch one or two women under the guise of helping them. I watched as he caressed Bertha Mae's neck while he talked about relaxing her neck and shoulders in the seated spinal twist and then held her hand while stroking her arm during the child's pose. Each time he came near her, Bertha Mae simpered like a schoolgirl meeting her favorite rock star for the very first time.

Terranova ended our yoga session with a two-minute meditation on the color yellow. When the meditation had ended it was clear that most of the class members were in no hurry to leave. Three or four gathered around the watercooler to refill their bottles while others put away their mats, but the majority of the class gravitated toward Martin Terranova, asking yoga questions or for meditation advice. He was polite but determined to shake off his followers as he headed in our direction.

He came and stood directly behind Bertha Mae, rested his hands on her shoulders, and began a gentle massaging of her neck, all the while looking at Evelyn and me. "So, tell me, ladies, how did you enjoy your first morning of Perfection?"

Before I could say so much as the first few words of a flattering but noncommittal response, Evelyn jumped in. "It was far more enjoyable than I expected. And my old muscles feel wonderful. I'd love to talk to you about making this class part of my regular fitness regime."

Martin unzipped a hidden pocket on the side of his green jacket and pulled out business cards, handing one to Evelyn and one to me, but he still spoke directly to Evelyn. "I have a class starting in a few minutes, but please call me so we can get together later to plan a series of classes that will meet your needs."

Bertha Mae turned around and stroked Martin's cheek. "Evelyn, believe me—following this man to better health is the absolute best thing you will ever do for yourself."

He beamed a smile as bright as the yellow sun he had described for our final meditation, and said, "It's friends like Bertha Mae who help me continue to feel so positive about what I do here. Now, if you'll excuse me, my weight lifters are coming in."

We stowed our mats and turned to leave. I noticed several men were already in the room. Tim Purdy gave us a friendly wave, as did Walter Hendon. Peter Whitlock, the new driver for the Fruit and Veg, was talking to another young man. I was happy to see he was finding friends in his age group. We were nearly at the door when it opened and Dan Andrews walked in with our town mayor, Jim Shevlin. While Jim gave us a loud hello, Dan nodded sheepishly and kept walking.

Once outside, we said good-bye to Bertha Mae, who turned "Good-bye" into "See you at the next class."

Maureen had barely started her car's engine when Evelyn whooped, "Well, that was a gold mine of information."

"In what way?" Maureen signaled for a turn she was about to make. "I do think I got a much better handle on my posture for a couple of the yoga poses, but otherwise . . ."

"I mean about Bertha Mae. Clearly she is besotted with this Terranova. And that is super dangerous. He's a first-class gigolo."

"Granted, he is flirtatious," I said, "but I don't believe he would go any further. After all, both his home and his business are here in Cabot Cove, and if word of that kind of behavior got spread around, it would ruin him. You should be careful what you say and to whom you say it. You could be trashing a man's reputation for no reason."

As she was inclined to do, Evelyn dug in her heels. "I am telling you, Jessica, that Bertha Mae is mesmerized by Terranova and he encourages it because he is after her money."

"Bertha Mae's money? What money? I mean, she does have a lovely home, but she is an aging widow and she once told me that she admires my work as a writer because I will never be forced to live off my life savings. That implied, at least to me, that she was describing her own financial situation. She is far from poor but I do suspect she needs to be careful," I said.

I've long known that when Evelyn disagrees with someone, she is queen of tossing a quick, snappy retort, so it surprised me when she remained mute for a second or two before she said,

"Believe me, I know," and folded her arms across her chest. The subject was unmistakably closed.

Maureen said she was surprised to see Dan Andrews show up for the class. "He does ride his bicycle all over town, but I never thought of him as the muscular type."

Evelyn laughed. "I asked Dan to join a class and try to get friendly with Terranova. Before I leave Cabot Cove I am going to find out the true cause of his interest in Bertha Mae."

"And that is the exact same reason that you were angling to go back to Perfection to meet with the gym owner to discuss buying a membership. You're on a news hunt," I said as Maureen stopped the car in front of my gate.

Evelyn chortled. "Jessica, you got it in one. Me? A gym membership? Please! After this morning's exercises, my whole body is crying for a cup of coffee and a nap. The only reason I would crawl around on the floor like that is a story, and my gut says Terranova is a story."

"Well, then you ladies better come inside," I invited. "I can't provide naps but I definitely have coffee."

We were gathered around the kitchen table enjoying our first sips of fresh-brewed coffee when there was a knock on the door behind us. My neighbor Maeve O'Bannon held up a dish-towel-covered plate so that we could see it through the glass panel in the top half of the door. Maureen, who was closest to the door, opened it and said, "Something smells delicious."

Maeve put the plate in the center of the table and pulled off the towel as though she was the magician in a carnival magic show. "I saw you ladies come in and I thought you might enjoy some raisin scones. And, as it turns out, I have some unbelievable news to go with them."

Chapter Five

She'd whetted our appetites for both scones and local gossip. While I got the butter out of the fridge, Maureen got another coffee cup and some dessert plates out of the cupboard.

I was pouring coffee into Maeve's cup when Evelyn said, "Come on, Maeve. Out with it. If there is fresh Cabot Cove news, we want to be in on it."

Maeve held up a hand as though she was a traffic cop, took a sip of her coffee, and complimented me on its flavor, and only then did she reply, although she didn't get straight to what I assumed to be the core of the gossip.

"So, there I was, trying to remedy what the winter had done to my poor rosebushes in my front garden, when along comes Oscar Cisneros—" Maeve began, but Evelyn interrupted.

"Do you mean Oscar the junk man? The guy who rides around in that beat-up old convertible with no top, filled to the brim with odds and ends? I remember him. Never bothered anybody. Goes about his business." Evelyn was happy she'd matched a face with the name.

"Exactly. The very man. Well, there I am on my ratty old rubber knee pad looking for signs of severe damage when I hear a sheriff's car make that short *whoop-whoop* sound as they sometimes do. So I look between the slats of my fence, and there is Oscar's car stopped, and that nice deputy Andy Bloom is getting out of his car and walking toward Oscar, wishing him a good morning," Maeve said, and then stopped to take another sip of coffee.

I could see that Evelyn was getting antsy enough to explode, so I tried to move the story along. "Maeve, did you happen to hear Andy say why he stopped Oscar on the street?"

"Of course I did. I told you they were right in front of my garden, so I could hear every word. Andy was looking for something that was missing and wanted to look through Oscar's things, and Oscar, being the gentle soul he is, told Andy to come along and look all he wants. Said he could take his time about it."

Evelyn could wait no longer. "Do you know what Andy was looking for?"

I could tell by the glint in Maeve's eye that she was enjoying herself. She was never beyond a bit of teasing and Evelyn was a perfect target. "Oh yes, I do know now. Of course, I didn't then. I did hear Andy ask Oscar to drive back home. Andy wanted to look in that broken-down storage shed behind his house where Oscar keeps his odds and ends. And off they went."

"That's it? Your unbelievable news is a traffic stop?" Evelyn scowled, and took a large bite out of her scone as if to keep herself from saying more.

"That's only the beginning of the story. A while later my phone rang and it was Doris Ann from the library. She told me that the latest Rhys Bowen book I'd been waiting for was finally available. Long waiting list for that one. Then she said that everyone coming into the library could talk of nothing else but the arrest. I didn't know what she was talking about, and I said so. That's when she told me that Oscar Cisneros was under arrest. Deputy Andy Bloom had found stolen property in Oscar's shed and arrested him. Now, isn't that unbelievable?"

"Oh, that can't be right. It just can't be. Oscar has been a Cabot Cove fixture for, well, just about forever," I said. "There's never been the slightest suspicion that he is anything but honest."

Maureen pulled out her cell phone and hit speed dial. Mort must have answered on the first ring. She said, "I know you're busy, hon, but is it true about Oscar? . . . That's so hard to believe. I know. See you at home."

Sweeping her eyes around the table as she put down the phone, Maureen said, "Mort says it's true. He's holding Oscar in a cell."

Evelyn stood. "I hate to break up the party but, Maureen, I need a ride back to the Hill House to swap out these sweats for my investigative-reporter clothes. I better call Dan. We need to talk to whoever in town knows Oscar best."

I wasn't sure she realized that she was reciting her to-do list out loud. She swiped a scone from the serving plate, held it up high, and nodded to Maeve. "Delicious. Really delicious." And she bolted out the kitchen door.

Wide-eyed, Maureen said, "I guess we are leaving. I'll call you later, Jessica." And she followed behind Evelyn.

"Well, that was a sight to see. And what does Evelyn intend to investigate? She doesn't even live in Cabot Cove anymore, never mind that she doesn't work on the *Gazette*," Maeve said. "Of course, the entire town is shocked. Everyone likes Oscar, but the deputy did find stolen goods in his shed."

"That may be true," I said, "but the real question is, how did the stolen property get there?"

Maeve gave no reply. Good neighbor that she was, she simply continued to help me straighten the kitchen, and then went home to continue to work on her roses.

My plan was to spend the day slogging through a mountain of research material for my next book, but I knew I wouldn't be able to focus. Better to clear my mind before I settled down to work.

I pulled out my bicycle and set out for the sheriff's office. The weather was a bit blustery but the sun was strong enough that a fair number of people were outside, either checking out their gardens as Maeve O'Bannon had been doing or scouting their fences, sheds, and other outdoor amenities to see what repairs might be needed after a long winter.

Most waved or said hello and kept on with their work. The first to lean over his fence as I pedaled by was Charlie Evans, who used to run the gas station just outside of town. Now he mostly gardened and gossiped.

"Stop by a minute, Jessica. Tell me what you know." Charlie pulled off his denim work gloves, draped them on a fence slat, and then slid his eyeglasses out from under the brim of his navy blue Boston Red Sox hat.

"Well, I do know Evelyn Phillips is back in town for a visit," I said as if I had no idea of the topic that was on his mind.

He began to clean his glasses on the hem of his blue and gray plaid flannel shirt. "That's old news. Everyone in town knows Evelyn's around, lugging one of those big, heavy bags of hers. Probably looking over Dan Andrews's shoulder at every word he types." Charlie snickered. "The real news is at the sheriff's office and there's not a person in town who don't know how close you and Metzger are, so tell me true, what is the story on poor ole Oscar?"

"I can honestly say I don't have any idea. I am as stunned as I am sure the rest of the town is," I said.

"The sheriff ain't talked to you? Word around Mara's is that he never makes a serious arrest without checking in with you." Charlie had finished wiping one lens and was now polishing the other.

"Well, if that's true, I can tell you that if Oscar was arrested, it shouldn't be considered serious, because the sheriff has not spoken about it to me." I didn't see any reason to mention that I was with Maureen when she talked to her husband about Oscar's arrest, nor that I was on my way to Mort's office.

Crestfallen at my lack of information, Charlie put his glasses back on and reached for his work gloves. Interrogation over.

I rode the rest of the way without having to answer any questions other than the relaxing hometown questions I was used to, such as *How are you doing?* or *How you liking this sunshine?*

I parked my bicycle, and just as I was going into the sheriff's office, Joe Turco, a nice young man and a very smart lawyer who had represented me a few times in civil matters, was coming out of the building. I smiled a cheery greeting, but his step never slowed and his "Hello" was clipped. He seemed tense, all business. And I noticed he was wearing a jacket and tie, a sure sign that he was working. Clearly he had something serious on his mind.

Inside the office Mort was sitting at his desk while his deputy Floyd McCallum leaned over his shoulder. They were looking at some papers. Mort motioned for me to come to his desk. "Hey, Mrs. F., did Joe Turco send you in as the second assault team?"

"I don't know what you mean. I did meet Joe outside, but he seemed to be in a hurry, barely said hello," I said.

"Oh, I suppose he is off to the courthouse." He swiveled in his chair toward the deputy. "You hungry, Floyd? It's early for lunch but I've had a heck of a morning. I could use a Reuben sandwich from the deli counter at the Fruit and Veg. And Andy is buried under paperwork—see if he wants something, and don't forget to check with Oscar. We may not be allowed to question him, but we can certainly feed him. What about you, Mrs. F.? How about a sandwich?" Mort leaned back and crossed his legs at the ankles, his feet resting on his desk. "Heck of a day, and it's barely eleven o'clock."

Floyd went to round up lunch orders while Mort and I sat, not talking, since he clearly didn't want any conversation. I was hoping a few minutes of quiet would help him simmer down. When Floyd returned, he asked if I had decided on a sandwich, and when I declined he said, "Sheriff, I'm ready to call in the order. Did you want anything else?"

Mort dropped his feet to the floor. "Now that I think of it, I'll take a nice slice of the pie of the day. Maureen's not here to count my calories. And since the Fruit and Veg has been buying their pies from Charlene Sassi's bakery, slices to go are always fresh and tasty. And I could sure use fresh and tasty."

"Okay, Sheriff, I'll call it right in."

When Floyd left the room, Mort seemed finally ready to talk to me. He held up one hand. "Before we start, I know how you and most of the folks in this town feel about Oscar Cisneros, but it's just like I told Maureen. Andy found stolen goods in Oscar's shed."

"Would you mind telling me what Andy found?" I asked gently.

"Yeah, a couple of antique candlesticks. Bertha Mae Cormier identified them. Said they went missing from her house a few days ago. She was so excited that we found them, because they'd once belonged to her grandmother. Poor Bertha Mae almost cried when I couldn't let her take them home because I have to hold them as evidence."

I still didn't quite understand. "Had Bertha Mae reported them missing? And what on earth inspired Andy to look in Oscar's shed?"

"Now, that is a funny story. Nothing to laugh at, mind you, just odd. That Perfection guy, Martin Terranova, came in to report that he had seen a pair of antique candlesticks stashed amid the pile of castoffs in Oscar's convertible that he was sure belonged to Bertha Mae. He hadn't asked her if her candlesticks were missing, because he didn't want to upset her, but he thought we should know, maybe look into it," Mort said as he stood, coffee cup in hand.

"I need a refill. Can I get you a cup, Mrs. F.?"

"No, thank you, but tell me, Mort, why did you decide to investigate?"

"It was just routine. People come and tell us all sorts of things. We look into them. Andy drove over to Bertha Mae's house. If she pointed to her candlesticks sitting on the mantel or said she had given them to Oscar—case closed," he said.

"But that didn't happen," I ventured.

"*Oh, no,* it did not." Mort settled back in his chair. He took a sip and continued the story. "When Andy mentioned the candlesticks, she told him that she had been looking for them for days. She even said she thought her former housekeeper, Greta, had stolen them. But Andy already had a suspect."

"Oscar," I said.

Mort nodded. "Andy searched Oscar's car, and then asked if Oscar would mind if he took a look in Oscar's shed. Well, you know Oscar; he is as agreeable as the day is long. He said sure. It took Andy about ten minutes to find the candlesticks stashed behind some cartons of dusty old books. He had no choice but to bring Oscar in here."

"And what did Oscar say?" I thought that would be the most critical point of the entire episode.

"Oscar said he never saw the candlesticks before and he has no idea how they got into his shed. He might have said more, but Joe Turco came busting through the door and told us he was Oscar's lawyer. He ordered us to cease and desist any questioning immediately. He actually said that, 'cease and desist,' like on one of those Judge What's-the-name TV shows. Lawyers usually just tell us they want us to stop." Mort shrugged. "He's on his way to court to get a judge to make me release Oscar, and Andy hasn't even finished the paperwork. I think for some reason Oscar is really important to Joe. Darned if I can figure why."

"Maybe he simply believes Oscar is innocent," I said.

When Floyd came back from the Fruit and Veg, I left Mort to enjoy his Reuben sandwich and pie of the day, which Floyd said was apple. I'd spent enough time on our little Cabot Cove mystery. If Joe Turco was helping Oscar, there was certainly nothing more I could do. As I pedaled home my brain was sorting through my research material, preparing for my next few hours of work. When I got to my gate, Evelyn Phillips, now dressed in her "investigative reporter" outfit of jeans, a plaid shirt, and a windbreaker, was standing next to Dan Andrews at my front door. Clearly my research would have to remain on hold for the next little while.

Chapter Six

Where've you been?" Evelyn asked. "Dan already spoke to Metzger and got the whole story about Oscar."

I said nothing, but I thought it would be interesting to learn if Dan and I had heard the same version.

Always soft-spoken and well-mannered, Dan said, "Good morning, Jessica. I hope we are not intruding."

I managed a smile as I assured him they were not.

When Evelyn, the self-described rolling stone, had decided it was time for her to begin roaming the country to visit friends and relatives whom she'd neglected for far too long, she invited her longtime friend and former colleague at the New York bureau of United Press International, Dan Andrews, to take her place as editor of the *Gazette*. Extremely diligent when it came to his job, and always pleasant when dealing with people, Dan had fit seamlessly into our placid community. He was a regular at Mara's for breakfast and never badgered other patrons while they were trying to enjoy their blueberry pancakes or their sausages and eggs, as Evelyn had been known to do. Their personalities were so different that I marveled that the two reporters had remained close friends for so long.

Evelyn dropped her enormous brown tote on my couch and flopped into my recliner in such a way that the yellow and orange afghan draped across the top slid to the floor. She waved Dan toward the couch and left me to choose my own seat, which was noteworthy since this was, after all, my house.

Without any preliminaries, Evelyn said, "Danny, tell Jessica what you found out."

Dan took a notepad from his jacket pocket and began to read its contents aloud. They were basically a repetition of what Mort had told me, except Dan didn't seem to have learned about Joe Turco's involvement in the case. He must have gotten to talk to Mort before Joe arrived and offered to represent Oscar.

After Dan finished, Evelyn said, "So, what do you think, Jessica? Did Oscar Cisneros become a thief recently, or has he been stealing from folks around here for forever and a day but no one noticed until now?"

"Evelyn, neither of those scenarios seems even remotely possible. I can't believe Oscar would steal so much as an empty pop bottle to redeem the deposit, much less take anything of real value that belongs to someone else. And you would be the first to admit that Bertha Mae, even at her best, certainly makes for an extremely unreliable witness."

"But what about the witness? The finger pointer?" Evelyn was getting to what was, in my mind, the crux of the matter.

"Ah yes, Martin Terranova. His involvement has been nagging at me. What possible reason could he have for examining that rickety old rust-bucket car of Oscar's and reporting the contents to the sheriff? And . . ." I hesitated, organizing my thoughts.

"Yes?" Evelyn prompted.

"How was it that Terranova claimed to have seen the candlesticks in Oscar's car, yet Andy found them in the shed, and Oscar denies that they were ever in his possession?"

Dan picked up my point. "That's easy. Someone is lying."

I nodded. "And I have a great deal of difficulty believing it's Oscar."

"On that we agree," Dan said, "but I am stuck trying to figure out what possible reason Martin Terranova could have to lie about Oscar. And, to take it further, if he is lying, then it stands to reason that he must have been responsible for the hoax of the disappearing and reappearing candlesticks. To what point?"

Dan's questions clicked everything into place for me. I stood. "Dan, can you drive me back to Mort's office?"

"Oh, I like the sound of that. So that's where you went on your bike ride. You've already talked to Mort and now you have one of your ideas. C'mon, Dan. This is going to be good." Evelyn rubbed her hands together with the relish of a gambler placing a bet on a sure thing.

Within minutes the three of us were sitting in front of Mort's desk. I explained Evelyn's original concern, which I shared to a small degree, that Bertha Mae was far too taken with Martin Terranova for their relationship to be a healthy one.

"Yeah, I already got that," Mort said, "but what has Bertha Mae's crush on a man young enough to be her grandson got to do with the stolen candlesticks?"

"Everything, if Martin Terranova is the person who stole them," I said.

"What?" Mort leaned forward and dropped his elbows on his desk. "If he stole them, why would he then report Oscar to our office? And why hide the candlesticks in Oscar's shed? You're not making sense, Mrs. F."

"Oh yes, I am, very much so. Think about it. We have been assuming that Bertha Mae's crush, as you call it, is a result of her brain being addled by time and the presence of a handsome young man who now lives next door. But suppose—just suppose—that Terranova is an emotional predator, slowly seducing her, not physically but emotionally, with a great deal of attention and flattery. Maureen, Evelyn, and I visited his class and witnessed for ourselves how he treats his older clients. He oozes cloying charm from every pore, and the older ladies are mesmerized." I winced slightly at the memory.

"I am confident that he has been in Bertha Mae's house quite often and is familiar with her family treasures and knows which items are most important to her." I sat back in my chair, assured that I had made my case.

Mort nodded. "I am beginning to see where you are going with this. He steals the candlesticks, plants them on Oscar, reports the theft—"

Evelyn jumped in. "Andy recovers the candlesticks and Terranova makes sure that Bertha Mae finds out that he was the one who reported Oscar as the thief. His already positive stature increases and he becomes even more of a hero in Bertha Mae's eyes. Jessica, I think you nailed it. Sheriff, it's time to let Oscar go. You have the wrong man."

I raised my arms. "Hold up, everyone. This is only a theory. We don't have one iota of proof. Not a shred. Everything we are saying is pure speculation."

"Well," Mort said, "on the bright side, Joe Turco asked a judge to order me to release Oscar on the grounds that his mental state was deteriorating rapidly while being locked up. And since we still haven't been able to get Bertha Mae to sign a formal complaint, the judge agreed."

"Why won't she sign?" As usual it was Dan who asked the most logical question.

"Because she's Bertha Mae." Evelyn rolled her eyes.

Mort pointed to Evelyn. "You got it in one. Bertha Mae won't sign the complaint until she gets her candlesticks back, and we can't return them until there is a disposition to the case. Technically, without Bertha Mae signing the complaint, we have no proof that the candlesticks don't legally belong to Oscar. Bit of a stalemate."

Dan said, "If what we are surmising is correct, giving Bertha Mae back her candlesticks would end this whole affair. That is beginning to sound like justice in this particular situation."

"Nonsense," I said. "You'd be right, Dan, if Oscar were a transient and would be gone and forgotten in a week or less. But he has lived in Cabot Cove all his life. He makes his living because the townspeople give him castoffs, which he sells at flea markets during tourist season. This is his home. It is not a question of setting aside the arrest. More importantly—"

"We have to find a way to clear his name." Dan finished my sentence.

But none of us could come up with a way that we could definitively do so. Evelyn suggested that Mort bring Terranova into the office and question him repeatedly until Terranova tripped over himself in trying to keep his answers straight.

I advocated for a more direct route. "Perhaps Evelyn and I

could visit Bertha Mae tomorrow and tell her that the sheriff's office made a mistake. That it is very likely that Oscar did not take her candlesticks. If she repeats that to Terranova, it may cause him to do something that would show his hand."

"What do you think he would do?" Dan asked.

"That's just it. I have no idea." I sighed.

Mort threw up his hands. "This is getting us nowhere, folks. Why don't you all get out of here so I can get some work done, and maybe one of us will dream a bright idea in our sleep tonight?"

I asked Dan to drop me at Seth Hazlitt's office. When I am writing a mystery novel, I often find that if I am stumped on a plot point, Seth, with his no-nonsense down-east attitude, has a way of seeing through the haze and pointing out what is right in front of me. I was hoping that his pair of fresh eyes would help us clear Oscar.

Seth's office waiting room was bright and cheerful, with sunlight streaming through the windows. The only patient waiting to see him was Ideal Molloy, who was thumbing through a magazine.

She looked up and gave me a smile. "Do you suppose that Doc Hazlitt would fuss at me if I tore the recipe for fudge jumbles out of this *Women's Weekly*? It's an old issue, from last winter. I am surprised no one took the recipe before now. The jumbles look luscious."

And then, without waiting for me to reply, she answered her own question by tearing the page from the magazine and slipping it into her purse.

Ideal dropped the magazine on the table next to her chair.

"Imagine Oscar Cisneros a thief. All these years I've been so kind to him." She began ticking items on her fingertips. "I gave him my old curtains, flowerpots, kitchen chairs, even some of my jewelry, and it wasn't junk jewelry either. Now I have to wonder what he stole from me."

"Oh, Ideal, you can't really believe that Oscar stole anything from you. Why, you have known him all your life. I've dropped by your house when you and Oscar were in the kitchen drinking coffee and eating some of your homemade cake."

Ideal said, "That may be true, but doesn't it just make the whole thing so much worse?"

The door to Seth's office opened and a young woman with short blond hair came out. I recognized her as a new teacher at the elementary school. I introduced myself and was asking how she liked Cabot Cove when the door opened again and Seth called Ideal into the examination room.

She stood, but before she followed Seth, she said to me, "All I can tell you, Jessica, is that Oscar Cisneros will never have cake and coffee in my kitchen again."

The teacher, who had introduced herself as Viola Shaw, said, "I heard about the theft this morning. Poor Mrs. Cormier. Imagine losing family treasures to someone you trusted. The whole episode puts me into something of a muddle. Perhaps you could advise me."

"I'll do my best," I said, even as I was wondering why she would seek advice from a perfect stranger. She'd been here for months and must have known someone in town she could talk to about whatever was bothering her.

"When I arrived in Cabot Cove, just before school began last autumn, I rented a small, lovely apartment in a two-family house over on Maple Street. You probably know my landlord, Eleanor Greenwood. She lives downstairs."

"Why, yes, I do. In fact, we serve on the Joshua Peabody Day committee together."

"Well, I didn't have much money when I got here. Still don't, to be honest," Viola said.

I raised my eyes heavenward. "Teachers' salaries. I get it. I absolutely get it."

"Eleanor said she had a friend who deals in secondhand goods and she offered to ask him to help me. I was able to get a few small tables, a really comfy living room chair, and a kitchen set, not to mention pots, dishes, and two pretty paintings for my bare walls."

"Sounds like you did quite well," I said.

A worry wrinkle crossed her brow. "I felt like I did at the time, but the man Eleanor introduced me to was Oscar Cisneros. Now I find out that he is a thief . . . I can't help but wonder, if I invite a new friend to my apartment am I going to serve them a snack in a bowl stolen from their house?"

This was a problem I hadn't foreseen, Cabot Cove residents wondering if the bric-a-brac they bought from Oscar at the last church tag sale had been stolen from neighbor or friend.

I told Viola that I firmly believed Oscar was an honest man and I was sure we would soon discover that the entire episode of Bertha Mae Cormier's candlesticks was nothing more than a complete mix-up. And when she said good-bye, she seemed much relieved.

On the other hand, I was far more worried about the consequences for Oscar of the Cabot Cove rumor mill than I had been when I arrived in Seth's waiting room.

Ideal opened the inner door and said to me, "I always feel better after Doc Hazlitt gives me a once-over. Of course, he complained about the few pounds I gained since my last checkup. If he doesn't want his patients gaining weight, he shouldn't have magazines in the waiting room with such yummy recipes. Am I right?"

As with so many of the questions that Ideal proposed, I was stumped for an answer.

On her way out of the building, she promised to let me know how the fudge jumbles turned out.

Seth stuck his head through the door and waved me into his office. "Come in and sit a spell. You're not here medically, are you?" he asked.

"I almost wish I were. If I had the flu or another virus, I'd feel better than I do right now. It's this business with Oscar Cisneros."

I told him briefly of my day's adventures and the recent conversation I'd had with Evelyn, Dan, and Mort. When I was done, Seth played with the penholder on his desk for a while, and then he said, "Jessica, I like Oscar as much as you do. He's a fixture here in Cabot Cove, but did you ever stop to figure out a reason why Terranova would want to get close to Bertha Mae?"

"Honestly, no, I can't. But Evelyn confided in me that Bertha has far more money than any of us would suspect. I tried to get more information about it, but you know Evelyn, tight-lipped when she wants to be."

We sat, each with our own thoughts, and then Seth said, "How's this for a plan? I will drive you home. You will provide dinner. Afterward, a game of chess."

I perked up immediately. That sounded like just the distraction I needed.

"I have leftover chowder and brown bread from Evelyn's welcome dinner, if that will do," I said.

Seth replied, "That'll do fine."

In the car Seth deftly changed the topic to the library fundraiser. I knew that dinner, chess, and even talk of the fundraiser were his way of clearing Oscar's troubles from my mind, but I couldn't shake the uneasy feeling that the worst was yet to come.

Chapter Seven

Early the next morning I was certain that a bracing bike ride on my favorite path overlooking the harbor would help me put Oscar's troubles on my back burner. I couldn't afford to fall behind in my research. I needed a ride to clear my brain. I pulled my bicycle out of the shed and walked it to my front gate.

I had one hand on the gate, about to open it, when Dan Andrews's car stopped right in front of me. Evelyn Phillips popped out of the passenger seat, shouting, "Dan's got a major front-page headline. *Martin Terranova is dead!* Can you believe it?"

I was so startled by the news that my hand slipped off the bicycle and it clattered to the ground, unfortunately crushing a couple of crocuses that were nearly ready to bloom.

"What? Are you sure?" I asked. "How did it happen?"

"Invite us in for coffee and we'll tell you everything," Evelyn said.

"Coffee? We have no time for coffee." I looked at her incredulously. "Let's find out what information Mort has. Dan, will you drive us to the sheriff's office?"

Dan didn't hesitate. Evelyn and I got into the car and he made a U-turn. As if he wanted to blunt any disappointment we might feel if we got no real information at the sheriff's office, Dan said, "I don't know what you think the sheriff can tell us. From what I understand, a couple of fishermen showed up for the predawn weight-lifting class that Martin holds once a week. They found his body in the gym. He was cold and lifeless. He probably died sometime last night. All I know is that it had something to do with the weights. Maybe he was stacking them or rearranging them and conked himself on the head."

I couldn't accept that theory. "Perhaps, Dan, but I think there has to be more to it. He was a young, healthy man—"

Evelyn interrupted. "Jessica, even young, healthy men have accidents, but I have to say, if he had one, Terranova's must have been a doozy."

Dan turned into the sheriff's parking lot and I was glad to see that Seth's car was already there. I'd definitely want to get his take on Terranova's injuries.

"I just don't understand it," Dan said. "During the classes I attended, Martin was really careful and he was constantly cautioning us to be vigilant when handling weights, especially the heavier ones."

As Dan turned off the engine, Evelyn said, "Well, I admit, I am relieved. I won't have to worry any longer about Terranova flimflamming Bertha Mae."

"Evelyn! How can you be so callous? The poor man should have had many decades of life ahead of him." Although I'd known her for more years than I could count, Evelyn had not lost her ability to shock me.

When we entered the office, Mort was sitting behind his desk and Seth was in a chair opposite him. They both had their hands wrapped around coffee mugs.

Mort said, "Can you tell me, Doc, why I am not surprised to see this group parading into my office so early in the morning?"

Seth stood up. "No surprise to me either. Can I offer you ladies a chair? How about you, Dan? Make yourselves comfortable."

As we were settling in, Evelyn said, "I have to admit, I don't recall ever being greeted so cordially when I lived here. Sheriff, your attitude toward the press has changed for the better."

"I haven't changed a whit, Evelyn. Let's get something straight. You are no longer editor of the paper or a resident of the town. If you three have come here to find out what we know so far about Martin Terranova's death, we can have a conversation. But Dan has to agree that our little talk is strictly off the record, and you and Jessica have to agree not to repeat anything you hear outside these four walls."

Evelyn started to bluster. "Well, I never . . ." Then she must have realized she had no argument with any strength to it, and she stopped talking.

Mort looked at the three of us. "Do we all agree?"

When we did, he relaxed. "Here is what we know. Martin Terranova was bench-pressing sometime last night. He must have slipped somehow and was killed when a barbell landed on his neck."

Dan shook his head. "That doesn't make sense. In the few classes I attended he was exceptionally careful. He emphasized that we should never lie on a bench and lift a barbell without

someone acting as a spotter in position above us. He unequivo-
cally convinced me, and from what I saw, he got the message
across to everyone in the room. Why wouldn't he follow his own
rule?"

"Maybe he was following the old axiom 'Do as I say, not as I
do'," Evelyn said.

"Ayuh, Dan," Seth said. "I'm inclined to see this as something
more than an accident. I think it is possible, even likely, that
someone forced the barbell down hard on Mr. Terranova's neck,
crushing his larynx and most of the bones in his neck, including
the hyoid. While those injuries are significant, they aren't neces-
sarily fatal. We are awaiting the coroner's report, but I'd bet
strangulation was the cause of death."

"I'm not sure I understand. How can you be certain it wasn't
an accident?" I was puzzled.

Seth looked to Mort, who answered, "Mrs. F., I haven't lifted
weights in years, but I clearly remember that when I bench-
pressed, just like Dan says, I always had a spotter, you know, to
be safe. You're kind of vulnerable lying on your back with weights
coming at you from above. Well, there was a time that I dropped
the bar and my spotter grabbed it in the nick of time, or it would
have hit me for sure. But it would have landed just below my
shoulders, nowhere near my neck.

"In Terranova's case, if the bar slipped and he couldn't catch
it, then it would land on his chest. Even if it rolled to his neck, it
might have caused some damage but, according to Doc Hazlitt,
unlikely enough damage to crush his hyoid, much less cut off his
air supply, given the small amount of weight that was hung on
the bar. It seems likely he had only begun lifting and was using
his warm-up weights."

"So what you are saying is Martin Terranova was murdered," I said.

"Doc and I think someone, maybe one of his students or a friend who Terranova asked to spot him, waited until he was lowering the bar, and then they grabbed the bar, pushed it down on his throat with tremendous force, and . . . that's all she wrote.

"We are waiting for the full coroner's report, but in the meantime, I'm treating it as a suspicious death. Andy and Floyd are out interviewing the neighbors right now to find out if anyone heard or saw anything last night around—what time did you say, again, Doc?" Mort turned to Seth.

"Pending the coroner's report I'd say between eight and ten o'clock last night. That's not exact but close enough," Seth said.

"Bertha Mae!" Evelyn said. "We have to go to Bertha Mae before Andy or Floyd ring her doorbell. She needs to be told gently and by a friend."

"Calm down, Evelyn," Mort said. "When the ambulance team arrived and saw the situation they called for us. That's standard procedure. Andy was first on the scene. He took down witness names and sent for Doc Hazlitt. When Andy called to update me, I realized that Bertha Mae might have a problem handling the, ah, news, so I asked Maureen to go with Andy to break the news to Bertha Mae. When Andy left Bertha Mae's house, the two of them were having tea and talking about yoga."

Seth picked up the tale. "After I finished examining the body, I stopped at Bertha Mae's. I pretended to express my condolences, but at Mort's insistence I was checking to be sure she was doing all right. Then I called her doctor, Arnold Becker, and he promised he would stop by to check her later today."

"Well, that is a relief," Evelyn said. "I was afraid this would really send her off the deep end, but with Maureen she should be fine. Maureen has a way with her."

"My wife has a way with most people." Mort beamed. His pride in his effervescent and always thoughtful wife was evident.

"Mort, I was wondering . . . about Oscar." I hesitated, not sure how to proceed without stirring up potential trouble.

"What about him? The last I seen of him was when Joe Turco waltzed him out of here yesterday afternoon. Yeah, I guess we'll have to check his whereabouts around the window of the time of death." Mort rocked back so his chair was balanced on its rear legs. "I can't see it, though. We never mentioned Terranova to Oscar. All we did was ask to look in his car and in his shed and Oscar readily agreed."

"As any thief would," I said dryly.

"That's not fair, Mrs. F. Oscar had no idea that Andy was looking for something in particular." Mort tilted forward and the front legs of his chair hit the floor with a thud. "Now, I have a lot of work to do."

We were clearly being dismissed.

As soon as we got into the car, Evelyn began to complain about Mort. "Everything's always a big secret with him. Like the words 'freedom of the press' have no meaning in this town. And you"—she gave Dan a backhanded slap on his upper arm—"didn't even argue when he ordered you to keep everything we heard off the record."

I expected Dan to respond, and when he didn't I said, "Evelyn, you do realize that until they have the coroner's findings, everything that Mort and Seth discuss is their opinion, not to be taken as factual until confirmed."

"I've always found that as long as we in the press couch our words carefully, the public is happy to put their own spin on what we have to say." Evelyn sounded a bit too smug for my taste, so I enjoyed Dan's response.

"The thing is," he said, gently but firmly, "you are not the press anymore, Evelyn."

"Humph. So I guess you'll handle the story your way." Evelyn folded her arms, and in order to move as far away from Dan as possible, she leaned against the passenger-side door with such force, I feared she would push it open and fall right out.

Dan stopped the car in front of my house and I quickly opened my door. I thanked them for the ride and strode down my front walk without a backward glance. I fired up my computer and went into the kitchen to put the kettle on the stove. Right now I craved a strong cup of tea to help me shake off the news of the morning, and then I planned to throw myself into research that was fast becoming overdue.

Teacup in hand, I was heading back to my computer when I noticed the message light flashing on my telephone. A brief message from Doris Ann at the library said she was looking for me but didn't say why. I took a sip of tea and called her back.

"Jessica, thanks for getting back to me so soon. We have a bit of a problem with the Friends of the Library meeting. I scheduled it for Thursday, only to learn that the custodian has finally been able to book the painters to come and brighten up that dingy meeting room. The only problem is they are painting on Wednesday and doing finishing touches, molding and trim and the like, on Thursday."

"I see. Of course we'll have to cancel our meeting." I was secretly overjoyed to have more free time for research. "That's perfectly fine with me."

"Oh, canceling is a given. I'm calling about rescheduling. We are looking at next Wednesday or Thursday and will go with whichever date works for the most committee members. So what do you say?"

"Right now, either date works for me," I said.

"That's a relief. I was considering earlier in the week but the custodian said it would take a while to air out the paint fumes, so I thought midweek would be best, and most of the committee members seem to agree." I could almost see Doris Ann putting a check mark next to my name.

"Sounds perfect," I said. "Well, I'll see you then."

"Jessica, there is something else." She paused and then lowered her voice. "It's about Oscar Cisneros."

"Now, Doris Ann, you really don't believe that he—"

She quickly cut me off. "No. Not for a minute. Oscar is no thief, but what worries me is that he was in here as soon as we opened, and he scoured the travel section. He borrowed the Fodor's travel guide for Maine, Vermont, and New Hampshire and left without a word. You don't think Oscar is planning on leaving Cabot Cove, do you?"

"Oh, I hope not. I can't imagine where he would go. He's lived here his entire life. His neighbors know him and—" I was about to say *trust him* when I realized that might no longer be true. Not knowing what to say, I ended with, "Let me look into this."

I sat at my computer and stared into space while I finished my tea. My brain was scrambling in a thousand directions. *One thing at a time,* I said to myself, and I opened my research file.

I'd visited San Diego, California, any number of times, but through my years as a writer I had learned that no matter how

"I feel the same," I said, hoping to put Tim at ease.

"Along the way I often see friends and neighbors running, walking, or biking. Haven't I seen you fairly often, Jessica, and we shared a hello or a smile?"

I nodded my agreement, not wanting to interrupt again.

"That day was just another morning. I got winded earlier than usual and my jog was down to a sluggish trot by the time I reached Oscar's house. I passed by as I always do, and a few yards down the road I saw Martin Terranova doing a slow jog toward me, and he was carrying something under his arm."

"What was he carrying?" I asked.

"Honestly, I didn't pay attention. All I recall is a brown paper bag. Well, I got to my turnaround spot, the corner fence of the Miller property, and took a hasty drink from my water bottle before heading home.

"It wasn't long before I saw Martin Terranova jogging toward me. He must have reached his own turning point, and he was a lot peppier on this leg of his jog. This time we both said, 'Good morning,' and kept going."

Tim raised his teacup to his lips and took a drink. "I didn't think anything of it at the time, but when Maeve told me Oscar was arrested because he was suspected of stealing some candlesticks— well, I hate to accuse anybody of anything, but I am highly suspicious that for some reason I can't fathom, Martin Terranova framed Oscar for the theft of Bertha Mae Cormier's candlesticks."

"What makes you think that?" I asked Tim.

"Once I took the time to focus on what I'd seen that morning, I realized that when I passed Martin the second time, he wasn't carrying anything. There isn't much out there besides Oscar's ramshackle house and shed. When I first saw Martin—you know, when he was carrying the package—for the next mile in the direction he was going there was nothing but Oscar's property, followed by Clark Proctor's cow pasture. To pass me again on his return trip, I assumed his turnaround point must have been somewhere along the pasture fence. So, unless Martin Terranova threw the package in the pasture, he had to have left it somewhere on Oscar's property. Why not the shed?"

Why not indeed? I thought.

Tim visibly relaxed his shoulders, which, while he was talking, had tightened and reached nearly to his ears. He'd stretched his hand toward the cookie plate when Maeve reminded him that he was not quite done.

"Tell Jessica what has you so fidgety. Tell her why you need her advice," she prodded.

Tim sighed and put the cookie down on his saucer. "This morning I was having breakfast in Mara's and I heard that Terranova is dead. There's a rumor that he was murdered. Last night I thought my information could help prove Oscar isn't a thief, but with Terranova dead, if I tell the sheriff what I saw, isn't it possible I will get Oscar deeper in trouble? I mean, suppose he knew that Terranova framed him and he, well, took his revenge."

"I'm certain that whatever happened to Martin Terranova, Oscar Cisneros had nothing to do with it, but I am equally certain that Mort needs to have all the facts," I said in my best matter-of-fact schoolteacher voice. "And you have a responsibility to speak to Mort as soon as possible. It is important that he know any and all facts that concern the accusations against Oscar as well as Martin Terranova's death." I stopped to let that sink in.

"I guess you are right. It's best I get this off my chest." Tim's voice wobbled a tiny bit.

To shore him up I said, "I'll go with you. Hard-to-do things are easier when you have a friend at your side."

Even knowing how loyal she was to those she considered to be friends, I was surprised that Maeve opted to go with us. I supposed she felt that since she had encouraged Tim to talk to me, she should stay by his side until he'd told his story wherever it needed to be heard.

The parking lot at the sheriff's office was quite full, so I feared we might have a long wait. Sure enough, when Tim opened the door and we saw more than half a dozen men sitting and standing around the waiting area, he shrank back as if willing himself to magically be in his car driving anywhere but here.

I took his arm and whispered, "You got this far. If you don't talk to Mort now, you'll only have to come again. Let's get it over," I said.

My saving grace was that Deputy Floyd McCallum was already walking toward us. "Morning, Mrs. Fletcher. As you can see, the sheriff is a mite busy right now. Gorry, there haven't been this many people packed into our office since the sheriff called for volunteers to search the woods and the waterways when young Nathaniel Allen went missing. Gave the whole town quite a scare. Turns out he skipped school to avoid a math test and then realized too late that the school would probably call his mom, so he crawled up into Proctor's hayloft and fell asleep. That was quite a day."

"I remember it well," I said. "I was one of the searchers who scoured the top of the cliffside. But this?" I motioned at the men sitting and standing restlessly looking at their watches or scrolling through their cell phones. "What has brought all these men together?"

Floyd lowered his voice. "It's about Martin Terranova. Andy found his file of class registration forms and the sheriff asked us to round them up. He actually used the words 'round up.' I can tell you he sounded like the French policeman in that famous old movie—you know, the one where he says, 'Round up the usual suspects.' Anyway, Sheriff wanted us to find everyone who was registered for any of Terranova's weight-lifting classes. And find 'em we did." Floyd puffed out his chest.

"And Mort is going to speak to every one of them?" I fretted.

That was distressing. I was afraid Tim would throw up his hands and say, *Well, I tried.* And march on home.

"Floyd, could you bring a note in to the sheriff for me?"

"Do my best, Mrs. Fletcher," Floyd said.

I pulled a pen and an old receipt from Mellow's Notions from my purse and wrote:

MORT, I AM IN THE PARKING LOT WITH TIM PURDY. HE HAS IMPORTANT INFORMATION ABOUT TERRANOVA AND OSCAR.

I handed it to Floyd, told him we would wait outside, and ushered Tim and Maeve into the parking lot.

"So, that's it. We can leave?" Tim sounded so hopeful I almost hated to answer.

"Not quite yet," I said. "I've asked Mort to meet us here, if he can get away."

By the look on Tim's face I knew he wasn't happy, so I decided to remind him that he was here for a good reason. "I'm sure Oscar will be grateful when all this is over and he can go back to his normal, quiet life. Don't you agree, Maeve?"

"That I do, Jessica. That I do. He is a grand man and a wonderful neighbor." Maeve began to list Oscar's finer qualities, and then she stopped and pointed.

Mort and Floyd were coming around the corner from the rear of the building.

"Mrs. F., whatever it is, we gotta make it quick." Mort gestured back toward his office. "As you can see, we are swamped. In fact, Floyd, why don't you go inside and start the next interview?"

"Will do, Sheriff." Floyd turned on his heel and disappeared behind the building.

I hoped Tim would take charge of the conversation, but when he remained mute, I explained to Mort that Tim had been witness to something that could cast some light on exactly how Bertha Mae's candlesticks wound up in Oscar's storage shed.

Mort moved into what I always thought of as his interrogation stance. Arms crossed, feet apart, eyebrows raised, lips pursed.

Seconds ticked by before Tim realized he had no choice but to speak. "You see, Sheriff, I jog the same route every day . . ."

When Tim finished explaining what he had seen, the relief on his face was palpable. He didn't anticipate that Mort would have a question or two.

"How can you be sure that the package you saw Martin Terranova carrying contained the candlesticks?" Mort asked.

"I can't, but what else could it have been? I mean, I saw Terranova jogging near Oscar's house with a package and coming away from it without one. Then it was later that same morning your deputy found the candlesticks in Oscar's shed. If Oscar didn't put them there, who did? I'm not trying to make things look bad for Oscar now that Terranova is dead, but I do believe Martin Terranova planted the candlesticks, although I can't say why he would do such a thing."

Mort asked a few more questions, trying to pinpoint the exact time and location of Tim's encounter with Terranova. Then he thanked Tim and sent us on our way.

Once we were in Tim's car, Maeve and I lavished praise on him, but he remained quiet until he pulled up in front of my house. He threw the gear in park, placed both hands on the top of the steering wheel, and looked straight ahead as if he were still driving. "Ladies, I know that in theory my talking to Sheriff Metzger was the right thing to do. I hope my information was valuable but I cannot help believing that I have painted an X directly on Oscar's back. If he is arrested again, it will be my fault."

"Tim, justice can never be served unless the truth is known." Although I'd taught high school English, even to my own ears I sounded like an American history teacher. "I am sure that Mort will resolve precisely what happened to Martin Terranova and that Oscar will be found completely innocent of any wrongdoing."

Maeve supported me. "Tim, if you had decided to keep what you saw a secret, you wouldn't be the man that everyone in Cabot Cove thinks you to be."

After a few more rah-rah speeches from the two of us, Tim perked up just enough that I felt comfortable saying good-bye.

I could hear my telephone ringing when I opened my front door. I ran and picked it up, apparently just in time. "Woman, where have you been? I was just about to hang up. I already left one message this morning. I seem to remember that you were dedicating your entire day to working on . . . I believe you called it 'extensive research' for your next book. And now I find that you've been out gallivanting."

"Now, Seth, you're not the least bit humorous. I did plan on spending the day researching San Diego International Airport and the San Diego Padres baseball team. And I intend to get to it as soon as I hang up this phone."

"Don't be too quick to hang up. You'll want to hear my news. The coroner's office has determined that Martin Terranova's death was not an accident. It was deliberate. Someone pressed that barbell on Terranova's throat with enough force to prevent air from reaching his lungs and blood from reaching his brain. It may have taken him a few minutes to die, but I guarantee that about ten seconds of severe pressure on his carotid arteries and on his jugular would knock him unconscious. Then the killer could press away with no resistance from the victim."

"That sounds awful," I said. "And I also have news that isn't very cheerful."

I told him everything I had learned from Tim Purdy.

"Does Mort know?" Seth asked.

"Yes. I was at his office, along with Maeve O'Bannon. We were Tim's moral support."

"Well, after all our news gathering this morning I suggest that I pick you up tomorrow morning for some breakfast and murder-free conversation at Mara's. Say eight o'clock?"

I agreed and hung up the phone. I poured myself a glass of ice water and sat down to work. Little did I know that by tomorrow morning there would be another widely discussed suspect in Martin Terranova's death, and I wouldn't believe that person could be guilty any more than I could believe Oscar was.

Chapter Nine

I should have realized there was something amiss the next morning when, as soon as Seth and I walked through the door, Mara set her coffeepot down on the counter, grabbed a couple of menus, saying, "Good morning, Jessica, Doc. Come right this way," and led us to a booth in the farthest corner of the room, the most isolated seats possible.

"Mara"—Seth stretched his neck to turn and look across at his favorite table, which was midroom and near the counter—"I don't suppose we could . . ."

She shook her head firmly and lowered her voice a smidge. "Trust me. This is the table you want today." Then, after announcing in her breezy, hostessy voice, "Coffee coming right up," Mara turned and left before Seth could argue.

Once we'd slipped into the booth, sitting opposite each other, Seth leaned across the table and asked, "What on earth was that all about? I feel like a kindergartener who broke a school rule and now has to sit in the naughty corner."

"I have no idea, but I am sure we'll find out sooner or later. We may be in the corner, but we have menus. I haven't actually looked at one in ages. I wonder if Mara has added any interesting breakfast dishes lately." While pretending to study the menu, I held it in front of my face and turned slightly toward the counter. It didn't take long for me to put the menu down.

Seth was still grousing about being put in the corner, so when Mara came back with our coffee, I couldn't resist baffling him by saying, "Mara, thank you so much. You saved us from such an annoyance. I think I will have a short stack of blueberry pancakes to celebrate."

"What happened to 'watching your waistline'?" Mara joked.

"Not today," I said, and we both laughed.

She stuck her pencil behind her ear and said, "Two short stacks coming right up. I know, I know, Doc—extra butter."

Seth said, "Jessica, please tell me what you and Mara are celebrating that I seem to have missed."

Just then a loud burst of laughter came from closer to the front of the restaurant. "Turn around and take a look, Seth. The catalyst of that boisterous group of fishermen is Hilly Davis. He has been going from man to man leaning over shoulders and whispering in ears. And they are all at the counter right next to your favorite table."

"Ayuh, now I see. Mara steered us out of harm's way. I don't understand how you caught on so quickly." Seth peered at me over his glasses. "Ah, the menu. You weren't looking at the menu."

I smiled in acknowledgment. "I will admit, as soon as we

walked in the door, I did notice that the usual morning-at-Mara's chatter was louder than usual. So a quiet corner did look inviting. Then, when I saw who was causing so much of the noise . . ."

When Mara came back with our pancakes, Seth thanked her for seating us in a cozy corner, and then he asked, "What is the uproar over there? How is Hilly so popular all of a sudden? I try to avoid him. Most of the people I know do too. Now here he is, the center of attention. No sense to it. No sense at all."

Mara leaned down until her head was bent over the center of our table, with her nose nearly touching the creamer, and said, "One of my cooks is out sick, and we've been so busy this morning that I haven't had time to pick up what's going on. All I can tell you is that while I don't know exactly what the joke is, the butt of it is Evelyn Phillips."

"Evelyn? What could Hilly have to do with Evelyn?" I said.

Mara stood up straight and, as she shifted her eyes to her left, said, "I think you are about to find out. Enjoy your pancakes, folks."

She rushed past Hilly Davis, who was barreling in our direction, fluttering his arms while the hood of his dark brown ski jacket bounced along behind him. He stopped at our table sporting the biggest Cheshire cat grin I'd ever seen and said, "Morning, Doc. Morning, Jessica. Being you're both such good friends of Mort Metzger's, I suppose you heard the latest 'bout your other friend, that nosy body Evelyn Phillips."

Seth immediately lifted his coffee cup to his lips and held it there as if he couldn't get enough caffeine. He wasn't interested in any conversation with Hilly, especially one that involved Evelyn.

I was curious and took the bait. "Good morning, Hilly." I kept my voice as neutral as possible. "I will say it's been delightful to have Evelyn back in Cabot Cove for a visit."

Hilly chortled loudly enough to get the attention of the entire room, and when he was sure he had it, he boomed, "*Delightful?* You think having a murderer holed up right down the road in the Hill House is delightful? Jessica, you been writing those mystery books of yours for so many years that you can't tell fact from fiction no more."

"Now, just one minute there, Hillard Davis . . ." Seth half rose and began to slide out of the booth, ready for a confrontation, but I reached across the table, grabbed his arm, and stopped him. I was perfectly capable of handling Hilly myself.

To frustrate both Hilly and the crowd of onlookers who were waiting for a long and loud battle to begin, I spoke as softly as I could without actually whispering. "Now, Hilly, I am not sure what motive you think Evelyn could have to kill anyone—"

Hilly opened his mouth as if to interrupt but I didn't allow it.

"And if you are referring to the tragic death of Martin Terranova, well, I did hear that you have been telling anyone and everyone who would listen that ever since he moved to Cabot Cove, Mr. Terranova had been encroaching on your land. I wouldn't toss the word 'murderer' around quite so lightly, because you never know when it might bounce back in your direction."

Hilly furrowed his brow and pursed his lips so fiercely that I was sure he was scrambling for a snappy comeback. When he couldn't find one to suit, he went back to his original premise. Using what was for him a normal tone of voice—loud, but not ear piercing—he said, "Go talk to Sheriff Metzger. We'll see who's right then, won't we?"

He drew a slouchy gray knit hat from his pocket, pulled it down over his balding head, and without looking to the right or the left, marched out the front door.

The usual level of chatter resumed throughout the room immediately, although whether the topic had changed, I couldn't say. It didn't take long for Mara to come back with a full coffee carafe.

Although Seth and I both declined a refill, Mara stood at the side of our table, and asked, "Is that what Hilly is up to? Trying to make Evelyn Phillips out to be a murderer? Why would he do that? I mean, he's crazy as a loon, but I never thought he was that crazy."

I shrugged. "I have no idea."

I deliberately neglected to say that, whether in fiction or after a real crime, the person most likely to vehemently accuse someone else of an unsolved murder is quite often the killer. Hilly would do best to stay quiet and let Mort's investigation take its course, but I knew keeping quiet was never Hilly's way and he surely wasn't about to start now.

As soon as we were outside and away from prying ears, Seth said, "So, what do you think?"

"I think that we'd better get to Mort's office and find out exactly what Hilly is talking about," I said.

Seth held up his hand and jangled his car keys.

When we walked into the sheriff's office, Andy Bloom was leaning on the counter, reading something in an open file folder, which he closed as soon as he saw us. "Dr. Hazlitt, Mrs. Fletcher, what can I do for you this morning?"

"Actually, we'd like to see Mort for a few moments if he is not too busy," I said.

A perplexed look crossed his face as if he was deciding what he could say. "Sheriff is kind of busy right now. I could have him call you later, or if you want to have a seat . . ." He indicated the visitor chairs in the waiting area. "I'm not sure how long he will be."

Seth looked at his watch. "I have patients coming in shortly, Jess."

"You go along, then, Seth. This is too important. I have some time to spare. I'll wait. It's critical that I speak to Mort before this murder business gets out of hand."

Just then the door to the back offices opened and Evelyn Phillips pushed through, her head twisted behind her as she grumbled, "Don't trouble yourself, Sheriff. I can see myself out."

Mort was right on her heels with a snarky command. "I guess I don't have to tell you not to leave town."

Evelyn turned to face him, her arms akimbo, her fists planted firmly on her hips. "I wouldn't dream of it. While you are wasting your time harassing the innocent, I still have plenty of investigating to do."

When she spun around and headed for the door and saw Seth and me, she directed her next tirade toward us.

"I keep telling *your* sheriff that I am still and always will be a reporter and my nose for news tells me that there was something hinky about Martin Terranova and his whole gym setup." She crossed her arms for emphasis and gave us a defiant glare, as if daring either of us to challenge her.

The tension in the room was so palpable that the only thing I could think to do was to separate the combatants. "Seth, didn't you say you had patients coming in shortly? Perhaps you could give Evelyn a ride wherever she needs to go. Ah, I can talk to Mort about the faulty alarm on the library security system. You and I can catch up later."

Seth looked confused but Evelyn jumped at the opportunity. She said, "Doc, could you? I'd love a ride back to the Hill House. Thoughtless people dragged me out of bed before I even had a chance to eat my breakfast."

Seth rose to the occasion. "I don't see why not, but we have to leave right now. Can't keep my patients waiting."

As Evelyn went out the door, Seth tossed me a look and mouthed, *Later.*

I raised my eyes heavenward. I knew from past experience that look meant that Seth wasn't saying, *I'll see you later.* He was saying, *You'll pay for this later.* The last thing he wanted was to be alone in his car with a foul-tempered Evelyn Phillips.

In the meantime, I had to contend with a sheriff who was just as irritated.

Mort walked to the coffeepot, mug in hand. "Sorry you had to witness that, Mrs. F., but Evelyn Phillips is as ornery as ever. Still never happy with how I do my job. I'd rather deal with a nor'easter. Now, what's this about the library alarm?"

"Seth and I had a—I guess I would call it an unsettling encounter in Mara's this morning, but I didn't want to mention it in front of Evelyn, and, well, that cranky old alarm system at the library was the first thing that popped into my head," I said.

"Smart thinking. There is no sense in giving her anything else to play 'investigative reporter' about." Mort started to walk to his desk but then hesitated.

"Can I offer you a cup of coffee before you tell me what

happened?" Mort turned toward the coffeepot, but when I declined his offer he relaxed deep in the chair behind his desk. "Ah, this is more like it. A civilized conversation with a normal person."

"Mort, I am afraid what I want to talk about is more complicated than you might expect. I had a rather strange experience this morning."

He leaned back, crossing his feet on the desktop, and said, "After the morning I had with Evelyn Phillips, you'll be hard-pressed to convince me that your morning was worse."

"I'll let you decide. Seth and I were in Mara's and Hilly Davis was roaming from table to table accusing Evelyn Phillips of murdering Martin Terranova," I said flatly.

Mort dropped his feet to the floor so abruptly that he spilled coffee on his shirt. He called Andy, who was still shuffling through papers at the counter. "Go find Floyd. I need the two of you to listen while I explain to Mrs. Fletcher exactly what happened this morning. I want to make sure I get things right."

Within a minute Andy had pulled up a chair and sat next to me while Floyd leaned against the wall.

Mort spoke slowly, stressing the importance of getting his story exactly right. "Once the coroner declared that Martin Terranova's death was deliberately caused by a person or persons unknown, we knew we had a murder investigation on our hands. The coroner also confirmed Doc Hazlitt's estimate of time of death, although he tightened it to somewhere between eight o'clock and nine thirty the night before the body was discovered.

"We had already interviewed everyone who attended Terranova's Pilates class, which had ended a few minutes after seven. Even the hangers-on were gone by seven thirty, and, as luck would have it, everyone traveled home in groups of two or three. No lonely stragglers to draw our attention."

"What about private sessions?" I asked. "I've heard Terranova did a fair amount of one-on-one teaching."

Mort shrugged. "There was nothing on his calendar. Andy talked to Austin Carpenter, who picked up his wife and daughter from the gym at seven twenty. Austin said that when he went in to tell them the car was outside, all three of them waved good night to Martin, who was on the phone, and there was no one else in the gym."

"And I suppose the phone call was no help?" I wondered half-aloud.

Mort shook his head. "We sent to his service provider for his call list. Far as we can judge by the time Austin gave us, Terranova was on the phone with the Fruit and Veg. Probably something about kale, if I was to guess by the contents of his fridge. Floyd did go over there to double-check and found that Terranova had a delivery scheduled for the next afternoon. No one remembered speaking to him, but he could have been updating or checking on his order. Likely routine stuff."

While Mort was giving me the rundown I noticed that Floyd began fidgeting, and Andy was twisting and turning in his chair so frequently that I knew the most interesting part of their adventure was yet to be told.

Chapter Ten

Last night I sent Andy and Floyd to scout Terranova's neighborhood between seven and ten to see who might be around, like joggers, dog walkers, lovers out for a stroll, anyone at all. I widened the time frame because there was a chance that some of those people might have been on the street near or during the coroner's window on the night Terranova was killed. People never know what they might have seen until someone asks 'em about it." Mort nodded to Andy. "You want to tell Mrs. F. what you found?"

Andy pulled a notepad from his pocket and began to read. "Floyd and I met nine people and we took turns doing the interviews. Four of them said they had been on the street during the night in question. Irene Dunlap told us that, to give her daughter a break, she pushes her colicky grandson every night from around seven thirty until he finally drops off to sleep. Boy, does that kid have a set of lungs. Anyway, she didn't see anything out of the ordinary. Eventually the baby fell asleep and she wheeled him home. Two boys from the high school track team were getting in some extra practice every night this week. All they remembered was the baby crying every night. Then Floyd came upon our star witness."

At the sound of his name Floyd straightened up and stood directly in front of Mort's desk, as tall and straight as if he were reporting for duty as a deputy for the first time.

"Sheriff, like I told you before, when I first saw him, Hilly Davis was crouching down on the ground and measuring distances between the fence around Terranova's property and all sorts of trees and bushes, some inside the fence and some outside. I watched him for quite a while. Gorry, I couldn't figure out what he was doing." Floyd looked at the three of us as if perhaps we had an explanation.

Mort motioned with his hand, trying to pull the story from Floyd a little faster.

Floyd took a deep breath and went on. "When I asked him what he was doing, Hilly looked at me like it was so obvious that he couldn't understand why I asked. He said he was measuring to see how much of his land Mr. Terranova had stolen. Said he does it every night. Didn't make much sense to me for Hilly to keep on measuring once Terranova was dead, but I wasn't going to argue."

"And then . . ." Mort spoke through gritted teeth. His patience was wearing thin.

"Then I asked, was he there about this same time on the night that Terranova died and had he seen anyone or anything unusual? And, like I told you, he had." Floyd smiled, pleased that he'd gotten his story completed.

"Floyd, I know you told me. Now tell Mrs. F. what Hilly saw."

Floyd looked at me, slightly abashed. "I'm sorry, Mrs. Fletcher. I figured you knew. Hilly's been all over town telling anyone who will listen that he saw Evelyn Phillips walking around in the woods along Terranova's fence on the night that Terranova died. Hilly thought it was odd, her tiptoeing in the dark like that all by her lonesome. Then he saw her walk off toward the gym building—you know, the old pool house—and he figured maybe she was in cahoots with Terranova to steal more land."

"Then, when Terranova's body was discovered, Hilly . . ." I said.

"Hilly decided to tell me, the sheriff, and all and sundry that from what he'd seen Evelyn Phillips must have done the deed," Floyd concluded.

"Oh yes, you are right about that, Floyd. Hilly certainly has been spreading the word. I heard him myself this morning at Mara's referring to Evelyn as a murderer." I turned to Mort. "Surely you can caution him to be more . . . temperate in his choice of words. Perhaps you could remind him that slander might lead to his being liable for civil damages." I was looking for any way to squash the rumors and innuendo that were spreading through Cabot Cove like a flash flood.

Mort got the pensive look on his face that usually preceded his telling me I was off target. "Here's the problem, Mrs. F. On the whole, it is really looking bad for Evelyn. Without a shred of evidence she has been shrieking to anyone who will listen that Martin Terranova was trying to con Bertha Mae into giving him large sums of money. During her interview"—he waved an arm toward the back rooms of the office—"she spent half an hour trying to convince *me*, when all she has is unfounded accusations.

Now, I can look into Terranova's finances—he's a murder victim—but I can't just go ruffling through Bertha Mae's bank accounts on Evelyn's say-so."

I acknowledged that he certainly had a point there. "Perhaps I could talk to Bertha Mae. Just as a chatty neighbor, you understand."

"Well, I guess that couldn't hurt, might even help clear things up. But I gotta tell you, Mrs. F., I know you and Evelyn Phillips are friends but she is in deep weeds here. I am going to talk to her another time or two, but if nothing much changes I may have to declare her a person of interest in this murder case." Mort stood up and came around his desk. "Now, unless you need my help with something else, the library alarm system, for instance . . . ?"

I stood as well. "No, nothing at all. I know how busy you are."

"Floyd, would you give Mrs. F. a ride home?" Although Mort phrased it as a question both Floyd and I knew it was a directive, and I was glad for the ride, although I had another destination in mind.

As we pulled out of the parking lot, Floyd said, "You have no idea how the sheriff has struggled trying to interview Mrs. Cormier, but she can be a real stubborn lady. It was mighty nice of you to offer to talk to her, neighborly like. Maybe find out something we can't. Could turn out you are doing the sheriff quite a favor."

"Why, thank you, Floyd. And now I need a favor from you. Instead of going home, I'd like to stop and see Dan Andrews at the *Gazette* office. Would you mind dropping me there?"

"I'll just make a left at the next corner and have you there in a jiffy." Floyd gave me a knowing smile. "I guess you are thinking about helping the sheriff in more ways than having a little talk with Mrs. Cormier."

I thought it wisest not to answer.

Dan was sitting at his desk with his landline phone receiver tucked on his shoulder, a pen in one hand and a container of coffee in the other. When he gave me a nod to come in, the phone almost slipped and he jolted it back in place with his chin.

Behind his desk was the poster I always admired, the one that reminded everyone sitting in a visitor's chair that kindness is not weakness. I thought it was so appropriate. Although Dan was an extremely nice and gentle man, he was proving to be a hard-boiled reporter who was diligent in searching for facts—and that was the trait I was counting on this morning.

"Yes. Thank you . . . I appreciate it . . . Okay . . . Good-bye." Dan put down the phone and gestured to a chair. "Good morning, Jessica. I am in the middle of an investigation, so if my phone rings I have to answer it, but I always can steal a few minutes for you. What brings you by this morning?"

I decided to start at the beginning. As soon as I mentioned Hilly's name, Dan's face clouded over, and he continued to stare at his hands, which sat side by side, thumbs touching, on his desk while I described the scene in Mara's.

When I finished, he linked his fingers, turned his palms outward, and stretched his arms straight in front of him. "I haven't been here very long, but in that short time I've learned that Hilly Davis is bonkers. Why would anyone take him seriously?"

I agreed in part. "I am not sure that the townspeople are taking Hilly's accusation against Evelyn as gospel, but I can tell you that Mort Metzger believes that Evelyn has put herself in a tight spot by spreading around what Mort called 'unfounded accusations' that Martin Terranova is some sort of financial gigolo. He is considering naming her a person of interest in Terranova's murder."

"Just a minute there, Jessica. I have known Evelyn far longer than you or Mort or anyone else in Cabot Cove and I can guarantee that, as irritatingly loud and aggressive as she is, there is not a thread of violence in her." Dan's normally pale face turned redder than I'd ever seen it.

"I agree. That is why I've come to see you. Together we can find out more about Martin Terranova. His life didn't begin when he bought his house and set up shop in Cabot Cove. I recall that there was quite a buzz when he first arrived here. The girls in Loretta's were interested in the history of the eligible bachelor who'd come to town. The scuttlebutt was that he moved here from South Berwick. Perhaps we could drive down there—it's not that far—and ask around. Find out what people remember about him." I stopped short of begging.

Dan considered for a moment; then he picked up the receiver of his landline. "I have a story that may break as soon as today. Let me forward my calls to my cell phone, and then we are free to go."

He must have heard the relief in my voice when I thanked him. Certain as we both were that Evelyn Phillips was not a killer, we needed some evidence to overpower that of an eyewitness, even one as delusional as Hilly, and to counteract Evelyn's own behavior. I hoped we could find something or someone in Terranova's former hometown that could tell us something about him that could help us clear her name.

Dan set the GPS and plugged in his cell phone and we were off, riding south on an early spring day. Many of the roadside trees and bushes were beginning to show a small promise of the beauty that was soon to come.

Normally Dan was rather quiet, which I found surprising for a newspaper person—or perhaps I was so used to Evelyn's gregariousness that Dan's frequent silences jarred me.

I sat in the passenger seat admiring the roadside for miles on end before I decided to break the silence with an entirely different topic. "You mentioned a story that may become public today. Am I correct in assuming that it has nothing to do with Terranova or Evelyn?"

"I was wondering when your curiosity would get the best of you." Dan laughed, so I knew he wasn't annoyed by my question. "It's a much smaller story than murder, but it has the makings of a news story just the same. Someone I don't know well came to me a while ago with an uncertainty. One of those *Is this news or not?*"

"And is it?" I asked.

"At first I wasn't sure. The information was sketchy and the informant was edgy, two factors that could lead a reporter down the road to nowhere. Either the information turns out to be smoke and mirrors or the informant up and disappears." Dan sighed. "It's the nature of the business. A lot of the leads we get never come through."

"Oh, I understand completely. As a writer I often get what I think is a brilliant idea right up until I start to put words on paper, and then all the problems with the story line jump out at me like a flurry of snowballs flung by schoolkids who are hidden among the trees." I chuckled. Both events had happened to me far more than once. "You seem excited about this lead. How is it coming along?"

"For a while it did seem like we'd hit a dead end but lately when we speak, I sense the other person is more relaxed. We are getting close to what will be either a real front-page story or a few sentences in the back pages. Time will tell."

I asked more questions and commented politely on Dan's circuitous answers. I knew he was trying to protect his source and his story. Eventually we lapsed into a comfortable silence. It wasn't until we passed a sign that read WELCOME TO SOUTH BERWICK that I became super alert, anxious to learn what lay ahead.

Chapter Eleven

Two-story clapboard houses were scattered along the roadside, and it wasn't long before we hit what appeared to be the main business district, with shops on both sides of the street. Dan parked the car. The ride had taken longer than I thought it would, so I was glad to be on my feet and have a chance to stretch.

Dan raised his hand to shield his eyes from the sun, and turned his head this way and that. "What do you think, Jessica? Eeny, meeny, miny, moe. Into which store shall we go?"

I laughed. "Why, Dan, I had no idea you had the soul of a poet."

I looked at the storefronts across the street and said, "Well, a man who surrounds himself with all that workout gear is bound to own a few tools. Let's try the hardware store."

The store was jam-packed with every gadget, tool, and machine a handy or even a not-so-handy person might require. A half dozen shiny hand lawn mowers to the left of the door caught Dan's eye, which was enough to get the attention of the shopkeeper, a bulky man with a gray goatee who propelled toward us from behind the counter with lightning speed. "How do, folks? New in town, are you? I'm supposing you are going to need a lot of help to get your vegetable garden ready for spring."

"Actually"—I wanted to stop him before losing the imaginary sale he'd built up in his mind would make him unwilling to talk to us—"we're just passing through and thought we might stop to inquire about an old friend who lives here in South Berwick. Martin Terranova? I can't for the life of me remember his address. Neither can Dan."

I side-eyed an exasperated glance at Dan, who hung his head guiltily and shrugged. When a look of sympathy flashed across the shopkeeper's face, I knew our little charade had worked. In order to save a fellow man from the wrath of the woman in his life, the shopkeeper would cooperate in any way possible. I was sure the episode would give Dan and me a chuckle or two later on, but for now we were happy to be able to start the conversation that interested us.

The store owner stroked his beard as if he was pondering something wildly important. Then, at last, he shook his head. "Sorry, ma'am, but I've owned this store for nearly forty years and nobody by that name has ever bought so much as a thumbtack here. You might go next door to the dry cleaner's. Sooner or later everyone has to have his Sunday-go-to-meeting suit cleaned and pressed. I bet Jenny or Toby could help you out."

We thanked him and visited the dry cleaner's, followed by two take-out restaurants, one that served Mexican food while the other served mostly hamburgers and fries, with a few prewrapped sandwiches and pastries. We struck out everyplace we went. Not one person had ever heard of Martin Terranova.

When we got to a convenience store, the teenage counter girl, whose name tag read HI, I'M CHARLOTTE in bright blue letters on a white background, tried to be kind to two people she evidently thought were confused old folks who'd wandered into her store but should really find their way back to the nursing home before dusk.

"You know this is South Berwick, right? Is it possible your friend lives in North Berwick? Or even plain ole Berwick?" She twisted one of her shiny black braids around her index finger.

"I am reasonably certain he lives in South Berwick, or at least he used to. But I've forgotten my address book," I said while trying to look as helpless as possible.

"Well, I don't know who he might be, but I think if you went to the library, they might be able to help you. I mean, who doesn't have a library card? Besides, I don't know how they do it but—" She leaned across the counter and said in a highly confidential tone of voice, "Librarians know everything."

It was all I could do to keep from laughing. This was one conversation I definitely would have to share with Doris Ann, Cabot Cove's library director, as soon as I got back home.

Charlotte directed us to the library, which, once we turned the corner, was barely three blocks away.

As we walked along, Dan said, "Doesn't it strike you as odd that no one at the local shops knows Terranova? I mean, he didn't have a common name, and with all his focus on exercise, wherever he went he was likely to stand out in a crowd."

"I agree. You know, it is possible that he spread the word in Cabot Cove that he had moved from South Berwick when he never lived here at all. I mean, do you really think that everyone who knew you in your old neighborhood in New York would have forgotten you so quickly?"

"I certainly hope not. I'd like to think I left some impression, be it good or bad." Dan chuckled as he opened the library door. "Let's see what the people who 'know everything' have to say."

The library was a large tan building that looked like a church. Once we were inside, it was clear that the library had in fact been converted from an impressive, well-designed church. The main floor was bright and airy and the vaulted ceilings were trimmed with brown wood that emphasized the height of the arches. Long research tables were set up alongside computer pods, and comfortable-looking chairs were scattered around, inviting readers to settle in for an hour or so with their choice of thousands of books.

Several people, either checking out books or returning them, were on line at the circular librarian station, but we quickly found the information desk positioned between the display of gardening books and the beginning of the nonfiction stacks.

An attractive middle-aged woman with sepia skin, gray streaks in her curly dark hair, and wire-framed eyeglasses hanging on a chain around her neck asked in a clipped Caribbean cadence, "May I be of assistance?"

"I certainly hope so . . ." I was about to plunge into my looking-for-an-old-friend story line when a blowsy woman wearing a faded blue bucket hat and a New England Patriots sweatshirt pushed herself in front of me waving a copy of *Murder in a Minor Key*.

"J. B. Fletcher! I'm right—that's who you are, ain't you?" she demanded, and she pointed to my picture on the back cover of the book.

"Miss Laurette here introduced your books to the Tuesday Afternoon Book Club years ago, and now here you are in the flesh, as they say. Are you gonna do a readin' for us?"

"I'm sorry, no. Actually, I am here—"

Now the librarian interrupted. She stood and extended her hand. "Please, Mrs. Fletcher, forgive me. I didn't recognize you."

"There's no reason why you should. I am not here as an author, but merely as a neighbor from a few towns away looking for an old friend," I said as we shook hands. "Perhaps you know him? Martin Terranova?"

But the Patriots fan wasn't about to be left out of the conversation. She thrust her hand at me. "Iona Landers here. I am so happy to meet you, J. B. Fletcher."

Her handshake was so hearty that for a moment I thought I might end up with a dislocated shoulder. She talked nonstop about my books, mentioning both the killers and the detectives, amateur or otherwise, from at least three different story lines. She ended with "So, if you're not going to do a readin' today, when are you going to come for a nice long visit? We serve cupcakes at the Tuesday Afternoon Book Club, don't we, Miss Laurette?"

By now the librarian had come around her desk. "We certainly do, Iona." Then she turned to me. "And we'd be honored to have you attend our book club meeting. We would arrange to meet at any time that is convenient for you, but of course we realize how busy you are . . ."

I knew when she trailed off that I was supposed to respond, so I said, "I would be absolutely delighted to come back at a mutually convenient time to talk about mysteries with your book club members, who are, I am sure, as delightful as Iona."

I put as much wattage into my smile as I could, and then re-phrased my earlier question. "By any chance is my friend Martin Terranova a book club member?"

Laurette crinkled her brow and frowned. "No. He is not. In fact, it is possible he doesn't even have a library card. I don't recall ever hearing his name. Just let me take a look."

She went back to her desk and hit a few computer keys. "I am sorry, Mrs. Fletcher, but if your friend lives in South Berwick, he is not a library patron."

Once Laurette had given me her business card and I had promised to call so we could arrange a date for me to come to the library and do a reading, she said good-bye and offered to help a woman who'd been standing patiently behind us waiting for as-sistance.

Iona was not that easily evaded. She followed us, chattering all the way. I was sure she would have walked us to the car and per-haps tried to climb in, but when we reached the front door, she looked crestfallen when she realized that she held some library books that she'd not yet checked out and if she took another step the books would set off alarms.

As Dan and I left the building the last words we heard were Iona's reminder, "You promised to come back for a longer visit, J. B. Fletcher. I'm gonna hold you to it."

Dan, who had been quiet throughout our library visit, chuck-led. "The young lady at the convenience store was right. Librari-ans do know everything, and they are quick to teach their patrons about everything they know—especially the work of the famous writer J. B. Fletcher."

I tutted and said I didn't find him funny, but actually I did.

On the way back to Main Street, where we'd left the car, I was running out of ideas. I thought of the post office, which I was sure would be near the business district, but then I noticed a dental office across the street.

I pointed to the sign—SOUTH BERWICK FAMILY DENTISTRY—and asked Dan if he thought it was worth taking a chance.

Dan laughed. "Oh, definitely. I am sure my former dentist, Dr. Michaels back in Sunnyside, has never forgotten me—not with all the money I paid over the years to keep my teeth in shape."

The waiting room was quiet. A young man with earbuds firmly in place was seated in a visitor's chair and tapping his cell phone. A receptionist dressed in pink scrubs greeted us cheerily from behind the counter. "Welcome. How can I help you today?"

When I explained our mission, she hesitated for a few seconds and then leaned down and began to hit the keys on her desktop computer while muttering to herself. "Terranova. I know I've seen . . . Ah. I'm sorry. I thought the name was familiar, but our patient is a Joseph Terranova. We have no Martin listed." She sighed regretfully.

I, on the other hand, was elated at this first sign of real progress in our search for a connection to South Berwick. "Joseph! That must be the Uncle Joe that Martin speaks of so frequently. Perhaps if we could have his address he could help us get in touch with Martin."

Dejected that she had come so close to being helpful but couldn't actually complete the mission, she said, "I can't do that. Patient confidentiality. Dr. Sandusky would have my head on a plate."

"Well," I ventured, "perhaps we could wait to speak to the doctor? When I explain the circumstances, he might grant us some sort of exemption."

"I'm afraid that won't be possible. Mr. Dw— That is, the current patient only went into the exam room a few minutes ago, and Doctor is performing a lengthy procedure." Her tone turned brusque. "I am sorry I couldn't be more helpful. Good day."

When she dropped her head and began aimlessly shuffling papers on her desk I realized we had to surrender, so Dan and I headed out the door.

We were halfway home before I was able to admit to Dan how discouraged I was becoming. "I did think that the easiest way for us to get Mort's attention off Evelyn or Oscar or anyone else from Cabot Cove was to find someone in Terranova's past who had a grudge, a problem of some sort that could be considered a motive for murder. But as it is, we can't even ascertain that Martin Terranova *had* a past."

"We aren't giving up just yet, Jessica. I promise, at the first chance I get I will see what I can find out about Joseph Terranova who lives in South Berwick. Thanks to Dr. Sandusky's office we know he exists. He has teeth and a dental chart. Looking for him is a big step forward. We are no longer looking for a phantom."

Comforted as I was to know I wasn't alone in the search, I was so deep in thought trying to find a solution that I barely noticed that we had pulled up in front of my house until Dan said, "Looks like you have company."

Greta Pacyna was pacing nervously back and forth on the road by my front gate.

My instant response was "What now?"

Then I thought of Bertha Mae. Had something happened to her?

Dan asked if I wanted him to come in with me but I declined. "I took you away from your story investigation for too much time already. You'd best get back to it. Greta probably wants my help in getting her job back, or perhaps in getting another job altogether."

I got out of the car confident that a cup of tea and a ten-minute talk would have Greta out of my kitchen and on her way home. As I would soon learn, I was wildly off the mark.

Chapter Twelve

G reta, how nice to see you. I hope you weren't waiting too long," I said as Dan drove away.

"No. No. Mrs. Fletcher, it is fine. I need advice." Greta turned her head this way and that as if afraid she would be overheard. "I don't know who to trust but everyone in town speaks of you as honest, helpful, and kind. Right now I need a friend with all those qualities."

Her face was flushed with anxiety and her eyes pleaded for a rescue. In spite of the fact that I had my own worries, which were compounded by my fruitless trip to South Berwick, there was nothing for me to do but invite her to come inside.

I put the kettle on the stove, and when I offered, Greta opted for green tea rather than Earl Grey or Irish breakfast.

I set the table, and while we waited for our tea to steep I observed that she seemed to be somewhat upset, and that was the opening she needed.

"Oh, Mrs. Fletcher, I am so worried. I don't know what to do. If anyone can guide me, I think it is you." Greta began to cry with great, heaving sobs.

I went to the cabinet for more napkins, placed them in front of her, and sat quietly, waiting for her tears to subside and her story to begin.

It took a while, but eventually her crying slowed down. After two or three hiccups, she dropped the napkin she'd been shredding between her fingers and picked up a fresh one to wipe her eyes. Then she took a sip of tea.

When she was silent, I said, "You mentioned that you need guidance and you think I may be of some help . . ."

"Oh yes, yes, I do. Mrs. Fletcher, you travel around the country, around the world even, and in the books you write murders are committed and killers are brought to justice. So many people here in Cabot Cove have a narrow vision. They believe traveling to Portland is a long trip or that snatching a doughnut from Charlene Sassi's cooling tray is a capital crime. You are not like that. You understand a bigger world."

She relaxed ever so slightly, as if she had explained everything to me and I could take it from there.

I was more befuddled than ever. Why wait in front of my house only to say that she believed me to be more cosmopolitan than most of my neighbors?

"That is kind of you to say, Greta, but I am wondering, how is it you think I can be of help to you?" I needed her to unravel my confusion.

"Mrs. Fletcher, I think you know my husband, Lucius," Greta began, then stopped dead.

As soon as I realized I was supposed to answer, I did. "Of

course I do. He fixed my back fence after that last hurricane flattened it. And he did a superb job."

Greta gave me a grateful smile. "Oh yes, Lucius is very good with his hands. Give him some tools and a few pieces of wood and he can make miracles."

"Is there a problem about some work he has done? Does Lucius need a reference?" I was perplexed. Why were we embroiled in so much drama if all Greta wanted was to ask for a note that I would have no qualms about writing?

"Oh, no, this problem is much more difficult." Greta brought the napkin to her eyes once again, and then said, "It is about Martin Terranova, the man who was killed. There was an . . . incident."

This was going to be far more serious than I'd first thought. "Take your time," I said. Although I was anxious to get the facts, I wanted to get them in perfectly straight order.

Greta nodded, wiped her eyes, and said, "I know I shouldn't have told him, but he could see how shaken I was . . ."

I reached over and gave her a gentle pat on her arm. "I always find that the beginning is the best place to start."

"You know that Bertha Mae and Martin Terranova were very friendly, don't you? He walked in and out of her house as if he lived there. And she—well, she gushed over him as if he was . . . I honestly am not quite sure what she thought of him, but I can tell you I'm pretty sure it was not the way a woman of her age thinks of a man his age.

"One day I was gathering Bertha Mae's laundry and when I went to the kitchen to round up the napkins and dish towels I was not completely surprised to find Martin standing in front of the refrigerator holding the door wide open. When he saw me he asked why there was no beer. I told him Bertha Mae doesn't drink beer. You know, Mrs. Fletcher, she likes a glass of sherry or sometimes a little wine, but she has never favored beer."

"That's very true. I've never seen her drink a beer," I said. "Did the lack of beer in the refrigerator make him angry?"

"Wicked angry, and also mean. He grabbed me by the arm and said that he told Bertha Mae he liked a cold beer now and again. He was sure she added it to her shopping list, so where was the beer? He asked if I drank it. When I tried to pull away he pushed me up against the dishwasher and tried to kiss me. I tried to push him away but he is—was—so strong. Then he said that I better be careful how I treated him, because Bertha Mae did whatever he asked her to do. He told me he would not have to say much to get me fired."

I was appalled. "How terrible for you. How did it finally end?"

"He was trying to pull me closer and I was pushing away when we heard a knock at the back door. It was that nice young delivery boy from the Fruit and Veg, Peter something. Anyway, I ran to the door, and when I let Peter into the kitchen, Martin had disappeared. He went to some other room, and by the time I finished putting away the groceries and looked for him, Martin was nowhere in the house. Believe me—for my own safety, I checked."

"Did you tell Bertha Mae about this?" I asked.

"No. I didn't want to upset her, and to be honest, I was afraid she wouldn't believe me. It turns out I did something much worse. When I got home, I told Lucius." A tear rolled slowly down her cheek.

Now I could clearly see why Greta thought she had reason to worry. "What did Lucius do?"

"It was awful. I still have nightmares when I think of what could have happened. I never should have told Lucius. He flew into a rage and practically pushed me into the car. He drove like a madman from our house to Terranova's. When we got there, the gym was dark but the house was well lit, so Lucius banged on the front door, and as soon as Martin opened it Lucius growled like a grizzly bear and threatened to kill Martin if he ever touched me again." Greta buried her head in her arms and began wailing. When she looked up again, she said, "Oh, Mrs. Fletcher, what did I do?"

"You can't blame yourself for anything that happened. If anyone behaved badly it was Martin Terranova. He had no right to threaten you and absolutely no right to touch you. It wouldn't surprise me to learn that, wanting some sort of childish revenge, he put the idea of firing you into Bertha Mae's head."

"I never thought of that, but you are right. I bet he hid Bertha Mae's medicines and whispered in her ear that I was trying to kill her." She shuddered. "It's too late now to do anything about that, but I am worried about Lucius. He might have a bit of a temper, but I *know* him. We have been married for nine years. He would never knowingly hurt another human being, no matter what that person had done."

"I see." And from what I'd seen of her husband, I was sure Greta was right. "Greta, it would probably be best for you and your husband to stop by and tell Sheriff Metzger what happened."

She began shaking her head violently.

"Settle down. Hear me out," I said softly. "We don't know yet exactly what happened in Terranova's gym the night he died. But I am confident that the sheriff will resolve this case before long and that it will have nothing to do with you or your husband.

Still, wouldn't you rather speak to Mort now and be done with it than wait for some neighbor to recall hearing Lucius threaten Martin as he did?"

"I guess that does make sense," Greta whispered, more to herself than to me.

"That's the girl. Now finish up your tea and go talk to Lucius. You will both feel better when you get this story off your chests and into Mort's notebook."

We finished our tea and Greta went home, a much calmer woman than she'd been when I found her pacing by my front gate. I kicked off my shoes, poured myself another cup of tea, took an orange from my fruit bowl, and began to peel it. I needed a moment or two to plan the rest of my day, but when I heard a knock on my back door and Maeve O'Bannon popped her head in, I knew planning would have to wait awhile longer.

"Are you too busy for a bit of a chin-wag?" she asked.

"Not at all. I was just about to have my second cup of tea and an orange. I know you are not partial to green tea, but the kettle is still hot and I have some Irish breakfast tea."

"Now, that is a cuppa I would fancy." Her smile broadened.

Maeve sat down, and when I'd put her teacup in front of her she waited for me to settle back into my chair before she spoke. "Wasn't that Greta Pacyna I saw leaving a few minutes ago? I've been hearing around and about that she is in some sort of trouble with Bertha Mae. What's worse, I heard that her husband had a run-in with that gym instructor Martin Terranova, who was killed sometime after."

Maeve was only repeating what, I guessed, the entire town

knew. Still, it bothered me that such strident gossip had found its way to my kitchen table.

I measured my words carefully. "There was some sort of mix-up regarding Bertha Mae's medicine, which appeared to be missing but actually wasn't. Mort's deputy Floyd McCallum and Greta found the missing meds scattered around Bertha Mae's house, but by then Bertha Mae was totally agitated, so she dismissed Greta, who was an easy target. I'm sure she would have tried to get Mort to terminate Floyd if she thought she could get away with it. We all know how she gets when she is in a tizzy."

"And there, you've made my point." For emphasis, Maeve smacked the tabletop lightly. "Bertha Mae needs someone to keep an eye on her. So I ask you, now that you've had a nice little chat with Greta, do you think she'd be interested in regaining her old position as Bertha Mae's housekeeper? Nothing so very different from how it was until a few days ago. Greta would continue to arrange her own hours, do her household tasks in the order she finds suitable, and, more to the point, she would keep an eye on Bertha Mae for a varying number of hours most days a week."

"Given the circumstances, that is quite a difficult question to answer," I said. "I never even considered the possibility."

"Ah, but has Greta considered it? That is the real question," Maeve replied.

I shook my head. "I am afraid it is not that simple. Greta is not the one in charge. Bertha Mae would have to offer the job before Greta could even think about taking it."

Maeve raised her eyebrows and stared at me for close to a minute as if she was waiting for the light in my brain to dawn. When she realized it hadn't, she sighed. "Don't you worry about Bertha Mae offering Greta her job back. I am sure I can see to it that the offer will come, but not until I am sure that it would be warmly received."

At that point I was dumbfounded. To my knowledge they were casual acquaintances. What made Maeve think she would have that strong an influence on Bertha Mae? "Maeve, I agree with you that Bertha Mae needs to have someone check in on her, as well as help with the household chores. The only person who doesn't agree with you is Bertha Mae."

Maeve pushed back her chair and stood. "Jessica, as soon as you can tell me that Greta will agree to go back into Bertha Mae's employ, it will take me less than two shakes of a lamb's tail to arrange for the offer to be made. I am already working on it. Now, it is past time that I get back to my sewing. I promised Dr. Leung that I would make puppets of doctors, nurses, and technicians for the children's wing at the hospital, and I am a day or two behind. Can't let the children down. Thank you kindly for the tea." And she was gone.

After she left, I sat staring at Maeve's empty chair. If Maeve could wave her magic wand and get Bertha Mae to call Greta back to work, I was fairly certain that Greta would be glad to return, at least until doing so gave the scandalmongers of Cabot Cove a reason to rev up the gossip about the nasty confrontation she'd caused between her husband, Lucius, and the now-deceased Martin Terranova.

Chapter Thirteen

I admit to feeling distracted for the rest of the day. Try as I might to focus on my research, my mind kept drifting back to South Berwick. If that was Martin Terranova's residence before he moved to Cabot Cove, why didn't anyone there remember him? And who was Joseph Terranova? Were they related?

I was able to focus on my work only after I promised myself that I would devote an hour or two the next morning to what I was starting to think of as "the Mystery Man of South Berwick."

I had a restless night, but whether it was because of all the chaotic thoughts scrambling around in my head or the unrelenting thunder that began shortly after three o'clock, I couldn't be sure.

Rain was still coming down in torrents when I realized I had no hope of further sleep and got out of bed. The clock on my nightstand read six twenty but it felt more like four a.m. I pulled on my bootie slippers and fleece robe and went downstairs to raise the thermostat a notch or two and put on a pot of coffee—extra strong.

In my recliner I snuggled under my old and worn but much-loved afghan, sipped my coffee, and tried to put my thoughts about the Terranova murder in order. If this was in a book I was writing, my protagonist would always have a list of suspects, complete with clues aplenty, so I decided that writing one would be my first step. I picked up the notepad and pen that were on the coffee table, flipped over the top page, which held the few scrawled lines of a half-completed grocery list, and wrote *SUSPECTS* across the top of the next clean page.

Unfortunately, I didn't have much information to sift through. I was sure that Evelyn Phillips was Mort's number one suspect. She had been both loud and hardheaded about her distrust of Martin Terranova's excessively fawning behavior toward Bertha Mae. Personally, I thought Bertha Mae's response was more of a problem. Although none of this made Evelyn a suspect in my book, I wrote her name, followed by a question mark.

The next name that came to mind was Oscar Cisneros. I wrote his name under Evelyn's, although I was far more worried about his being labeled a thief than a murderer. But after hearing Tim Purdy's story, I had to admit that Martin Terranova had ample opportunity to steal Bertha Mae's candlesticks and plant them in Oscar's shed, since everyone knew that Oscar spent his days wandering around Cabot Cove and the surrounding area looking for resale items. And if Oscar had learned that he'd been set up by Martin—well, I couldn't believe Oscar was capable of murder, though I was sure some people thought he was.

I would not even have considered Lucius Pacyna, since his disagreement with Terranova was a private, nonviolent one, except for the fact that yesterday Maeve mentioned that she had heard that Lucius "had a run-in with" Martin Terranova, so if it hadn't already, word of the incident would eventually reach the sheriff even if Greta hadn't followed my advice and gone to speak with Mort.

I walked back to the kitchen and refilled my coffee cup. I had written the names of three people on my list, but I wouldn't seriously consider any one of them to be a stone-cold killer. There had to be someone else.

I settled back into my recliner, picked up the pad, turned the page, and wrote *UNKNOWN ADVERSARIES* in large letters. Perhaps someone had gotten seriously injured while training at Terranova's gym. I could ask Seth if he'd heard of any such incident. I wrote *gym members* next to the number one.

For my second unknown, I focused on money. People have been known to kill one another to clear debts, retaliate for thefts, secure inheritances—all sorts of reasons. I decided I would stop by the bank and see if I could find any information about Terranova's finances. Then I thought it was unlikely that any banker would give out any information about a client. I might have better luck talking to Jasper Boxley, who was, to my knowledge, Cabot Cove's sole loan shark—although he preferred the term "private banker." If Terranova was in dire need of cash, Jasper— or Jazzy, as he preferred to be called—would know about it.

My third unknown was the elusive Joseph Terranova. I wondered if Dan had some luck finding any information about him. I glanced across the room at my telephone, then realized it was far too early to call. Anxious as I was for information, I did remember Dan had his own hot story that he was investigating. I had dragged him away from it yesterday; perhaps I should give him a little breathing room today.

I put my notepad aside and drained my coffee cup. It was time to get ready for the day. As I headed upstairs to shower and change, I wondered if Mort or the coroner's office had been able to locate Martin Terranova's next of kin.

When I came back downstairs the rain showed no sign of letting up. My morning exercise would have to be indoors. Hoping I had timed it right, I turned on the television and was pleased that an episode of *Step It Up with Steph* had just begun. Today's workout was one of her energy boosters, and I was able to get right in pace with the ladies.

By the time the session was finished, my energy was indeed boosted and my brain had organized my day in some semblance of order. I did a few extra stretches for good measure and was washing my coffeepot when the telephone rang.

"Jessica. How dare you and Dan Andrews go on an investigation without me?" Evelyn Phillips. I supposed I should be grateful that the ferocious rain and wind had prevented her from rousing Demetri at some ungodly hour to drive her here.

"Hello, Evelyn. What can I do for you this morning?" I said as pleasantly as possible.

"You can assure me that the next time you and Dan go scouting for clues and criminals you will take me along for the ride," she said.

Rather than apologize for a spontaneous trip that produced no news whatsoever regarding Martin Terranova, I merely said, "Of course, Evelyn. We'd be happy to have you."

"Good thing. Dan may be the editor of the *Gazette*, but Cabot

Cove will always be my town. I told Dan this morning that I am the investigative reporter on the Terranova murder case and he'd better not forget it."

And she hung up, which was just as well, because I was totally irritated and not at all sure what I would have said next.

I sat with my hand still on the telephone receiver and realized there was one call I should have made yesterday. I dialed Joe Turco's office.

Young as she was, Joe's assistant, Lena, had a voice that was both professional and cheerful, a combination that many secretaries with far more experience had yet to achieve.

"Oh, Mrs. Fletcher, I am sorry, but Mr. Turco is in court this morning. Is there any message?"

I thought carefully about how to phrase what I wanted, and I decided to turn it into an offer of help instead.

"Yes. Please tell him that I understand he is representing Oscar Cisneros, and that I called to offer assistance in any way that I can, perhaps with fees or some such."

I was sure my offer surprised her, but she maintained her composure, recorded my telephone number, and hung up.

At that moment my cell phone rang. I tracked the sound to the kitchen counter and answered.

Seth Hazlitt said, "Morning, Jessica, and it's a nasty one, but rain or no rain, I have to ask, how did you manage your morning bike ride?" And without giving me time to answer, he laughed, acknowledging how ridiculous his question was.

"Seth, you're just being foolish." I tried to sound stern but he knew better and came back with an appropriate rejoinder.

"So, tell me, Jess, if you are so very busy researching your latest book, how is it you had time to go a-rambling practically to the Maine–New Hampshire border yesterday? Half of my patients expected to see a full report in this morning's *Gazette*, but I guess you and Editor Dan failed to come up with a scoop. So as a last resort they are asking me, because even the likes of Margaret Jacobson heard all about it before I did. Something about her book club meeting."

"I have no idea how word of our trip spread throughout Cabot Cove, but I am not the least bit surprised. Why don't you drop by tonight about six and I'll fill you in?" I said, and added as an enticement, "I'm making roast chicken and vegetables for dinner."

"With carrots?" he asked.

"Plenty of carrots."

Seth asked me to hold on and I heard him put down the receiver, and when he came back he hurried me off the phone. "I have to learn to lock the front door when I'm between office hours. I knew I heard someone walking around the waiting room. It's Pierce Collymore. I'd better find out what he wants. See you later, Jess."

I'd made a spontaneous offer to make one of Seth's favorite dishes in the hope that during our dinner conversation he could offer some wisdom when I told him how odd our trip to South Berwick was.

I took a quick look at the contents of my refrigerator and pantry. While I did have a cut-up roaster ready to go, I was going to need fresh rosemary and thyme, baby red potatoes, and a large bunch of carrots if Seth was going to be happy with the dinner.

As I was writing my grocery list I remembered how Mort raved yesterday about the pies that the Fruit and Veg was ordering from Charlene Sassi, so I added *pie of the day* and called in my order.

Jenny, the Fruit and Veg telephone clerk who often took my order, promised me delivery by three. "I hope that is all right, Mrs. Fletcher. Normally with orders called in this time of day Peter would have it to you lickety-split, but in this cold, wet weather we are getting more calls than usual. I am afraid we may even wind up with a backlog."

"Three o'clock will be fine. I have met Peter several times and he strikes me as unflappable, so I am sure the deliveries will go smoothly," I said.

In fact, I thought to myself, three o'clock would leave me a wide swath of time to finish my research on San Diego and its surroundings. I might even have time to begin outlining my synopsis.

I went into the dining room, powered up my computer, sat down, and got to work. I had no idea how long I had been immersed in the sunny skies and the bright blue Pacific Ocean of the beach at La Jolla Cove when my telephone rang and startled me back to wet and gloomy Cabot Cove.

"Jessica, hi. It's Joe Turco. Lena said you wanted to speak to me regarding Oscar Cisneros. If you have something to say that can help with his case, I'd rather we speak in person."

I was surprised that after his cheery hello he turned business-like immediately. Generally we chatted for a few minutes before we got down to serious conversation, but perhaps that was only when I was speaking as his client. In Oscar's case I was clearly an interloper.

"Oh, Joe, I only wish that I could be helpful in the way you mean, but sadly, I have no information that could help you clear Oscar. The reason I called is that Mort told me you were instrumental in getting Oscar released from custody." I hesitated. I didn't want to offend Joe, so I was careful in phrasing my thoughts. "I know how valuable your time is and I am perfectly willing to pay any and all of Oscar's legal fees."

"That is very kind of you, and I will be sure to let Oscar know that at least one person in this town has faith in him, but you needn't worry. I am taking on Oscar's case pro bono. I assure you, if I didn't my father would spin in his grave so fast and furiously that the world's seismologists would think there was a major earthquake in the cemetery of St. Luke's Episcopal Church."

"Your father? I don't understand," I said. I remembered Joe's father, Henry, quite well. We served on the library board together until he became ill. From what I recalled, he had grown up on a dairy farm just behind Clark Proctor's. He graduated from the University of Maine School of Law and set up what became a prestigious law practice in Augusta. The Turco family spent most weekends in a saltbox up on the ridge overlooking Cabot Cove for as long as I could remember until first Joe's father and then his mother passed away.

"Although their adult lives took very different paths, my father and Oscar were close friends since childhood and remained so until my father passed," Joe said.

To say I was taken aback would be an understatement. If memory served me correctly, I could not recall ever seeing Joe's father and Oscar so much as exchange a nod of hello.

I said, "Well, then, I am doubly sure Oscar is in good hands. Just remember that should Oscar's expenses become too much for you to handle, my offer stands."

Joe thanked me again for my concern and hung up before I could ask any further questions. And I certainly had some.

Chapter Fourteen

Although my conversation with Joe about his father's relationship with Oscar had left me a bit disconcerted, I pushed it out of my mind and went back to finishing up the day's research. I worked for a while, but questions about the relationship between Oscar and Joe's father kept popping into my head. Questions like why one was so successful while the other spent his life being known as "the junk man." And what kept their friendship as solid as Joe claimed it to be? None of this had anything to do with Martin Terranova's death or Bertha Mae's candlesticks, but still they niggled at my brain and interfered with my work.

In the hopes of finding answers to clear my mind once and for all, I picked up the telephone and dialed the library. When I got Doris Ann on the line, I told her about my conversation with Joe Turco.

"When I offered to help financially, Joe refused my offer in no uncertain terms and told me that his father and Oscar were life-long friends, so he was honor bound to represent Oscar pro bono."

"Well, I think that was truly kind of you, offering to help Oscar like that when so many of our townspeople are eager to hang him from the yardarm, but if Joe declined, I suggest you leave well enough alone," Doris Ann said in her best "meeting adjourned" tone of voice.

"Oh, I agree wholeheartedly," I said. "Joe is an excellent lawyer and I am delighted that he wants to help to clear Oscar of any wrongdoing, but what I am wondering about is the family history. You knew Henry so much better than I did. Do you recall what drew Oscar and Henry together so that they remained close friends for all of Henry's life? What could have happened between them in their past? What was so strong that Henry handed the mantle and the responsibility of friendship down to his son?"

"Two men, the same age, who grew up in the farmlands on the edge of town. They probably were classmates as well as playmates. I remember a time when that would be enough to forge a lifelong bond," Doris Ann said.

When I thought of the high school and college friends with whom I still kept in reasonably close contact, I had to agree with her.

Doris Ann reminded me of the change in dates for the Friends of the Library meeting and ended the call.

I walked to my front window, pulled back the curtain, and watched the rain splat against the glass. There hadn't been a moment's letup all day. I told myself that the deep soaking the ground was getting now would do wonders for my roses come late May, early June. I'd done all I could to decipher the mystery of Henry and Oscar. I was determined to move on with my research chores, and I decided I needed a cup or two of tea to get me through the rest of this gloomy afternoon.

I went into the kitchen and put the kettle on the stove, then took out a much-favored teapot festively decorated with hollyhocks, and my trusty hot plate. I filled my tea infuser with a strong blend of black and green tea that I'd picked up at the last fundraiser for the new children's wing at the hospital. It was surprisingly bold and strong. Just the ticket for a day like today. Once I'd dropped the infuser into my teapot and poured boiling water up to the rim, I set the pot on the hot plate to steep.

I thought I'd done enough reading about San Diego for today. I was sure I had the details for the setting of the story firmly in my head. It was time to move on to the actual crimes. At this stage of planning I was certain there would be two murders committed by the same person. I already knew that the murderer would bludgeon his first victim in the colorful and historic Cabrillo National Monument Park. That murder would cause a citywide stir.

As the story moves along a character who was a friend of both the murderer and the victim believes he has discovered a number of clues and hints that point to the killer, and he confides his fears to a close friend. Unfortunately that friend happens to be the real killer. Once that conversation takes place the killer decides he has no choice but to kill victim number two and settles on poison as his weapon. As it turns out, victim number two had the wrong person in mind but realizes that only with his dying breath as he sits across the kitchen table from the killer. I hadn't yet decided whether it would be too dramatic to have as the victim's dying words *It was you . . . but I thought it was . . .* I'd have to reflect on that awhile longer.

In any event, I needed to choose a poison that would suit the scene as I envisioned it. I poured myself a cup of tea, gathered several books about poisons from my bookshelf, and sat in the recliner, reading and making notes. I'd narrowed my possibilities to three different flavorless, easy-to-dissolve poisons so I could avoid that good old standby arsenic, when I heard a *rat-tat-tat* on the back door. I looked at the clock: ten minutes to three. My food delivery.

I hurried to open the door, and when I saw how cold and wet he looked, I insisted Peter Whitlock come in out of the rain at least for a few minutes.

"Oh, no, Mrs. Fletcher. Here, please just take the box of groceries. I'm soaked. I'll drip all over your floor," Peter said.

"You never mind my floor. Come in. You can put the box on the table." I pulled a substantial wad of paper towels off the roll hanging under my cabinets. "Dry your face and blot your hair while I pour you a nice, hot cup of tea."

Peter dried his face and head as best he could with the paper towels. "Thanks, Mrs. Fletcher, but I haven't time for tea. Plenty of other folks are still waiting on their food. I better get going."

"Well, if you don't have time to sit and warm up, I have an insulated water bottle we can use." I reached into the cabinet next to the sink, then held the bottle high. "I'll fill this. You can take it with you and drink your hot tea on the road."

"I couldn't possibly—" Peter began, but I cut him off.

"You certainly can and you will. I am in no hurry to have this bottle back—I have several more. You can drop it off the next time you bring my groceries by."

"This is awfully kind of you. I started my rounds with a full container of coffee, but that didn't stay hot for very long," Peter said. "Speaking of kind people, Oscar—you know, the one they call the junk man—was really generous to me when I first got to town. I rent a room at McNulty's Boardinghouse, but it's really sparse. Oscar sold me some doodads and necessities, like a reading lamp and a cushy chair, that made my place take on a homey atmosphere, and when he saw I was low on cash, he let me have some items on credit until I got settled in this job. Didn't even charge me interest.

"Mrs. Fletcher, I've heard around town that you spoke up to Sheriff Metzger for Oscar. I'm sure it will help him to have someone of your stature on his side." He wavered for a few seconds, then, decision made, took the insulated bottle, said, "Thanks for the tea," and was gone.

While I put the groceries away I smiled as I thought about Peter's interaction with Oscar. It reminded me of Viola Shaw's experience and made me all the more certain that every town needed an Oscar Cisneros. Then I dove back into my research until it was time to start preparing the roast chicken and vegetables for dinner.

The pungent floral and woodsy aroma of rosemary and citrus thyme drifted from my oven and gave the kitchen a comfortable feel. I finished setting the table just as Seth came through the back door, looking as though he'd swum all the way from his office to my side gate. He pulled off the bucket hat that he generally wore only when he went fishing and looked around for a place to put it.

"Here, let me have your hat and raincoat. I moved the coat tree near the fireplace and lit a fire about an hour ago. Your clothes should be dry and toasty by the time you're ready to head home," I said.

Seth rubbed his hands together and moved closer to the stove. "'Dry and toasty' sounds as good as this kitchen smells."

He opened the oven, peeked inside, and drew a deep breath. "Smells ready to eat, woman. Don't tell me I'll have to wait any more than a minute for my chicken and carrots." He moved to the sink. "Should be ready by the time I finish washing my hands."

"Seth, you can see for yourself the oven is set on warm. Dinner has been ready for a good fifteen minutes," I said, even though I was well aware that "Where's My Food?" was a game that Seth always enjoyed playing.

We sat at the table, and before I had finished my salad Seth had inhaled his chicken and vegetables and was asking for more. "Heavy on the carrots, please."

I filled his plate, and when I set it in front of him I couldn't resist saying, "Save some room for dessert."

"I thought you spent the day knee-deep in research for your next book. Are you telling me that you had time enough to bake?" Seth looked surprised but pleased.

"There was no need for me to bake. The other day Mort mentioned that Charlene Sassi has begun supplying the Fruit and Veg with fresh-made pies, so I asked to have whatever the pie of the day was added to my order. You'll be pleased to know it was one of your favorites—coconut cream."

As if by mutual agreement, after we finished our dinner Seth cleared the table while I poured the coffee and sliced the pie. Seth said, "You know, Jess, after the day I've had, I really needed to relax with delicious food and a good friend. Now, this would be a perfect evening if you'd give me a chance to beat you in a game of chess."

I immediately asked for a rain check. "I'm afraid I wouldn't be much competition. I spent the day stretching my brain from here to San Diego and back again. Why don't we take our coffee and pie into the living room and enjoy the fireplace?"

I curled up in the recliner while Seth took his usual spot on the couch. We both stared at the fire, which I always found mesmerizing. Fearful that I would nod off, I sat up a little straighter and asked Seth if he knew the history of the close ties between Henry Turco and Oscar Cisneros.

"Why, Jess, I'm surprised you don't recall. About fifteen years ago Oscar had a medical scare. Turned out to be appendicitis. Anyway, he stopped in to see me and I determined that with the snow coming down at a fierce rate and another six to eight inches in the forecast, it was too chancy to transport him to the Veterans Administration hospital in Togus, so I admitted him to Cabot Cove Hospital and John Davidson did the surgery. Oscar was fit as a fiddle in no time." Seth took a sip of coffee and continued.

"The day after the surgery, Henry Turco came to see me. Offered to pay Oscar's medical bills. I told him there was no need. I'd already sorted everything with John and the hospital. Oscar didn't owe a penny. That's when Henry told me the story. It seems that one Saturday morning when they were eleven years old, Henry and Oscar decided to go ice fishing over on Taggert Pond. When they got there they found that, due to a couple of warm days about midweek, the Department of Inland Fisheries had posted 'No Fishing' signs and 'Thin Ice' warnings all around the pond. But the boys were eleven and they were invincible."

I could see the story was leading to some sort of calamity.

"Long story short, the boys walked toward their favorite fishing spot, about twenty yards out, and were halfway there when the ice broke and Henry went down. When his head bobbed up, he was a good three or four feet from the edge of the ice hole his fall had opened. He was scared and he was freezing. He looked around and there was Oscar, lying on the ice and sliding his fishing pole toward Henry. Oscar was screaming, 'Grab on! Hang on!' Henry told me he was too cold to even yell back and his hands felt frozen, unable to move. But Oscar kept shouting and inching closer and closer to the rim of the ice. Henry said his brain finally snapped to reality when Oscar yelled, 'If you don't come out, I'll come in there after you.' That's when Henry was finally able to force his hands around the fishing pole and Oscar pulled him to safety."

"So Oscar Cisneros saved Henry Turco's life all those years ago. I had no idea," I said.

"Most people don't. Anyway, Henry told me that since that day he'd always tried to live a life worth saving. And throughout their adult years, although Oscar always refused any money or help of any kind, Henry always kept an eye," Seth said.

"Sort of like a guardian angel," I mused. "And that is why Joe Turco is determined to save Oscar now."

I sat, lost in thought, for a minute, and then I sighed. "Seth, I can tell you one thing. Joe may be able to keep Oscar out of jail, but saving his reputation so that he can continue his placid life here in Cabot Cove is going to be a lot more difficult."

Chapter Fifteen

By the time I glanced outside the next morning, the sun was shining brightly and the street was as dry as if it hadn't rained in months. My yard and garden were an entirely different matter. I pulled on my rain boots and tramped around in the mud checking for damage to my plants and bushes.

Maeve O'Bannon waved from her yard. "Early morning to you, Jessica. How's the garden looking after yesterday's storm?"

"Not nearly as bad as I feared it might. And yours?"

"Same good news here. We had a lucky go of it—that's for sure," Maeve said.

I agreed and then we both continued about our business, picking up broken twigs and fallen leaves while trimming the partially broken branches hanging from bushes here and there.

Curious as I was about whatever secret weapon Maeve believed she had that would entice Bertha Mae to rehire Greta Pacyna, I decided not to ask about it just yet. I'd promised Mort

Metzger that I would talk to Bertha Mae and try to discover more details about her relationship with Martin Terranova. I didn't want to agitate her by unintentionally bringing up anything I might learn from Maeve.

Once my yard was tidied, I left my rain boots by the back door and decided the day was so glorious I would ride my bicycle to Bertha Mae's house. Although the round trip would be quite a bit longer than my normal morning ride, I thought it would be a good opportunity to work off that delicious coconut cream pie Seth and I had enjoyed last evening. And since I did have a mission to accomplish, getting in some extra exercise on my way was a win-win.

Following the advice I'd once given to Evelyn, I waited a good three or four minutes between each tap I made on the ancient push button that rang Bertha Mae's doorbell before I finally heard her ask, from behind the still-closed door, who was ringing the bell.

I tried to sound as cheery as possible. "Bertha Mae, good morning. It's me, Jessica Fletcher. I thought we might have a cup of tea and a chat."

I heard the lock disengage and Bertha Mae opened the door, but barely. She held it less than a foot wide and stood back away from the sunlight that was pouring in through that small opening. From what I could see, her hair was no longer circled in a scarf-wrapped bun; rather, it was tousled as if it hadn't been combed in a good while. Her face was pasty and wan, which made her red-rimmed eyes stand out like those of the Chinese tree viper snake I'd once researched as a murder weapon.

"Jessica, good of you to come visit, but I am not up to company just now." She started to close the door, but once I touched it with my outstretched hand the door went still. Bertha Mae was clearly out of strength.

"I am sorry to hear that," I said, putting as much sympathy into my voice as I could. "To be honest, I rode my bicycle here all the way from my house and, well, I am far too tired to ride home again without stopping for a rest."

I counted on my feeling that Bertha Mae was too well mannered to close the door in the face of my entreaty. It took only a few moments for her to prove I was correct.

She opened the door and then turned, and with slumped shoulders and shuffling feet, she walked toward her living room. I followed and was surprised that the room, which was generally bright and sunny, was barely made visible by the artificial light from one lamp that sat on an end table. Heavy brocade drapes that usually stood as sentries at either side of the high, wide windows overlooking Bertha Mae's backyard were tightly shut, deliberately severing the indoors from the outdoors.

"The kitchen is messier than it used to be when Greta . . . I mean, when I had help. We will have to have our tea in here. I hope you don't mind waiting alone for a minute. Please make yourself comfortable. I'll be right back."

As soon as Bertha Mae left the room, I opened the drapes just a bit and peered across Bertha Mae's slate terrace and backyard. Martin Terranova's property looked quite forlorn, cordoned off as it was by crime-scene tape. I wondered how long Mort would keep it isolated that way. When I heard Bertha Mae's footsteps coming along the hallway, I let the drapes fall from my hands and scurried back to the couch.

"Our tea is steeping. I thought it would be rude to leave you alone for very long, so I fetched some slices of pound cake that

Evelyn Phillips brought me yesterday." Bertha Mae set the cake, along with two dessert plates, napkins, and forks, on the coffee table. Then she walked over to crease a fold in one of the drapes that I had misshapen when I closed them so hastily. "I don't know why people think Evelyn is so ornery. She has been very kind to me."

Of course she has, I thought. *Evelyn sees you as a source for what could be an explosive news story.*

Fortunately, Bertha Mae wasn't seeking an answer. She excused herself once more, and soon came back carrying a tea tray. She sat a few feet away from me on the couch and stared at the drapes. "I can't stand to look out those windows since—well, since it happened. I suppose I will never get used to the fact that the person who was destined to bring me so much joy at this last stage of my life is suddenly gone."

I chose not to ask whom she meant. I thought it best to be the listener in this conversation. How else could I hope to learn anything that could help Mort solve Martin Terranova's murder?

While she was pouring tea into our cups Bertha Mae asked me a very pointed question. "Jessica, have you ever felt that it is too much of a chore to even get out of bed in the morning?"

This could be difficult emotional territory. If Bertha Mae was going to talk to me about depression—well, as a widow, I will always remember the struggles of those early days of loss and loneliness. But if she was going to compare her loss of a young man who I was certain was an emotional predator to my loss of a beloved husband, the conversation was bound to get awkward.

"I suppose we all have those days," I said noncommittally.

"Oh yes. I have had them before but, well, I don't know how to explain it. When Martin came into my life, he made me feel young again, and attractive. He would caress my neck in an intimate way during class, or sometimes he would come over here for a private conversation over a cup of tea, just as you and I are having now. Martin and I were growing so close that eventually I began to realize that our age difference didn't matter. And now . . . all I can say is that I don't understand why he is gone. It should have been me. I should have died first." As she tried to set her cup down Bertha Mae's hand began to shake, and the cup clinked repeatedly against her saucer as she struggled to steady it.

Tears crept slowly down her cheeks, and then the floodgates opened. I reached for her and she sobbed on my shoulder until her eyes ran dry. After a while she sat up and said, "He was going to make my final years so happy. And in return I would leave him my money and everything I own. And you would all see my house become a major gym and spa. He would be able to take Perfection nationwide, if not worldwide, and it would start right here." She spread her arms wide and then brought her hands together, as if encircling her entire house.

In that minute, there it was: the absolute confirmation I needed that Mort would have to clear Oscar of any theft charges. As soon as I heard Tim Purdy recounting the tale of seeing Terranova carry a package while jogging toward Oscar's shed, I was convinced Martin Terranova had framed Oscar so that he, Martin, could be the hero who led to the recovery of Bertha Mae's family-heirloom candlesticks. It was one more phase of his continuing process to insinuate himself into Bertha Mae's life and make himself her champion, albeit at Oscar's expense. One more step forward for the emotional predator.

Of course, I wasn't sure how Mort would view it. With Terranova dead, would what I thought matter? How could I persuade Mort that what he might well think of as my mystery-writer psychobabble was rooted in fact? I needed evidence. And I knew where to look.

I sat with Bertha Mae awhile longer, but I was getting impatient while she spoke wistfully about the future she could have had. I was surprised but grateful when she stood and said, "I know I am a terrible hostess, but I really need to lie down for a while. I hope you will come back another time, when I am feeling better."

Before she had fully shut the door behind me, I was already planning how to get into Martin Terranova's house to see if I could discover something, anything, that would prove to Mort that Oscar had been set up. In order for Oscar's life to go back to normal, he had to be exonerated beyond a shadow of a doubt.

I walked my bicycle up the pathway to the juncture where Bertha Mae's front lawn met Martin Terranova's. I walked around the leatherwood bushes that bordered his lawn and left my bicycle wedged unobtrusively between two of them. A blue Subaru SUV was the only car in the driveway, and since it was there when I attended the yoga-and-meditation class, I thought it safe to assume that it belonged to Terranova and had been parked there since his death. I walked casually but purposefully toward the house, keeping a sharp eye on my surroundings. I'd rather not be surprised by Evelyn Phillips or, even more disconcerting, by Mort or one of his deputies while I was snooping, as Seth Hazlitt liked to call what was simply me trying to satisfy my curiosity.

And I certainly was curious about Martin Terranova. Why did he come to Cabot Cove? And why did he spread the word that he had recently lived in South Berwick when not one person in that town remembered him? And why did he choose Bertha Mae Cormier as the victim he would manipulate and bend to his own predatory will? Surely there were plenty of elderly women in town who had more money than she did.

Too many questions were rattling around in my head. I strolled directly to the front door and looked around, and when I was sure I wasn't being observed, I tried to turn the doorknob— but I suppose I should have expected the door to be locked. I took a few steps to peek in a window that gave me a good view of the living room and part of the dining room. I gave the window a tug, but no luck. I moved around to the side of the house and tried each window, unsuccessfully, all the while wondering: Even if I got one open, was I willing to crawl in and climb or perhaps fall over whatever furniture might be blocking my way on the chance that I might find answers to any of my questions? Yes, I probably was.

The back of the house faced the swimming pool and, beyond that, the pool house that had become the Perfection gym, all surrounded by yellow crime-scene tape. I tried two windows without luck, and then I grasped the knob on the back door and, surprisingly, it turned. I gave the door a light push and was elated when it opened. I didn't even stop to think if it was possible that someone was inside.

I opened the door, then came to my senses and cautiously called, "Hello?" No one answered, so I stepped inside and called a little more loudly. I was nearly in the dining room when I heard the footsteps of someone running down the stairs from the second floor. I flattened myself against the wall between the kitchen and the dining room, but the runner never came my way. Instead, he barreled right out the front door. I ran to the closest window and watched as Hilly Davis pushed his way through the trees of Terranova's side yard as if he were being chased by a pack of wolves.

My heart may have been pounding at a hundred beats a minute, but once I saw Hilly, I was certain that I hadn't been in real danger. When he heard me call out, he was probably more alarmed than I was. But he had added one more question to my list. What was he doing here?

I knew I should call Mort, but that would lead to my having to explain what I was doing inside the murder victim's house. In that sense I was as guilty as Hilly. I decided that I would tell Mort everything—after I had a look around.

Chapter Sixteen

In his mad rush, Hilly had left the front door ajar, so I firmly shut it and turned the lock. Confident that I was now definitely alone in the house, I went back to the kitchen, locked that door, and began to look around, opening cupboards and drawers that revealed nothing more than the usual kitchen paraphernalia and foodstuffs. There was a small half bathroom off the kitchen. The medicine cabinet was empty except for a box of adhesive bandages and bottles containing two different brands of pain liniment. Apparently, Martin Terranova had the same response to overexercising as the rest of us—an ache here or some stiffness there.

Since the freezer and the toilet tank were hackneyed but still popular hiding places in detective shows and books, I checked both, but didn't find anything out of place.

The only drawers I found in the dining room were in the sideboard. One held tablecloths and placemats. In the other I found candleholders, a box of taper candles, a long-necked lighter, and—unexpectedly, since this was the home of "Mister Physically Fit"—an ashtray.

I moved on to the living room, but my luck was no better there. Neither end table had a drawer or a shelf. What would have been a bookcase in my house Terranova used more as a whatnot, with a few track-and-field trophies and about a dozen framed photos scattered among the shelves. The closet by the front door was filled with jackets, coats, hats, scarves, sweaters, and boots. Everything you would expect to see in any closet in Maine this time of year. I checked every garment. One jacket had a five-dollar bill crumpled in the left side pocket. When I stuck my hand in the kangaroo pouch of a gray sweatshirt I found a receipt from Mara's. It seemed that Terranova had lunch there the day of his death. Lunch for two, by the look of the amount of the bill. I took out my phone and snapped a picture of the receipt. Mara might remember who his lunch companion was.

I hoped to have better luck on the second floor. The doorway to what appeared to be the largest bedroom was directly opposite me when I reached the top of the stairs. A queen-sized bed was neatly made with a forest green and navy blue plaid quilt. Matching tailored pillow covers rested against the headboard.

The navy blue drapes were open and sunshine bounced off the full-length mirror that hung inside the open closet door. The red oak highboy chest opposite the bed had doors that would normally be closed to protect the top two drawers, but now the doors were wide open and the uppermost drawer had been pulled out and was sitting on a table next to a green boudoir chair. A pile of papers was strewn on the chair, with a few stragglers spilled on the floor. It was my best guess that Hilly had been rummaging through Terranova's personal papers when my arrival caught him off guard.

From what I could see, most of the paperwork looked like ordinary bills dealing with supplies and equipment for Perfection. I also found an automobile title in the name of Martin Terranova for the blue Subaru parked outside, and some household bills. I sifted through the papers and found nothing unusual until I got to the drawer itself. When I picked up a handful of papers, a small card dropped to the floor.

I bent down to pick up what turned out to be a New Hampshire driver's license. The picture on the license was of the man I knew as Martin Terranova, but the name on the license was Joseph M. Terranova. I was tempted to put it in my purse, but I knew that everything in the house must stay as it was until I talked to Mort. Thank heaven for modern technology. Once again I took out my telephone. As I tapped the camera icon, the phone rang and I jumped. Dan Andrews's name popped up. I answered without thinking.

"Jessica. I was wondering . . . Er . . . Pierce Collymore is here. We could use your help. Might we come over?" Dan sounded both worried and businesslike.

Well, this was going to be tricky. "Actually, Dan, I am not home right now. I've been spending some time visiting Bertha Mae Cormier," I said.

It was not exactly a lie, and I knew it sounded a lot better than *I am busy ransacking the home of Cabot Cove's recent murder victim.*

"If you can excuse yourself, I can pick you up in five minutes. And if you are on your bike, that won't be a problem. I'm sure I can squeeze it in my back seat." To press this hard, Dan must really need to talk to me. And what could the new fire chief have to do with anything?

"Give me ten minutes and I will meet you in front of Bertha Mae's. But if I am not there, please don't ring her bell. She is nervous about opening the door since Terranova died." Another useful truth preventing me from telling an outright lie.

I ended the call and hurriedly took four pictures of the New Hampshire driver's license. Then I put it back in the drawer. I had no time left to examine the rest of the papers. I had no choice but to leave them.

I'd already locked the back door, so I decided I should leave through the front door as Hilly had. I opened and then relocked the thumb-turn lock on the inside knob so that once I left, both doors would be locked, which might be a surprise to Hilly if he came back to finish whatever it was he'd started.

I pulled my bicycle out of the leatherwood bushes, brushed off the few leaves that came along with it, and was calmly standing by the side of the road in front of Bertha Mae's house when Dan pulled his car up alongside me.

Once we were settled in the car, with my bicycle tucked across the back seat, I was about to ask why he and Pierce Collymore needed my help—and for that matter, where was Pierce?—but Dan started a different conversation. He inquired about Bertha Mae.

I gave him what I thought was an accurate account of her extremely melodramatic reaction to everything that had happened in the past few days.

"It sounds to me like you are starting to agree with Evelyn.

You think Bertha Mae has reached the stage in life where she needs to have someone to keep an eye on her much, if not all, of the time," Dan said.

"I wouldn't go quite that far. What I will say is that she is in a terrible emotional state since Martin Terranova died. I think that she needs professional help on that score, counseling at the very least. Although I do agree that having someone like Greta there a few hours most days would be a great help. Someone who sees Bertha Mae regularly would be likely to notice if she became more . . . erratic."

"Well, I can't disagree with that, but from what I heard about the way Bertha Mae carried on, accusing Greta of everything short of murder, I know I wouldn't want to work for her. I doubt anyone, even a professional from one of those home care services, would want to put up with that kind of abuse."

"As people get older, allowances have to be made. Greta was extremely patient with Bertha Mae until this latest incident. Perhaps she will be again." I changed the subject. "Tell me, now, what is going on that you and Pierce Collymore, of all people, need advice from me?"

"I don't think it is advice Pierce needs," Dan said. "It is information. He has some questions about the Cabot Cove Fire Department Developmental Committee. He came to me because I am a member of the committee, but the, ah, situation he has run into appears to be a long-standing one and I am relatively new, whereas you . . ."

"I have been an active member since the committee's inception nearly twenty years ago." I finished the sentence for him. "We have a meeting scheduled for a few weeks from now. Wouldn't it be best for Pierce to put his questions before the entire committee and get his answers? That way we will all be on the same page, so to speak."

Dan shook his head while he parked his car in front of the *Gazette* office. Then he turned off the engine and said, "This needs to be resolved before the committee meets again. I will let him tell you. Before we go inside, I want to say that this may be something, or it may be nothing. I think you, as a longtime committee member, will know whether or not we have a real problem as soon as you hear what Pierce has to say."

I didn't like the sound of that. Dan's comment reminded me of his "Sometimes it's news; sometimes it's nothing" observation. For the sake of the Fire Department Developmental Committee and for the sake of the town, I hoped Pierce Collymore's questions would end up meeting Dan's definition of "nothing."

When Dan opened his office door Pierce Collymore spun around to face us. It seemed clear to me that he had been pacing the wide space alongside Dan's desk, from the door to the window and back again.

"Mrs. Fletcher—Jessica—so nice of you to help out. Did Dan explain our problem? . . . Er . . . my problem, I guess."

"Not yet, but you can tell me . . ." I stopped because he looked stricken. I suspected that, having told his story to Dan, he didn't want to repeat it.

Always considerate, Dan opened the small refrigerator on the floor behind his desk and took out three bottles of water. "Why don't we sit down and have a drink"—he smiled and gestured with the water bottles—"and discuss this like civilized people?"

Nervous as Pierce appeared to be, he laughed. "Dan, you sound like one of those big-time lawyers on the television advertisements trying to calm a prospective client."

And he took a bottle and sat in one visitor's chair while I made myself comfortable in the other. Dan handed me a water; then he pulled out the worn leather swivel chair behind his desk and sat down. He took a little extra time opening his water bottle, and then sipped. Once he'd set the bottle down he looked at Pierce and said, "There is no reason to be worried. You are among friends. Jessica has been on the development committee since its inception and knows everything there is to know about its operation. Just explain it to her the way you explained it to me."

Then Dan leaned all the way back in his chair and waved his arm as if tossing an imaginary microphone to Pierce.

Pierce looked at me and said, "We don't know each other well, but I can assure you that I came to Cabot Cove with the intention of being a top-notch fire chief in terms of the big three: safety, supervision, and budget. I have been relatively successful with the first two as the townsfolk have come to know me and the firefighters have learned to trust me as they did Chief Billingsworth. So that is all going well, but I have to confess, the budget process has me baffled."

I could certainly understand why he might find the procedure to be somewhat chaotic, since purchases for a fire department were ongoing and included everything from inexpensive items such as dish detergent and paper towels for the firehouse kitchen right up to hook and ladder trucks that cost well over half a million dollars. There were bound to be some procedural intricacies that could cause confusion.

"What exactly triggered your problem with the process?" I asked.

"I signed my first purchase order shortly after I was sworn in as the chief of the fire department. Olivia Quigley, who is the supervisor of the town's budget office, brought me the forms, explained what we were buying—in that case, two-door metal lockers needed for storage. I clearly remember the paperwork was for five. When four were delivered I thought it was a supply or transportation problem, so I decided to wait a few days before following up. Imagine my surprise when a check made out to Angus Billingsworth arrived at my office. It was for exactly half the price of the missing locker, and the affixed copy of an invoice for four lockers had a note scrawled across the bottom that said *THANKS FOR YOUR BUSINESS.* I called Olivia immediately and she said it was some sort of error and she would fix it. I sent her the check and the paperwork and forgot about it until . . . it happened again."

"Really? Didn't you ask Olivia why any check would be made out to Angus rather than to the Cabot Cove budget department or to our Fire Department Developmental Committee?" The budget office had long been in disarray due to retirements and antiquated processes until Olivia Quigley was hired. She modernized the office systems and charted a course that the staff was happy to follow.

"In fact, I did ask, and she said there was a new clerk at the company we'd purchased the lockers from and he was confused. Being new myself, I accepted her explanation. Over the next few months I signed maybe a half dozen purchase orders and never had a problem, until yesterday, when I received a similar check, made out to Angus, for a much larger amount." Pierce took a long sip of water, wiped his mouth with the back of his hand, and continued.

"I checked the invoice and it was for two water-rescue boats, the kind we use to transport our personnel and equipment to boats that catch fire at sea. I *know* we ordered three. But the invoice was for two and had a similar thank-you note. And I realized the check was for exactly half the price of the third boat."

"Did you call Olivia?" I asked.

"No." Pierce shook his head. "I thought it would be best to talk to a committee member, someone who understands how the finances should work, because I am afraid there is some serious hanky-panky going on—"

At that exact moment the door opened and Evelyn Phillips burst into the room. She dropped her humongous tote bag, which landed on the floor with a thud, and stood with her hands planted firmly on her hips. She swiveled her head, looking each one of us straight in the eye, then said, "Whatever you three are up to, I want in."

Chapter Seventeen

U p to? What could we possibly be up to?" Dan's puzzled look appeared genuine to me, but Evelyn had known him longer and better than I did, so I couldn't guess what she discerned. "Why would you think we are up to anything in particular?"

"Because"—Evelyn gave him an "Aha, caught you" grin—"I was on my way to check in with you, Dan, you know, just to chat about what's new in the world of the *Cabot Cove Gazette*. I was across the street, mere steps from your front door, when I was blocked by Doris Ann, who was very excited to tell me more than I ever wanted to know about the recent library fundraiser. Lo and behold, while Doris Ann was yammering away, I noticed you parking your car outside, and then to my surprise you escorted Jessica in here. Naturally, I wondered what the confab was about. As soon as I could shake Doris Ann loose, over I came. And when I saw Jessica's bicycle in the back of your car, I knew that you, Dan, had gone on the hunt, found our favorite amateur sleuth, and brought her here for a consult about the murder of the gym guy that has the whole town shook up. Am I right, or am I right?"

I could see by the way Dan was pressing his lips together that he was trying to figure out an answer that would get Evelyn out of the way so we could finish discussing the fire department budget issue, which was beginning to look like a crisis on its own. Pierce must have been thinking the same thing, because he swung into action by rising from his chair and extending his hand. "You must be Evelyn Phillips. I have heard so much about you. I'm Pierce Collymore, the new fire chief here in Cabot Cove."

Evelyn shook his hand and said, "I've heard about you from multiple sources. 'Come from away,' as they say around here. Some aren't too happy about that."

"Yes, ma'am. I know." Pierce laughed. "All the way from Vermont. Dan and Jessica are members of the Fire Department Developmental Committee and they have been kind enough to guide me through the intricacies of how we can be sure those meetings actually get anything done."

Disappointment flitted across Evelyn's face. If we weren't talking about Martin Terranova's murder, I'm sure she considered us to be a group of slackers who didn't seem to realize where the real action was. I decided to give her a tidbit that would keep her busy until I had a chance to sort out everything I'd learned in my visit to Terranova's house.

"Evelyn, as it happens, I visited Bertha Mae this morning," I said. "And I am beginning to believe you are right. I am still not convinced that she needs someone watching over her every move;

however, she is so very sad that I believe she does need a friend to lean on. Perhaps you could stop by and check on her?"

Evelyn gave me an "I told you so" smirk, pulled her cell phone out of her pocket, and tapped what apparently was a speed dial icon for our local cab service, because within seconds she said, "Demetri? I am at the *Gazette* office and I need to visit Bertha Mae. Thanks."

She pocketed the phone and said, "Sorry I can't stay longer, but duty calls." Then she fixed Dan with a hard stare. "You really should be interviewing Bertha Mae. Do you want to come along?"

"Sorry." Dan waved his hand over the stacks of papers on his desk. "I wish I could but I'm buried. But please let me walk outside and wait for Demetri with you," he offered, and followed her out the door.

Pierce said, "Well, that was a close call. From what I have heard about her, Evelyn Phillips would be the last person I'd want to learn that I had worries about whatever is going on with the departmental budget, especially if it turns out that my concern is unfounded."

When Dan came back into the office, he was laughing. "Well, I got a good three minutes of 'What kind of newspaper editor are you? Bertha Mae could have a great lead about Martin Terranova's murder.' Evelyn had out both the hammer and the tongs, lecturing me at high volume, when Demetri's speedy arrival saved my poor eardrums."

He stepped behind his desk, swiveled into the brown leather chair, dropped his elbows on his desk, and rubbed his hands together. "Now, where were we?"

I looked at Pierce, who was looking at me as if he expected me to get the conversation started. So I did.

"Pierce, why don't you give us a brief recap? And then perhaps Dan and I can make some suggestions," I said, although I already was certain that my recommendation would have the possibility of causing some distress at least to Pierce and the fire department and possibly to the entire town.

Pierce once again described the process and led us succinctly from his first purchase order, the one for the metal cabinets, to the most recent, the one for the water-rescue boats.

"And as I mentioned, those were the only two that I received paperwork on, along with the checks made out to Angus," he concluded.

That reminded me of the question he answered just before Evelyn came in.

"You said that you didn't bring the water-rescue-boat paperwork to Olivia's attention. Is that correct?"

He nodded. "Once the paperwork and the check made out to Angus landed in my departmental mailbox I remembered how cavalier Olivia was when it happened that first time, for a much smaller amount, so I decided to get an opinion from a committee member, and since Dan is the one I've gotten to know best in the few short months I have been here . . ."

"Of course. That makes sense." Then I turned to Dan. "And with the little we know so far, what action, if any, do you think should be taken?"

Dan didn't hesitate. "I would want to look at all the paperwork that is available and then I would want to talk to Angus."

"And not to Olivia?" I asked.

"Not yet," Dan replied. "Angus is the one who can tell us if there was a purpose for some refund checks to be made out in the chief's name—perhaps a petty cash fund, something like that. We may find that the only error here is that the checks should be in Pierce's name and someone neglected to tell him where he should designate the funds."

I believed Dan was on the right track and told him so, but I demurred quickly and energetically when he and Pierce invited me to join them in searching through the budget records and then visiting former chief Angus Billingsworth. Curious as I was about the bizarre pattern Pierce had come across in the funding stream of the fire department, I had more important chores on my mind.

Dan retrieved my bicycle from his car and set it on the sidewalk, resting it on its kickstand.

"Jessica, I can't thank you enough for taking the time to listen to Pierce's story. I know how busy you are and I hated to bother you. Experienced as both he and I are in this kind of matter, we are both very new to Cabot Cove," Dan said by way of explanation and, I suspected, apology for having involved me in the situation.

"Don't give it another thought. I was happy to do my part on behalf of the committee, but now I really must get on with my day," I said as I mounted my bike and headed for my next stop, Mara's Luncheonette.

I parked my bicycle in the rack at the end of the block, and when I entered I was happy to see that there was plenty of table space. With luck, Mara would have time to gossip a bit. I took a seat in the middle of the room, as far away as possible from any other occupied table.

Mara came over and set a glass of water in front of me. She

was holding a burger platter in her other hand. "If you have been riding that bicycle of yours around town, I figure that by this time of day you could use some serious hydration. Now let me serve this to Charlie Evans there by the windows and I can use the fact that I still have to take your order as an excuse to escape his unending theories about the Terranova murder."

Mara hurried toward the high, wide windows that gave a stunning view of the cove that led to our town's name. Out of the corner of my eye I could see her set Charlie's platter in front of him, and when he began to speak she pulled a pencil from behind her ear and motioned toward me while taking an order pad from her pocket. Charlie nodded and Mara walked back to my table.

"Wasn't I quick as a flash? Now, what can I get for you, Jessica?" she asked as she gave me a wink.

"How about a slice of wheat toast and a cup of green tea?" I said.

"Hmm, that sounds about right for you. Now, if it was Doc Hazlitt ordering, it would be *two slices, slightly burnt around the edges, and don't forget the extra buttah.*" She mimicked Seth perfectly. "Jessica, I'll be right back with your tea and toast."

True to her word, in what seemed like mere seconds Mara placed a chrome teapot and a green mug on the table in front of me. Next to the tea she set a plate holding a piece of wheat toast cut in half on the diagonal and two small pats of butter.

She took a white cloth from her apron pocket and began to wipe the unoccupied part of the table, a sure sign that she had a few minutes to talk, which she confirmed by asking in a super-low tone of voice what I thought about the Terranova murder.

For effect, I gave a slight shudder as if a sudden draft had crossed behind me. "Oh, it's terrible, of course. No one likes to have that sort of thing happen in their hometown. I stopped in to visit Bertha Mae Cormier today and she is beside herself with grief."

"As well she should be." Mara stopped pretending that she was at my table to clean off some invisible crumbs and stuffed the cloth back in her pocket. "From what I hear, that Terranova was all flirty with the older ladies who visited his gym. I can tell you that half the fishermen who breakfast here spent far too much time joking about how attentive he was to them all, but especially to Bertha Mae. I'm sure he was strictly in business mode, but nobody should be surprised that she's all torn up about his death, especially the brutal way he died. And right next door. I'm sure she could see that gym from most of the windows in her house."

You have no idea. I kept that thought to myself and said as casually as I could, "I heard down at Loretta's that Terranova was in here the day he died. Do you recall? Perhaps he was with somebody else. Maybe a stranger?"

"He was here all right. Stopped in most days for two of his specials—one to eat here and one to go." A look of regret crossed Mara's face, as though she suddenly realized that she'd lost a regular customer.

"What was this special he ordered so regularly?" I asked, partly to keep the conversation going but more to discern if the order matched the amount paid on the receipt I found. Busy as she often was, Mara might be mistaken.

Mara pointed to the chalkboard on the wall above the cash register. "Right there, third on the list. The Protein Power Bowl. Three scrambled eggs, sliced breast of chicken, grated cheddar cheese, and hummus. After he requested it a few times, some of the men in his weight-lifting class came in asking for 'Martin's Special.' Well, I wasn't having none of that. I name the specials in this luncheonette. So it went right there on the chalkboard as the Protein Power Bowl and that is how it has stayed." Mara harrumphed.

"A wise decision," I said.

"Come to think of it, the sheriff never mentioned whether his crew found that take-out container in the fridge. I figure Terranova must have eaten it before he died and tossed all the packaging in the trash; otherwise someone would have been talking to me for sure. If not the sheriff, at least a deputy." Mara sounded miffed that she hadn't been interviewed as a potential suspect.

I nodded and looked sympathetic, letting Mara go on with her thought that Mort should consider any evidence pointing to her, but I knew the very idea of her committing assault, never mind murder, was downright silly. Brusque and businesslike as she might be, Mara had a soft heart. Many a time I'd seen her quietly provide meals to folks in need. And I knew she volunteered at the shelter just outside town.

"Well, I guess they didn't bother with the trash, so they have no reason to interview me. Enjoy your tea, Jessica." Mara sounded disappointed as she headed for a corner table where a gentleman was signaling for her attention.

I was also disappointed, that Mara wasn't able to identify a second person having lunch with Martin Terranova on the day he died, simply because there was none. No help there. Still, I had the picture of Martin as Joseph Terranova on a New Hampshire driver's license. And I had interrupted Hilly Davis as he searched Terranova's house. And those two puzzle pieces were still in play.

I left my half-eaten toast on my plate and gulped down the last of my tea. I knew I couldn't stall any longer. It was past time for me to visit the sheriff's office and confess to Mort what I had done. I hoped the information I was bringing with me would override his annoyance at my sneaking into Terranova's house without permission.

Chapter Eighteen

Mrs. F., I can't believe that you, who I consider to be one of the smartest people I know, would do something so dangerously stupid!"

While I sat in a visitor's chair Sheriff Mort Metzger stood in front of me. His thumbs were tucked into his gun belt and he was drumming his fingers on the belt's leather. The constant tapping was somewhat unnerving and I guessed that was part of his interrogation procedure. I was not sure if it worked on criminals but it certainly was working on me.

When I had arrived at the sheriff's office half an hour earlier, our conversation started cordially, as it always did. I began by telling Mort that Dan and I had spent a few hours in South Berwick looking for any friends or relatives who might remember Martin Terranova. When I listed the various shops we visited I purposely left out the dentist's receptionist who did remember Joseph Terranova. I decided to outline my tale of travels chronologically and wait to bring up the name Joseph until I told Mort I'd discovered the driver's license, which I thought might lead to a bumpy conversation. (And I was certainly right about that.) I ended with the fact that there was no record of Martin as a member of the South Berwick library, which to me was proof positive that he wasn't a town resident.

"I don't know, Mrs. F. A guy whose job would require him to be out and about in order to drum up business, you would think everyone in town would know him. Are we sure he wasn't from one of the other Berwicks?"

"Funny that you should suggest that—it's exactly what Charlotte, the nice young clerk in the convenience store, said, and you both may be correct, but wherever he may actually have come from, one thing is certain. Martin Terranova wanted all of Cabot Cove to believe he was from South Berwick," I said.

"Mrs. F., you may remember how much teasing and often downright abuse I had to take because I was an outsider. People called me a foreigner. 'Come from away, did you?' asked with a hint of contempt was the most polite question thrown at me, and I was often told, 'You won't be happy here. May as well turn around and go back where you come from.' I took it because, hey, I'm from New York City, and small-town folks don't always like us big-city people. But, now, you look at Pierce Collymore. He's from right next door in Vermont and some folks around here treat him like he parachuted in from California. Maybe Terranova had heard what you Mainers are like and wanted to avoid the nonsense, so he picked a small town in Maine and used it as his former address when he set up shop here."

The second Mort mentioned our new fire chief, the conversation that Pierce, Dan Andrews, and I had less than an hour earlier started to replay, full-blown, in my mind. Was it possible that the fire chief was being framed in some bizarre plan to embarrass him into leaving Cabot Cove in order to make his job available to a local fire department specialist? It seemed far-fetched, but from what Mort described as his personal experience, I had to admit it was not out of the realm of possibility.

I pushed Pierce's problem to the back of my mind and returned to the topic at hand. "I get your point, Mort—I really do—but I can't help believing that Martin Terranova was hiding his past for more serious reasons. I don't think he was worried about being labeled an outsider. I believe that he was working hard to prevent anyone in Cabot Cove from discovering the kind of scams he had worked in his previous lives."

Mort rubbed his chin for a moment, and then said, "That would make sense, Mrs. F., if we had any reason to believe that Terranova was a scam artist, but he consistently appeared to be just what he presented himself to be, a physical fitness instructor who was working to build a business here in town."

"Mort, when you and I decided it might be helpful if I spoke to Bertha Mae, we both thought that she might be more comfortable speaking to a friend, and that perhaps I could get a better idea of her relationship with Martin Terranova," I reminded him. "So that is what I did."

"Now you tell me. While you were talking to Bertha Mae, did she happen to tell you that Terranova was some sort of Artful Dodger?" Mort raised an eyebrow, indicating he thought the idea was ludicrous.

As soon as I replied, "Oh, no, she absolutely did not," Mort relaxed his eyebrow and smiled. Then I told him what she did say as succinctly as I could.

"Bertha Mae told me that she and Martin Terranova were going to spend the rest of Bertha Mae's life together, and then, when she died, she would leave him all her worldly possessions and he would build Perfection into a nationwide, if not a worldwide, business venture, using *her capital* to do so."

Now both of Mort's eyebrows shot up until they nearly reached his hairline. "Are you telling me this wasn't one of Bertha Mae's fantasies? The two of them actually talked about this? They planned this . . . this life together, and as part of the deal Bertha Mae agreed to leave Terranova her entire estate? I mean, if she even has an estate. For all we know Bertha Mae's house is mortgaged to the hilt and she is living off a monthly Social Security check."

"That may be true but I can tell you Evelyn doesn't think so," I said calmly. "She told me that she has reason to believe that Bertha Mae has significant assets. Perhaps you should ask Evelyn how she knows anything at all about Bertha Mae's finances."

"Evelyn Phillips is capable of saying anything that she thinks will keep her out of one of my cells." He waved in the general direction of the door that led to the confinement area.

"Mort, really, if you continue to focus on Evelyn . . ." I knew I'd hit a nerve when Mort began to pace back and forth, so I thought it was time to let him know about my adventure this morning. "I suppose I should tell you that I visited Martin Terranova's house this morning, and I found this."

I held my cell phone up so he could see the pictures I took of Joseph Terranova's New Hampshire driver's license. But instead of thanking me, Mort lost his temper.

"Mrs. F., I can't believe that you, who I consider to be one of the smartest people I know, would do something so dangerously stupid!"

And that's when the interrogation began.

"Well, I—"

"Stop." Mort held up his hand, inches from my face, as if he was a school crossing guard stopping oncoming traffic. "Whatever you are going to say, there is no excuse. You went, unaccompanied, into a crime victim's home and did exactly what? *Searched* it? And now I should be happy that you took some pictures of whatever you came across that *you* consider to be evidence."

"Mort, if you would just calm down and look at my phone—" I said.

"Calm down! Calm down! Did it ever occur to you that we secure crime scenes and crime victims' homes for a reason? Suppose you strolled into Terranova's house only to find that you weren't alone. Suppose you stumbled across the killer."

Mort was apoplectic. I knew anything I said from this point forward would only further enrage him but I felt strongly that I had no choice but to continue. Truth will always out.

"Well, as it happens, Hilly Davis was upstairs, but I hid in the kitchen until he left. That was another thing I wanted to talk to you about. Why do you think Hilly was searching Terranova's bedroom?"

"Hilly was in the house? He was searching too? Now I have heard it all. Floyd," Mort bellowed, "get in here."

Floyd McCallum pushed through the door from the rear of the building so hurriedly that he nearly tripped over the threshold. "Yes, Sheriff."

"I want you to go over to Martin Terranova's house—the keys

are in the evidence box." Mort turned to me. "I suppose he will need keys?"

I nodded. "Oh yes, he will. I was sure to lock both doors before I left."

Floyd's eyes opened wide with disbelief. He got as far as saying, "Mrs. Fletcher, what—" before Mort glared him into silence and repeated, "The evidence box, Floyd. Get the keys. Go to the house. Stay there until I say you can leave. Don't touch anything."

"Yes, sir, Sheriff." Floyd touched his forehead in a snappy salute and disappeared into the secure section of the building, and we didn't see him again.

Once again Mort hooked his thumbs on his gun belt and started tapping his fingers on the leather. *Thwack, thwack, thwack, thwack.* And repeat.

"Okay, Mrs. F., from the beginning. What were you doing in Martin Terranova's house?"

"When Bertha Mae told me, quite definitively, about her plan to leave all her assets to Terranova so he could expand his business, it confirmed my suspicion that he was an emotional predator and that all his flirtatious and touchy-feely ways were part of his plan to separate Bertha Mae from her money. I think cajoling her into leaving him her resources after she died was step one. Once that was secure, he would slowly become the only person she could trust. I think Martin Terranova set up Oscar just as Tim Purdy described seeing, and since Terranova had such free and easy access to Bertha Mae's house, it is not unlikely that he juggled Bertha Mae's medicines, hiding them here and there so she would lose her trust in Greta. Which she did."

"Say all that is true. I still don't get what influenced you to decide to enter Terranova's house." Mort looked stymied.

"There I was, right next door, you see. And the more Bertha Mae talked about Terranova and their plans of a life together, the more sure I became that he had no intention of waiting to inherit. He was maneuvering to get his hands on whatever money he could." I paused. "May I have a drink of water?"

Mort stepped to the watercooler and then handed me a mug of water, which I sipped gratefully.

"Sitting in Bertha Mae's darkened living room, with her so sad and disheveled by my side, reinforced my belief that Terranova had to be a pro at this kind of deception. Bertha Mae is flighty in many ways but has always held any information about her assets close to the vest, even with people she has known for practically her entire life. I would find it difficult to believe that Terranova woke up one morning and decided to try his hand at swindling an old lady by working his way first into her will and then into her pocketbook."

Mort was following my train of thought up to a point. "Say I follow you on this—and I'm not saying I do. Say I even agree that everything you have said is likely. What has it got to do with you breaking into and entering Terranova's house?"

While his use of police terminology made me sound like a criminal even to my own ears, I skipped responding to the implication and said in as even a tone as I could manage, "When I left Bertha Mae, I decided to walk next door to take a look around Terranova's property. As it turned out, the kitchen door was unlocked."

"Unlocked or standing open?" Mort asked.

I saw where this was going. "Unlocked. And before you say anything else, of course I tried the doorknob—that was how I discovered the door was unlocked—so yes, I was trying to gain entry to the house. Now, if you will let me get to my point—"

"By all means. Don't let me stop you from making a full confession," Mort said with more cynicism than I could recall him ever using toward me.

I gave a rushed description of my search of the kitchen area and told him that when I called out to be sure the house was empty I was shocked that within seconds I heard someone come running down the stairs. "I flattened myself against the wall until Hilly Davis had run out the front door."

"And you are sure it was Hilly? I mean, did you see him on the stairs, or running out the door?" Mort leaned in, anxious to hear my answer.

"No, but I scooted to the bay window as soon as I heard the person leave by the front door, and I watched Hilly Davis run across the yard and disappear into the woods. Then I locked the front door securely and went upstairs. There were major signs that someone had been either searching or trashing Martin Terranova's bedroom when I arrived at the house and interrupted them. And the only person I saw was Hilly Davis."

"Hold it a minute." Mort pulled his cell phone from his pocket, hit a button, and said, "Floyd, are you in the house? Good. Now seal the bedroom. We're going to need to take fingerprints. Thanks."

He slid the phone back into his pocket and asked, "What else, Mrs. F.?"

Now it was my turn to pull out my cell phone. After what felt like hours of battling, I finally was going to introduce Sheriff Mort Metzger to Joseph M. Terranova.

Chapter Nineteen

I opened my phone, scrolled through the pictures I had taken of the driver's license. The third picture seemed clearest, so I spread it with my fingers to enlarge it. Joseph M. Terranova with an address in Dover, New Hampshire, which was only a few miles over the state border from South Berwick. The picture was of either our Martin Terranova or his twin brother. And I was betting on the former.

I handed Mort my phone and waited patiently while he examined the picture. After a while he asked where I found the license, and I told him about the open highboy with its contents scattered about the chair, the table, and the floor.

He shook his head. "I can't believe we missed this when we searched the house. We did our usual slow and careful look through. How did we miss a New Hampshire driver's license?"

"Quite easily, I am sure. It was tucked away in the midst of a large pile of papers, most of which appeared meaningless in terms of the murder. Every scrap was mundane. I saw things like bills from the power company and solicitations from charities. In fact, Terranova had made a note on the page he had torn out of the *Gazette* about the fundraiser for the children's hospital. He'd decided to pledge fifty dollars. It was an odd place to keep a driver's license, but that may have been exactly why it was there."

Then I followed up with, "It is possible that the only reason Hilly didn't find it before me is that my calling 'hello' basically scared him out of the house. When I went upstairs I saw that he'd disturbed so many of Terranova's personal belongings that I was convinced he was sure there was something worth finding. I hoped that because Hilly left in such a hurry, whatever he was looking for was still there for me to find. So I began searching through the mess Hilly had made."

Mort nodded but I could see that he was only half listening as his mind was racing to decide what to do next. He walked to the door that led to a nonpublic part of the office and called his deputy Andy Bloom.

Andy came in and gave me a wide smile and a nod, but then he was all business. "What do you need, Sheriff?"

"Take a look at this." Mort handed him my cell phone.

"But that's . . ." Andy looked at Mort with a question in his eyes. "Two Terranovas?"

"I don't think so. I think now we know why we've been having trouble finding a next of kin for Martin Terranova," Mort said. "I want you to make some calls over to New Hampshire. Is the license good? Is the guy real? I don't have to tell you what to do."

"Got it." As he turned to leave, Andy said, "Always nice seeing you, Mrs. Fletcher."

"She'll be here when you get back with the information." Mort pointed to my phone in Andy's hand. "That's her cell you are holding."

"Okay. Great. I will transfer the picture to our computer system and bring your phone safely back to you," Andy said.

"Andy, I'd appreciate your leaving a copy of the picture on my phone." Even with all the trouble finding the license had gotten me into with Mort, I still wasn't ready to give it away.

"No problem. Will do," Andy said, and then he disappeared into the back rooms of the office.

I saw Mort moving his jaw from right to left and back again, a sure sign that he was choosing his words carefully. "Of course, it's your picture and you can keep it, but I am wondering, Mrs. F., why exactly you think you need it."

"Oh, I don't need it. Let's just say it is an item of curiosity, and, well, once my curiosity is aroused . . ."

"I know that feeling," Mort said. "It's like an itch in the small of your back that you can't scratch because it is just out of reach."

"Yes, that's it exactly."

"Just do me one favor. When you are trying to scratch, please do your best to avoid searching vacant houses or wandering off by yourself to investigate. I got one dead body on my hands. I don't need any more." Mort crossed his arms as if his ultimatum had ended the conversation, but naturally, I had more to say.

I started by placating his biggest fear with carefully chosen words. "I promise you that I will make every effort not to go off on my own anywhere I consider dangerous. And I admit that wasn't my intent. I was in Bertha Mae's house, and Terranova's house was next door. The opportunity presented itself . . ." I shrugged. "Of course, when I heard the footsteps of someone on the staircase, I realized I was in a risky position, but once I saw Hilly fleeing, I couldn't imagine that he would harm anyone, especially me. What more would you like me to say?"

Mort heaved a sigh. "Let's drop it for now. No one in Cabot Cove would ever forgive me if you got hurt, or worse."

I was used to Seth worrying about me when I engaged in what he called my "snooping," but it had never really occurred to me that any of my actions would cause Mort to have that same concern. "I am sorry if I gave you reason to fear for my safety."

Mort looked at the floor. When he looked up again, he was smiling. "Well, you're here, so it wasn't nearly as bad as it could have been. Now, would you mind telling me any thoughts you might have about this murder? I have to tell you, unless Andy comes back with something, so far, I'm stumped."

As if on cue, Andy opened the door, stuck his head in the doorway, and looked at Mort, who asked, "What have you got? May as well say it out loud—I'm sure Mrs. F. will find out on her own if we don't tell her." And he gave me a wink to let me know he was teasing, which melted the remaining tension between us.

"It is a legitimate New Hampshire license that was renewed less than two years ago, and it is totally clean. Not so much as a speeding ticket. It looks like Joseph Terranova has no wants or warrants, but I'm still digging." Andy returned the thumbs-up that Mort shot his way, and then he went back to work.

Mort walked around his desk, slumped into his chair, and leaned all the way back so he could cross his feet on the desktop. He made a tunnel with his hands and looked over it at me. "Okay, now. So, this guy comes to Cabot Cove out of the blue. Buys a house, sets up a business, and gets himself killed. And as it turns out, we probably don't even know his legal name. So, tell me, Mrs. F., do you have any ideas? Right now I'd even take a few strong guesses."

"You are pointing out the obvious, Mort. Terranova bought a house—a very luxurious house by Cabot Cove standards—and he invested a nice sum of money in starting a business. Where did he get the money that enabled him to do all that?" I wondered aloud.

"I would think he sold an earlier business. You know how these entrepreneur guys are—they start a business, sell it, buy another, and so on down the road." Mort slid his chair back and dropped his feet to the floor, stretching his arms over his head as he did so.

"You have touched on exactly what is bothering me. Terranova didn't show up in Cabot Cove broke with his hat in his hand. He had to have come here with money, and I can't help but wonder precisely how much money, and where it came from originally. Was there a previous Bertha Mae in his life—an elderly woman from whom he cadged money?"

Mort stood and walked to the coffeemaker. "Can I offer you a cup of java?"

When I declined, he poured himself a coffee and sat in the visitor's chair next to mine, took a deep swallow from his cup, and then said, "So your theory is that this Terranova character wanders around the country scamming old ladies out of their last dollar and then moves on?"

"It's more a possibility than a theory. Although, based on what I saw of his personality, it is a strong possibility. I suppose you have checked his bank accounts?" I asked just as Andy came back into the room.

He handed Mort a sheaf of papers. "Here is what we have on Terranova so far. Funny you should mention his bank accounts, Mrs. Fletcher. Sheriff, check the second page from the bottom."

Mort shuffled through the papers, pulled one from the pile, and said, "Lookee here. We have two solid, outstanding banks right here in Cabot Cove, and yet, when Andy checked Terranova's finances, he discovered that Martin keeps his money stashed in one bank and one credit union in Portland, while Joseph has an account in a bank in Durham, New Hampshire. Maybe they are really twins." Mort laughed at what he clearly thought was a joke.

Andy took him seriously and was quick to answer. "Not a chance." He pointed to the papers in Mort's hand. "Look at the top page, Sheriff. It is one and the same man, who seems to go back and forth between names, and for all we know, between lives. He was born Joseph Martin Terranova. I did a deep-dive search and found business licenses in both New Hampshire and Maine issued in the name of Martin, but his Illinois birth certificate and that New Hampshire driver's license both have him as Joseph."

Filled with curiosity, I managed to wait silently while Mort looked over all the papers Andy had given him. Then he tossed them on his desk and swiveled his head between Andy and me. "So, now it looks like Joseph Martin Terranova believed he had some reason to live under two names. We need to figure out that reason."

That was exactly what I was hoping to hear. Now we could get down to business. I opened the conversation. "The most common reason people drop their given name is that they dislike it."

"I went to school with a kid named Cedar Wilson," Andy said.

"The only teacher who ever called him Cedar was Miss Hardy, who—believe me—lived up to her name. Everyone else, including the other teachers, called him by his middle name, Albert."

"Cedar, like the tree?" Mort asked. "Who would name a kid after a tree?"

"From what I heard, Cedar's dad insisted. Cedarwood is expensive because it's both beautiful and moisture resistant. Take a look the next time you drive through town. Half the fencing and decking you see is made from cedar purchased at Wilson's lumberyard."

"Ah, the kid was a good luck charm. I get it," Mort said.

We'd wandered so far afield that I decided to try another tack. "Mort, earlier we were talking about Terranova's money. Do you think Jasper might have some idea of how Terranova managed his finances?"

"Jazzy, the loan shark? Nah, I thought we agreed Terranova came with big bucks." Mort waved me off. "And we got other work to do. Andy, get the fingerprint kit. I need you to go to Terranova's house and dust the doors, windows, the banister, and every inch of his bedroom."

"We treating the house like a crime scene?" Andy asked.

"We sure are. And before you go, take Mrs. F.'s prints. You'll find hers all over Terranova's place." Mort grinned but I didn't find him as amusing as he found himself.

Andy was quite expert in fingerprinting, so in only a few minutes I was on my bicycle and pedaling toward home. Frustrated as I was because I didn't have the opportunity to go through Terranova's bedroom with a fine-tooth comb, I was sure that if there was anything else to find, Mort and his deputies would find it.

I had so many unanswered questions. I could only hope Mort

would share whatever answers they might find. I couldn't wait to get into my kitchen, put on the kettle, have a peaceful cup of tea, and refocus on my research for the book I was writing, but when I pedaled around the corner onto Candlewood Lane, I saw Evelyn Phillips leaning over Maeve O'Bannon's fence. I had no idea what they were talking about, but when Evelyn looked up and saw me, she boomed, "Good talking to you, Maeve. I'll let you get back to your garden. Here comes Jessica now. And high time, I say."

In that moment, although I knew I could still drink my cup of tea, I doubted it would be peaceful.

Chapter Twenty

Evelyn followed me into the house, settled herself at the kitchen table, and seemed grateful for the cup of tea I offered. She was patient enough to wait until I sat down with my own mug brimming with steaming hot black tea before she spoke.

"Bertha Mae told me that you stopped in to see her this morning, but she couldn't seem to remember why you were there or what you talked about." Evelyn picked up the creamer and poured a few drops of milk into her tea. "She's really not in the best of shape."

"I certainly agree, and as you keep reminding us all, she definitely needs assistance. Personally, I think a part-time housekeeper, while helpful, won't be enough. Bertha Mae should talk to a grief counselor, a professional who understands what she is going through and can—I don't know—guide her, I suppose, in dealing with the loss in a healthy way." I was a tad uncomfortable talking to Evelyn about anything to do with Bertha Mae or Martin Terranova. Evelyn had made it clear from the moment she came to town that she was on the hunt for a story, so even if her concern for Bertha Mae's mental health was genuine, Evelyn's primary interest now would be the murder. She always envisioned headlines, and I was sure today was no different.

"Strange thing. When Demetri came to pick me up at Bertha Mae's, just as we were pulling away from the curb, I saw a sheriff's car with Andy Bloom at the wheel turn into Terranova's driveway. I asked Demetri to stop, and I watched as Andy parked behind another sheriff's department car. He took some kind of bag—looked like a small suitcase—out of the car and went into the house. Didn't even have to unlock the door. Gotta wonder who else was in the house. Mort Metzger? Floyd? Or maybe Andy was meeting some law enforcement bigwig? Maybe someone from the district attorney or the courts?"

"I have no idea. I suppose there will be lots of routine coming and going from the gym and the house until Terranova's murder is solved." I took a slow sip of tea to punctuate that I wanted this to be the end of speculation.

But of course Evelyn wasn't inclined to let it go. "Jessica, do you suppose that they found something new? I am not stupid. I know Mort has his eye on me, and if he comes up with the slightest bit of evidence that could put a noose around my neck . . ."

"Evelyn, what could Mort find that could put you further in his sights? We know he already has a witness who saw you approach the gym on the night Martin Terranova was killed. What else could there be? Did you leave something behind? Pick something up?" I was honestly thinking of fingerprints, which I chose not to mention. I should not have been surprised when she answered.

"Well, that's just it, Jessica. I looked through the window of the gym and saw Terranova was walking around and straightening this machine or rearranging that one while he was cleaning them with a spray bottle and chamois cloth. It looked like he would be occupied for a while, so I decided to take a look around the property. I went into the toolshed, which was disappointing. I didn't find anything besides the usual gardening tools, along with a hammer, a few screwdrivers, cans of WD-40, and the like." Evelyn hesitated long enough for me to be certain that there was something she wasn't sure she wanted to mention.

"What did you do next?" I prompted.

"I went into the garage. And that is where I found this." Evelyn began rummaging through her oversized tote bag and came out with an envelope, which she passed to me. "If Terranova hadn't left his car in the driveway, I might never have seen this envelope. It was lying on the floor under where the driver's seat would have been if the car was in the garage. At some point he probably dropped it while he was getting into or out of the car."

When I lifted the flap of the envelope a picture slid into my hand. I recognized Martin Terranova sitting under a palm tree on what appeared to be a tropical beach. Cradled in his arms was a much older gray-haired woman wearing a caftan with a brightly colored bird-and-flower pattern.

"Go ahead. Tell me that's a young man vacationing with his grandma." Evelyn's tone dared me to reply.

I shook my head. "Whatever the relationship is between Terranova and this woman, it certainly appears to have a romantic touch. I wonder who she is?"

"That is exactly what I wanted to find out, which is why I took the picture with me. But before I could investigate, Mort Metzger pulled me into his office for a lengthy interrogation. Once I realized that, thanks to loudmouth Hilly Davis, Mort knew I was on Terranova's property around the time of the murder, well, it didn't seem like a good idea for me to say, *Nah, I didn't kill anyone. I only stole a picture.* And for that matter, while Mort is casting his net around, looking for murder suspects, why isn't he taking a closer look at Hilly?" Evelyn lifted her hand and smacked the table with such force that dollops of tea splashed over the top of her mug.

I automatically passed her a couple of napkins, and while she was blotting the tea from the tabletop around her cup, I said, "Evelyn, in all the years you and Mort worked here in Cabot Cove, I can't recall a time you ever worked together. And it was always you who was adversarial. Whenever a crime happened that you thought would be of great community interest, you behaved as though you and Mort were in a race. You were never cooperative for fear that sharing information with law enforcement would hurt your 'scoop,' as you liked to call those bold headlines you wrote so creatively. Am I right?" I looked her straight in the eye.

"Jessica, that's my job." She stared back defiantly.

I raised my hand, palm out, in school-crossing-guard fashion, and brought her to a full stop. "That *was* your job when you were editor of the *Gazette*, but now that is Dan's job. Let's be clear. You are a former resident who has come to Mort's attention for two reasons. First, you have been loudly bad-mouthing Terranova, who is now a murder victim, since you arrived back in Cabot Cove. Second, and definitely the more serious, you were seen at the murder site quite close to the time the murder occurred. You know Mort would certainly be in his rights to declare you a person of interest in this murder, and yet you persist in pretending that he is persecuting you, and all the while you withhold evidence from him."

"And if I give him this picture, then what?" Evelyn grimaced. "He nails me for trespassing and maybe even removing evidence from a crime scene, and I lose my opportunity to find this woman, who is the one person I am sure can tell us exactly what a greedy perv Terranova was and how he took her to the beach and scammed her out of every last nickel in her bank account."

I could see Evelyn was getting more agitated, so I switched my approach ever so slightly. "Has it occurred to you that Mort would have more resources to find the lady in the picture than you have? He has access to all of Terranova's personal and business records. Perhaps somewhere in his files there is another picture with a name. Or perhaps he has another means to identify her."

"You have a point there. Short of showing the picture to every newspaper editor in Maine—if I could even get their attention— I am at a loss as to how to identify this woman." Evelyn's shoulders slumped and she dropped her head, chin to chest.

We sat quietly for a couple of minutes. Finally, Evelyn sat up straight, picked up her mug, and finished her tea. Then she pushed her mug toward the center of the table. "Okay. Decision made. I'll call Demetri. He can drive me to the drugstore. They can make me a couple of copies of the picture in a matter of minutes. Then I will go to the sheriff's office and give Mort the original, and he can do his thing while I continue to do mine."

"Would you like some company?" I offered, glad to see she had come to her senses.

Evelyn smiled, a rare thing, and said, "You're a sweetheart, Jessica, but no, thanks. This is something I should handle by myself. I violated private property and, for lack of a better word, stole the picture. Time to fess up."

She hoisted her enormous tote bag up on her shoulder and headed for the front door. With one hand high over her head, she waved good-bye. "Take care, Jessica. I'll be sure and write from my lonely cell in the hoosegow."

She was laughing manically when I heard the door close behind her.

I could only imagine the contentious conversation that she and Mort would be having in a few minutes' time. And I was somewhat relieved that I wouldn't be part of it. I refilled my mug and set it next to my computer on the dining room table. It was past time for me to get some work done on my San Diego mystery.

I had already organized my research material into files: location, victim, first murder method, second murder method, etc. Now I wanted to integrate the information into cohesive story form in preparation for my synopsis. I was making so much progress that the jangling of my telephone startled me. I snatched the receiver off the phone, and without waiting for my hello, Mort Metzger began. "I don't know how you manage to do it, Mrs. F. Evelyn Phillips is the most irritating, cantankerous woman I have ever met, but today she comes marching into my office, calm and sweet as you please, to tell me exactly what she was doing on Terranova's property the night he was killed. How do you like that?"

"Why, that's—that's wonderful, Mort," I said.

"'Wonderful' is the word for it, and according to Evelyn, I owe it all to you. Although how you, or anyone, could talk that woman into doing a single thing that she's not inclined to do escapes me." Mort sounded as though he would be pondering for years to find that answer.

"Actually, I merely suggested—"

But Mort cut me off. "Let me tell you what your suggestion did. If Evelyn is being totally honest, and she sure sounds like she is, the time frame she gave me for her little adventure in the tool-shed and the garage matches the time Hilly said he saw her. So, with her seeing Terranova alive and well and Hilly seeing her at the same time, we are able to tighten the window for the time of death by about twenty minutes. That's provided Evelyn is not the killer, of course."

"Oh, Mort, you know as well as I do that Evelyn Phillips is all bluster and no bite," I said.

"Not sure I agree with you there, but in this situation, you are probably right. Evelyn spends her energy looking for the big headline, Pulitzer Prize kind of stuff. And if she turned out to be the killer, the headlines might be gigantic, but she'd be on the wrong end of them."

I had to smile at Mort's logic. "I agree. Evelyn's goal is to *write* the story, not to *be* the story." And then I asked, as nonchalantly as I could, "Have you heard from Floyd and Andy? Did they find anything of importance at Terranova's house?"

"Besides your fingerprints?" Mort laughed. "Only teasing, Mrs. F. I haven't heard from them, but I did tell them to turn every room over at least twice, so it will be hours before they come back to the station. With or without new information is anybody's guess."

I settled in my chair and reentered the world of murder and mayhem I was creating. By the time I finished working for the day, I was confident that tomorrow I would be able to begin writing my synopsis. How was I to know that an interruption of my morning bicycle ride would lead to a day of chaos?

Chapter Twenty-One

Early the next morning I started my favorite bicycle jaunt, pedaling up to the ridge overlooking the harbor. The ride was complicated by the occasional powerful gust of wind that made me feel as though the temperature had dropped momentarily by at least twenty degrees. Then the wind would calm down and I would glide along until the next gust had my teeth chattering. Still, the sun was strong and some early birds were singing. All in all it was a joyful morning in spite of the wind.

I made my usual turn around the flagpole and gave Old Glory a salute. I was on my way home when I recognized Dan Andrews coming directly toward me on his sporty new Hiland racing bike. As we got closer to each other, I slowed down, assuming we'd say a friendly "Good morning." I was surprised that Dan kept pedaling furiously until he skidded to a stop beside me.

I thought he was speeding to show off what the bike could do until he said, "I am so glad I found you. I need your help. I'm afraid I am in over my head. Pierce and I met with Angus last night and he had quite a story to tell. In fact, the main problem I saw was that the story kept changing.

"Anyway, the three of us were in my office haggling until the wee hours, and I didn't dare call you last night. Desperate as I am feeling, I'm not ready to go to Mort Metzger . . ."

Dan looked so helpless that I took pity on him. "Please, just tell me what you want me to do."

"I told Pierce and Angus that, as members of the Fire Department Developmental Committee, you and I would meet with them in my office this morning at nine sharp to discuss how we can fix this purchasing mess without getting the entire town in an uproar." He shrugged as if he didn't know what else to say.

I didn't like the sound of that and said so. "Oh dear, are you saying there is more to the issue than we were told yesterday?"

Dan pursed his lips and raised his eyes to the sky, and then, as though he'd made a decision, he looked back at me. "Much more. Will you come? I have to admit I need the support. Jessica, I am still too new in town to take the lead. Will you help me?"

I looked at my watch. It was nearly eight o'clock. I still had to bike home, shower, and get dressed for the day. "I'll tell you what. I can be ready and standing at my front gate at ten to nine. Would you be able to pick me up, or shall I call Demetri?"

For the first time that morning Dan smiled. "Jessica, you are a lifesaver. I will see you at ten to nine." And he pedaled off as swiftly as he'd arrived.

True to his word, Dan Andrews was parked in front of my house with his car engine running when I opened my front door.

On the brief ride to his office I tried to find out exactly what had happened last night and what kind of turmoil we were facing, but Dan was extremely tight-lipped. All he would say was that it was best to wait until we were all together.

Pierce Collymore and Angus Billingsworth were standing in front of the *Gazette* office when we pulled up. I was glad they were on time so I wouldn't have to wait much longer to find out what had Dan so roiled. I did notice that in the few months since I last saw Angus he seemed to have aged. He'd always been clean-shaven but now he sported a scraggly beard, and his eyes had a rheumy look to them; whether that was from age or illness, I had no idea.

Dan invited us to follow him inside and led us to seats at the conference table in the main room. He went into his private office and came back with four bottles of water, a stack of paper napkins, and a bowl of grapes. I thought that was a clever way of making this appear to be a normal developmental committee meeting even though everyone at the table knew it was not.

It appeared that each of us was waiting for someone else to start the conversation, because for the first few minutes, we sat in silence. Then Dan cleared his throat and said, "Angus, I know it may be difficult for you to repeat everything you told Pierce and me last night, but Jessica needs to understand the facts so she can help us decide how to resolve the problem."

Angus nodded but didn't speak.

Dan tried again. "Jessica is aware that there have been some problems with the Fire Department purchasing account. Angus, I'd like you, as the former chief, to explain to her how the trouble came to be."

Angus ran his fingers through his thinning, unkempt hair,

and then threw back his shoulders and stared straight at me. "The most important thing, Miz Fletcher, is that I want you to remember that Cabot Cove always had and still does have the finest kind of fire department. Well trained and courageous."

I instantly realized that whatever I was about to learn was deadly serious. In the twenty or so years we'd known each other, Angus had always called me Jessica. "Ms. Fletcher" sounded awfully formal to my ears.

"Now, Angus," I said as gently as I could, "you are among friends. Please, tell me."

"It was all a trap. I see it now, but at the time . . ." Angus shook his head. "Not sure why I was so dumb."

"A trap? Who set the trap?" I asked as delicately as I could.

"Why, that Olivia Quigley, o' course. Who else would have the gumption? Supervisor of the town's budget office! Ha! Town crook is more like it."

I must have looked as puzzled as I felt, and Angus decided he was out of his league. "This is a mite hard for me to explain. I'm feeling a bit gawmy. Dan? Pierce? Help a fella out?"

Dan sighed. "Okay, Angus. I will tell Jessica what we talked about last night, but I need you to jump in and correct me if I get something wrong."

"Ayuh, I will, and that is a promise," Angus said.

"Okay, so, Jessica, some of what Angus told us last night was totally unknown to me and to Pierce—"

"That'd be because you two come from away." Angus folded his arms and gave a brief but satisfied smile as if he had made a grand contribution to the conversation.

Dan shot him a look and then continued. "According to Angus, the main reason Olivia Quigley was hired as head of the budget office after her predecessor retired was that Mayor Jim Shevlin and the town council saw a real need for modernization, and of all the applicants, they thought Olivia filled the bill best. Does any of this sound familiar, Jessica?"

"Actually, I remember it quite well. In fact, Seth Hazlitt was on the hiring committee and he was quite keen about another applicant—a young man from Portland, I believe—but when all was said and done, they offered the job to Olivia and highlighted her computer programming savvy as the skill set that would streamline our billing and payment procedures." I looked at Angus, who gave me a slight nod as if I had scored one for the home team.

Dan continued. "According to Angus, Olivia spent some time with him, just as she did with the other department heads. She patiently explained the innovative procedures and taught him how to fill out the new purchase forms, which she said were less complicated than the old forms but Angus thought were . . . What did you say, Angus? That they were just as troublesome?"

"Ayuh, that's what I told her time and again." Angus turned to me. "You have to remember that all this was happening just about the time I lost my Sarah to the cancer. I had no room in my heart or my head to learn anything new."

I winced as I recalled Angus's wife's, Sarah Billingsworth's, long, torturous illness, and I remembered that, except for meeting his duties as fire chief, Angus barely left her side. I could see how learning a new billing-and-purchase system might have been one chore too many for Angus during that dreadful time.

Angus dropped his eyes to the tabletop. "Tell her the rest. No use holding back the evil part."

Dan hesitated for half a beat, and then said, "After a few

weeks, Olivia told Angus that the town was modifying the process."

"Called it a 'rebate procedure,' she did. If I didn't have my own troubles surrounding me, I might have questioned her, got a few answers, but that wasn't the way of it." Angus cradled his head in his hands. "You tell her, Danny. I can't say it all again."

"Olivia told Angus that she discovered that under the old method the town had inadvertently paid too much for a variety of fire department purchases, so she had arranged with the suppliers to discount some of the department's purchases and provide rebates for others."

Angus interrupted Dan. "Made sense to me. If we paid too much, we should get our money back, wouldn't you think? But the way of it—that is what should have got me thinking."

When Angus didn't continue, Dan picked up the thread. "As we discovered when Pierce began to receive checks made out to Angus, the plan Olivia devised was to return half the cost of a paid-for but unpurchased item directly to Angus. Olivia told him to cash the checks, put ten percent of the money in the fire department's petty cash fund, and pass the other ninety percent over to her so she could deposit it in the town account."

"Angus, did Olivia give you any reason for such an unusual process?" I asked. "It would seem to me that money being returned to the town should be in a check made out to the town, and then if they wanted to give part of it to any agency's petty cash fund, a check would come from the town's main account."

Pierce and Dan both nodded in agreement.

Angus looked at me with those sad, rheumy eyes. "I got no answer. She was the new budget lady and I followed what she said. Like I told you, I was more worried about Sarah, so this money stuff wasn't that important to me. And by the time that Sarah passed, well, Olivia's ways with the money had become routine. I just followed along, didn't think much about it. Once I retired, I thought all that would become Pierce's problem, but that wasn't the truth of it."

Pierce said, "In spite of my becoming chief of the department, Olivia continued to have these rebate checks made out to Angus, and he continued to cash them. I would never have known except that first one and then a second check made out to Angus were delivered to me amid copies of the run-of-the-mill paperwork. I came to Dan for clarification and we spoke to Angus. And now you are up to date."

I was perplexed. "Angus, just so I am clear, you continued to receive these 'rebate' checks *after* you retired? Can you tell me what you did with them?"

Angus's cheeks turned a fiery red and he dropped his eyes to the tabletop. "When I got the first one, I called Olivia. Told her a mistake was made. She drove over to my house lickety-split. I thought she come for the check. That's when she told me that all these years I'd been cashing what she called 'kickbacks'—you know, payoffs from the vendors. I couldn't believe it. When I threatened to go to the mayor and the sheriff and turn her in because, after all, she set up the plan and she got most of the money, she actually laughed right in my face."

Angus lifted his head and slued his eyes at the three of us sitting at the table. "Then she said all those checks from the different vendors were written to me. I cashed them. If I claimed I handed the money over to her, it would strictly be my say-so against hers. I was already a crook, so what could I do? I keep on cashing the checks, only now I give her all the money."

"No, Angus, you most certainly are not guilty of anything more than naivete. You were set up to take the fall. Olivia targeted you at a time when you were vulnerable because of all you were going through with Sarah. I am sure if we four put our heads together, we can find a way to shine some light on Olivia's crimes while making you the hero." I was determined to ensure that the real culprit was caught and punished.

Apparently so was Dan. He rubbed his hands together vigorously and said, "Let's get to it."

Chapter Twenty-Two

Within an hour we had a detailed strategy. Then it took the three of us a lot of persuading to convince Angus that he would not be in any trouble as long as he stayed calm and we all proceeded according to plan.

As time went by I became more and more anxious to get home so I could begin working on the synopsis for the book I now thought of as *Murder at the Cabrillo Monument*, so you can imagine my relief when we finally adjourned. We shook hands all around and reassured Angus we three would stand by him to the end, and then Dan and I got into his car for the short ride to my house.

In all the time since Dan had arrived in Cabot Cove, he had been so reserved that I was genuinely surprised by his effusive gratitude for my support. He was still gushing when he pulled up to my front gate. "Jessica, I really can't thank you enough for your help. After we talked to Angus, Pierce and I were in a panic.

Angus kept saying things like, 'I'll take my punishment. I know now that what I did was wrong, but I didn't know how to get out of it.' And now you have shown all of us a way."

"It's not over yet," I cautioned. "Angus is bound to be shaky. It is up to you, and especially to Pierce, to keep him calm until it is time for us to act."

"I understand, and I know Pierce does. Trust us. We will be alongside Angus every step of the way."

I opened the car door, climbed out, and then had a worrisome thought. I leaned on the door and stuck my head back into the car and said, "And for goodness' sake, don't let Evelyn hear a word about any of this. If she gets so much as a whiff, our plan is doomed."

Dan touched his chest with his index finger. "Cross my heart. Not so much as a syllable."

I hung my jacket on the coat tree, and then as I walked through the dining room, I tapped the control button to start up my computer. Once in the kitchen I put on the kettle and popped a piece of wheat bread in the toaster. My niece Donna had recently sent me what she liked to call a "because we miss you" gift. This package was from a farm on the eastern end of Long Island and contained half a dozen jars filled with jam made from different fruits grown on the farm. I hadn't yet tried the raspberry and I thought it might just hit the spot. I found it tucked between the jars of strawberry and mulberry in the pantry.

I had already poured my tea and was spreading the thick red jam on my lightly toasted bread when I heard a light tap behind me and the kitchen door opened. Seth Hazlitt came in carrying a small cardboard box with FLORIDA printed on the side, next to a picture of a fat, luscious-looking orange surrounded by bright green leaves.

"Lucky us, Jess, here it is, not quite spring, and one of my patients brought me a few of the fresh oranges he bought while visiting his mother in Tampa. He shared with me and I am sharing with you."

He set the box on the table and looked at my toast and jam. "And if you had anything you wanted to share in return . . ."

Seth was so obvious that I had to laugh. "Why don't you have a seat? The kettle is still hot, so I can make you a cup of tea. If you prefer coffee, that will take a few minutes longer. And I bet you'd like me to drop a slice of wheat bread in the toaster."

"Tea would be perfectly fine. As for the toast, two slices would do me better than one—I had an early breakfast and am feeling a little peckish." Seth patted his ample stomach as he pulled out a chair and took a seat at the table.

While I was fixing Seth's tea and toast he casually asked me what was new, and I made an instant decision not to mention anything about Angus's troubles. At this point I had no reason to tell him and I could see no harm in his not knowing.

"Well, it took far longer than I expected, but I've finally completed enough research for the San Diego book that I am confident I can move forward." I put his toast on a plate, set it beside his teacup, and slipped into my own chair.

"Of course you have. I had no doubt whatsoever. You always manage to get your books done on time, come fire or flood. Truth be told, what I am interested in learning about is the story behind the talk floating around Mara's this morning. It seems that you spent quite a bit of time at the sheriff's office yesterday. Word has it that later in the day Evelyn Phillips stopped by here to visit with you and then she spent time with Mort as well." Seth gave me a sly grin.

"And you're here because you want to know the latest gossip," I said.

"Not the gossip. Plenty of that going around Mara's, and it wouldn't surprise me to find it circulating at Loretta's, Sassi's Bakery, the check-out counters at the Fruit and Veg, and possibly the library reading room. I came here to get the facts firsthand. I'm surprised that whatever you, Evelyn, and Mort are all confabbing about, you didn't call to tell me first thing." He sounded miffed but I took that to be part of his teasing.

I was so relieved that the chatter around town was still centered on the Terranova murder and that there hadn't been a hint of the financial scandal that would soon be brewing around the town hall that I was absolutely cheerful while I brought Seth up to date on the results of my search of Terranova's house and Evelyn's search of his garage.

Seth looked at me with raised eyebrows. "Breaking and entering. I am amazed Mort didn't put handcuffs on the pair of you."

Now it was my turn to pretend to be offended. "There was no breaking. Evelyn and I were both fortunate enough to come across open doors. And besides, I told Mort where to find Joseph Terranova's driver's license, and I'm sure Evelyn gave Mort the picture she found on the garage floor. Our little finds were more than enough for Mort to send Floyd and Andy to recanvass the house, and now, I suppose, the garage."

"In hindsight, they should have treated the entire property as a crime scene from day one," Seth said, "but with the body in the gym, I guess that building would have been the main focus."

Since we were chatting so informally about Terranova's murder, I decided to ask once again a question that Seth had refused to answer in the past. "Completely between us—and you know I will never quote you—in your opinion, is Bertha Mae mentally agile enough to have avoided being completely taken in by Terranova?"

Seth leaned back in his chair and looked at the ceiling while he was deciding how to answer. Finally he said, "Let me share a common observation with you: There is no fool like an old fool. What do you expect me to say? That kind of matter of the heart is not a medical issue. I can only opine on the matters of the heart that can be detected with a stethoscope."

"Well, then I will ask you something that has been on my mind and would definitely be a medical issue. Among your patients or during your meetings at the hospital, have you heard of any serious injuries happening at Terranova's gym?" I had been considering that that might be an avenue that would lead us to people who might have wanted to hurt Terranova.

"You mean injuries more serious than José Ramos turning up in the hospital emergency room with a sprained ankle after he fell off the treadmill while working out at Perfection? Not that I've heard." Seth shook his head. "Why are you looking for other potential murderers here in Cabot Cove? You told me that you found a New Hampshire driver's license with Martin Terranova's picture but it has his name as Joseph. Woman, there's your clue. I am sure that by now Mort has called the local law in Dover,

New Hampshire, and gotten all the information on which Terranova that dead body actually is. Er, could you pass me an apple from the fruit bowl while we speculate on what Evelyn was doing in Mort's office? I think the whole town was surprised that once Mort had her, he let her leave."

While I was explaining to Seth my assumptions about the older woman in the picture and the odd place where Evelyn found it, the back of my mind was putting two pictures together, the one Evelyn found and the one on Joseph Terranova's New Hampshire driver's license. Rather than hope to discover what Mort may or may not have found out, I was optimistic that a road trip to New Hampshire could provide much desired information, and I was positive that, even if he had the time and the inclination, Seth wouldn't be the right companion for the trip.

"Once the killer is caught, there is still another problem to be resolved," I said. "How is Oscar Cisneros ever going to recover his reputation? Without it, his life here in Cabot Cove is over. Doris Ann told me he has been in the library looking at travel books."

"Maybe the killer will confess that he is the one who framed Oscar and all will be well," Seth suggested.

"Oh no, that will never happen. Based on Tim Purdy's seeing Terranova near Oscar's shed, first with and then without a package, I am inclined to believe that it was the murder victim who framed Oscar, not the murderer. It fits with Terranova needing to be sure that he was becoming the only person Bertha Mae would trust," I said.

"Well, if you're right about that, I suppose with him dead there is no way that we will ever know for sure." Seth drained his teacup and stood. "I've kept you away from your book long enough. I guess even with me here, that book is rattling around in your head, dying to jump out. In any event, I'll have patients lining up at my door in a few minutes, so I'd best get out of your way."

"Seth, I can't thank you enough for stopping by. Even though I am a bit preoccupied by my book, I appreciate having the opportunity to talk about all that is happening with the Terranova killing. How about we switch gears to a fun conversation tomorrow? Breakfast at Mara's? The usual time? On me?"

Seth laughed. "My favorite meal? At gossip central and at no cost to me? How can I resist? I will see you then." He opened the kitchen door, then looked back at the table and winked at me. "Don't forget to try those oranges."

As soon as the door closed I began tidying the kitchen, and in a few minutes it was presentable enough that I could move into the dining room. I picked up the top folder from the pile next to my computer and opened it, intending to skim through it one last time before I began writing. After the first few sentences, I realized that I wasn't the least bit focused.

I dropped the folder on the table and walked to the telephone and called the *Gazette* office. Dan answered on the second ring.

"Jessica, how are you?" He sounded loud and somewhat jolly. His next sentence explained why. "Evelyn is here, and she was just telling me how taking your advice got her out of trouble with Mort."

I let him know I understood. "So you can't talk."

"That's exactly right. If you are calling about the change in day and time for the Friends of the Library meeting, Doris Ann already notified us and there will be an announcement in the morning's paper."

"Call me when you are free. It's important."

"I sure will. Good-bye, now." And Dan clicked off.

In spite of the fact that she didn't live here anymore, Evelyn Phillips still had a remarkable ability to get in my way.

Chapter Twenty-Three

Disappointed as I was that I couldn't immediately lock Dan into a trip to New Hampshire, it did give me time to buckle down and work on the synopsis for my novel. I was satisfied with my progress during the several hours until my phone rang.

When I answered, Dan was buzzing over his conversation with Evelyn. "Jessica, I had a hard time believing it, but Evelyn was more upbeat than I had seen her in years. Her conversation with Sheriff Metzger went so well that I believe she now considers herself to be deputized, or at least a consultant to the department."

"I wish she'd shown some of that goodwill toward law enforcement when she was editor of the *Gazette*. That could have saved us all from dealing with continuous friction between her and Mort," I said.

"Jessica, I've known Evelyn for more years than I can count, and I can tell you that today's smile could easily morph into tomorrow's frown. We will have to keep our fingers crossed. Your earlier phone call has me concerned. Nothing wrong with our Angus plan, I hope?" Dan sounded fretful.

"I'd be the last to know. I thought you and Pierce were in charge of Angus. It's your primary responsibility to keep him calm until the moment comes. In the meantime I have other things that I want to take a look at. Would you be up for a car ride to New Hampshire anytime soon?" I asked.

"New Hampshire, eh? Why do I think your attention has moved from Angus to Martin Terranova?" Dan chuckled. "As I recall, South Berwick is right near the Maine–New Hampshire border."

"Yes. We were so close and didn't know it. Do you remember the receptionist in the dentist office saying that they had a patient named Joseph Terranova but declining to give us an address?"

"Don't tell me! You found his address and he is across the border in New Hampshire." Dan was beginning to share the excitement I'd been feeling since I first saw the driver's license.

"Even better. I have a picture of a New Hampshire driver's license that indicates that Joseph and Martin are one and the same, which is good, hard evidence, and I have already shared it with Mort but—"

"But all the same," Dan continued as though reading my mind, "you'd like to visit New Hampshire and examine every little nook and cranny for yourself. I can't wait to see the driver's license. Can you text me a picture? I have one small item to take care of here at the office, and then I am free for the rest of the day. What say I pick you up in half an hour?"

*   *   *

The ride to South Berwick seemed shorter than it had the last time we had driven there, but the shops and houses looked just as welcoming. We passed through the town and got on Highway 4, and as soon as we crossed the border into New Hampshire we were in the town of Dover.

"Wow, talk about back-to-back!" Dan said. "South Berwick runs along the Maine border, and Dover is alongside it as the New Hampshire border town."

"Wouldn't you say that is a convenient location for a person who is furtive about his identity? He lived in one state, got his dental care and goodness knows what else a few miles away in a completely different state. And perhaps no one in either state got to know Mr. Terranova very well," I said.

"Well, we are about to find out. Where would you like to start?" Dan asked.

"Since this is Central Avenue and there are lots of shops, let's just pick a few." I pointed to a small strip mall. "That's a good place to start. I doubt they would know him in the nail salon, but there's a barbershop, a convenience store, a shoe repair shop, and a smoke shop. He may have frequented one of them."

"If you say so, but I can't see Mr. Body Beautiful going anywhere near a smoke shop," Dan said.

"I would agree with you if I hadn't found an ashtray sharing space with candles and a lighter in a drawer in his dining room. Even if it was used only when he had company, he might have been the kind of host who provided cigarettes or cigars to his guests," I said.

"I don't see it," Dan said as he pulled the car into a parking spot. "Let's try that shop first and we will find out for sure."

"You mean we will find out which of us is correct." I laughed. "You're on."

It turned out Dan was right. Even if Joseph Terranova personally used the ashtray in his house, he wasn't a regular customer of the Smoke Shed on Central Avenue in Dover.

Our mission was a lot easier than it had been in South Berwick. Now we had a picture and an address rather than only a name as reference.

The craftsman in the shoe repair shop explained that he'd bought the shop only a few months earlier and apologized profusely that he was still getting to know his neighbors and customers.

The young lad in the convenience store said that Joseph looked familiar. "Did he ride a bicycle a lot? A guy who rode around town on a sharp-looking Redline kinda looked like this guy but I'm not really sure. Haven't seen him since I was a kid, so I can't tell you much more."

When we got outside, Dan let out the snicker he'd barely been able to contain. "When he was a kid? What is he now? Sixteen, eighteen?"

"You forget, I taught high school, and as I recall, the delineation in the teenage mind between 'kid' and 'grown-up' is decided by possession of a driver's license. And by that standard, as a teacher I know I was the butt of many a joke. I believe the driver's license age in New Hampshire is sixteen."

"Ah, got it," Dan said.

We walked past an empty store with a prominent "For Rent"

sign in the window and went into the barbershop. The lone barber was using a shiny silver clipper on a young man's neck and proceeded a few inches up the back of his head.

Dan nudged my arm and pointed to the two older men sitting in the back corner playing checkers. He whispered, "Like an old-time movie."

I smiled and fondly remembered that up until Jake Little retired and moved to Charleston to live with his youngest daughter, checkers and chess games were common in his barbershop a few doors down from Charlene Sassi's bakery.

The barber held a mirror so his customer could see how closely shaved the back of his head was. "Even the Marines would want you with that close cut. For sure you'll look snappy when you present your Eagle Scout project during your board review."

The teenager blushed, hopped out of the chair, murmured, "Thank you," as he handed the barber some bills, and bolted from the shop.

The barber turned his attention to us. "I'm Jonas Perkins. Can I help you folks?"

Dan stepped forward and introduced us both; then he held up his phone displaying the picture of Joseph Terranova's driver's license. "We are looking for someone we once knew. He lived here in Dover a few years ago and we know he is not at his current address. By any chance do you recognize him?"

The barber barely glanced at the picture. "Oh, him. Gus, Lionel." The checkers players looked up from their game. "You remember that fella, gym teacher of some sort. Way too fancy to get a haircut here. Used to drive all the way to Durham to get his cuts from some upmarket 'stylist' who had a shop near the university."

"Gym guy. Sure. Remember him, yep. Ain't seen him in

forever," one of the checkers players said, and they bent their heads back over their game board.

"Is there anyone who might remember more about him? Someone who might be able to tell us when he left Dover and where he went?" I smiled as though I was confident that he could provide the information I needed. And, luckily, he did.

"Your friend"—he looked at Dan's phone again—"Joseph, is it? Used to take a lot of meals at the diner down on Main Street. Seems to me that someone there should be able to help you out. Ask for Ollie. He's owned the place for twenty years or more. Ain't much he don't know."

Jonas gave us directions to the diner, wished us good luck, and wandered over to watch the checkers game before we'd even left his shop.

The diner parking lot was not overly crowded and that certainly buoyed my spirits. We had a good chance of finding Ollie when he had some free time to talk to us.

We sat in a booth by the tall, wide window overlooking the parking lot, with a view of the street beyond.

In an instant a middle-aged blonde with a smile that belied her years was standing beside us, holding a tray that had a coffeepot and two mugs on it. She said, "Hi, I'm Margo. Can I interest you in a cup of coffee?"

"You most certainly can," I said. "Margo, I feel as though you read my mind. I need a pick-me-up and coffee will do it."

She laughed. "There's no secret to it. Most folks that come in this time of day are either late lunch or coffee and a snack. I save myself a few steps if I show up with the coffee and mugs."

I nodded. "Back home in Cabot Cove, Maine, my friend Mara often walks around her restaurant with a coffeepot at the ready."

"Mara? The prizewinning-blueberry-pancake lady? Wait until my boss finds out you know her. He's been trying to wiggle her pancake recipe out of her for years. He'll be asking you to spy for him," Margo said.

"Would your boss be called Ollie, by any chance?" I asked.

"He sure would. Don't tell me Mara sent you to speak to him." Margo grew wide-eyed.

I shook my head. "No, she didn't, but I was hoping to talk to him about another matter. I am looking for information about someone who lived here a few years ago."

"Ollie is definitely your man. There is nothing and no one in Dover that escapes his eye or his ear. In fact, I can tell you that more business transactions take place in these booths than in most of the lawyers' offices in town. Before I get Ollie, is there anything else I can get for you? Maybe a pastry or a piece of pie? Apple crumb is today's special."

As delicious as that sounded, I declined while Dan opted for a piece of pie.

Margo was back in a flash. She set Dan's pie on the table, topped off our coffee cups, and said, "I told Ollie that you were friends of Mara's and wanted a word with him but that it wasn't about pancakes." She giggled. "I couldn't help myself. He harrumphed but said he would talk to you anyway. He is a really nice man."

Then she slipped back into waitress mode, looked at Dan, and said, "Enjoy your pie, sir." And she walked to the next table, coffeepot in hand.

Dan had nearly finished his pie and I was getting a bit antsy wondering if we would ever meet Ollie when a voice behind me said, "What's this I hear? Is it true Mara sent you down from Maine to wheedle the recipe for my apple crumb pie out of me?"

Chapter Twenty-Four

We heard a deep, enjoyable laugh, and a tall, rotund man with a neatly shaved head moved to stand at the side of our table. Ollie was wearing a white short-sleeved shirt and white pants covered by a long white apron hanging from a neck loop and tied at his waist.

I said, "You must be Ollie. Thank you for taking the time to speak with us."

Dan slid toward the window and said, "Please have a seat."

"Don't mind if I do. I take it you folks are visitors needing a hand and not actually recipe poachers, so how can I help?" Ollie's smile was warm and friendly.

We introduced ourselves, and then I told him we were looking for information about someone who had lived in Dover at one time. I held up my phone, and as soon as he saw the picture of Terranova's driver's license, he said, "Oh sure, I remember Joe. He ran a yoga studio two blocks down." Ollie waved vaguely to his right. "And he loved his salads with lots of added protein like meats, eggs, beans. The man loved his protein."

I made a snap decision not to tell him that Mara had said something quite similar. "What can you tell us about his business? And do you have any idea why he left Dover?"

"I am happy to tell you what I know and what I think, but turnabout is fair play, so first you can tell me why you are asking questions about Joe and how you came to have a copy of his license. You cops or something?"

"'Or something' fits us to a T. I'm the editor of the *Cabot Cove Gazette*." Dan had his press card at the ready. "Mrs. Fletcher here is my assistant. Mr. Terranova passed away recently and we are trying to gather all the background information we can for a Sunday feature about his life."

I chimed in. "Our local sheriff, Mort Metzger, authorized me to have the picture of the driver's license for identity purposes and I shared it with Dan." That was close enough to the truth that I didn't feel guilty saying it.

"Press, huh? Well, I guess if Mike from our own *Dover Daily* was asking these questions, I'd answer him straight and true, so there's no reason why I can't do the same with you folks. Fire away."

"We are interested in learning when he came here and what type of business he was in while he lived here. We're also curious when he moved from Dover, and we'd entertain any guesses you might have as to why he left." Dan was succinct in his questions, leaving plenty of room for Ollie's answers.

Ollie leaned back and rested one arm on the hard red plastic that edged the top of the booth. "It seems to me it was five or six years ago that Kaye Silverman closed up her what-knot shop and went off to one of those retirement communities in Florida. Why, I can't imagine, but I heard she's happy there, playing a lot of golf and such."

He slued his eyes from me to Dan and back again. Satisfied that he had our undivided attention, he continued. "A few months later I heard that some young fella bought Kaye's shop. We all speculated on what a young'un would do with a what-knot shop, but as it happened, he turned it into some sort of gym. He named the place the Ladies Gym and Yoga Studio and drew in nearly the exact same customers that Kaye had. Women of a certain age, if you catch my drift."

A worried look flitted briefly across his face and he looked directly at me. "By 'a certain age' I mean ladies older than you. Much older than you. I hope you didn't take offense."

I smiled reassuringly. "Of course not. Do you have any idea why he aimed his, ah, business model at that particular age group?"

"Darned if I know. 'Course, there was a lot of speculation at the monthly business owners' luncheons. Most thought he was foolish and inexperienced and would have to shut down in a matter of months or even weeks. He surprised us all when he managed to hold on for a couple of years."

"But he did eventually move on. Do you know why?" I asked.

Ollie grimaced and shrugged his shoulders. "Simple enough, I suppose. Like I said, Joe specialized in women clients, ones who'd been eligible for Social Security for a decade or more, and they don't have the longest of life spans. Nature took its course and Joe began losing clients. He held steady for a while, and then one day a moving truck pulled up and he was gone."

Dan and I exchanged a look. Terranova milked the Dover ladies for what he could get, and when the pool dried up he simply moved away.

Then Ollie asked, "Young guy like that—how'd he die, anyway?"

Since we were in a public place and Ollie was the proprietor, I practically whispered, "He was murdered," so as not to draw attention, but it was no use.

"Murdered?" Ollie's voice boomed throughout the diner. We could hear cutlery drop to the tabletops, and both Margo and a man whom I presumed to be the cook burst through the swinging kitchen doors.

Ollie realized he'd caused a commotion and speedily calmed everyone down by saying, "Sorry, all. We're talking about a television show. Plot was so good I got carried away."

There were several titters and guffaws scattered about the diner, and then everyone went about their business.

Ollie lowered his head as if talking to the table and asked, "How'd it happen?"

Dan explained that Terranova was found in his gym and had been killed with a weight bar.

"That's good. He went out like he would have wanted to—at his own gym, on his own equipment. I always tell my wife I want them to find me on a Sunday after the post-church breakfast crowd has gone home. I'll be in the back booth reading the Sunday papers. I hope when I go, my face falls splat on the comic section." Ollie gave a deep belly laugh, which I was happy to note drew very little attention. I supposed his customers were used to it.

Ollie refused payment for our coffees and Dan's pie, saying he couldn't have Mara thinking he hadn't treated us like the finest of company. He walked us to the door, and he didn't seem the least bit surprised when I asked him where we might find the office of the *Dover Daily*.

Ollie smacked his forehead. "I should have realized you two wouldn't be able to leave town without saying howdy to Mike. Why, he'd be insulted if you didn't stop in. Here, let me show you." He opened the door and we stepped outside. He pointed. "Follow Main Street to the traffic light where it turns into Central Avenue. Drive over Fifth Avenue, and just past the bank on the right you will find a storefront with *The Dover Daily* printed on the window in gold letters about yea high. You can't miss it. Ask for Mike Bélanger."

We shook hands all around and Ollie made us promise to come back to visit anytime we crossed the state line between Maine and New Hampshire. As soon as we were in the car, I said to Dan, "Can you believe it? I am certain that Terranova ran a financial scam on some of the elderly women of this town, and who knows how many women in how many towns before he arrived here."

"Agreed. Now, how are we going to approach the newspaper editor? You have to remember that a news story is a news story, and if he knows what we are looking for, he's going to want details and plenty of them," Dan warned.

"We haven't even met this man, and yet you describe him as though he were Evelyn Phillips," I scoffed.

"Jessica, he is a news reporter—just like Evelyn, just like me. For us it is always about the story. All I am saying is that before we set one foot inside his office, we need to decide what and how much we are going to tell him. Like Mara's restaurant, Ollie's diner may be the center of town gossip, but the newspaper is the center of town fact," Dan said as he guided the car into the parking lot of the *Dover Daily* and turned off the ignition. "I think it's best to know ahead of time exactly what we are going to say."

We sat in the car for a few minutes while I collected my thoughts and Dan patiently waited for my answer. When I finished sifting through all the facts as I knew them, I said, "We'll tell the editor everything we know so far. We can't stop him from printing what he wants, but if we are clear about the differences between what we know to be true and what we only think is true, then I believe if he is a fact-based reporter he would want to help our search for accurate details."

"Okay, then let's go." Dan reached for his door handle. I put my hand on his arm to stop him.

"I do have one hesitancy. Is there any way our being open with the editor of this paper could hurt you or the *Gazette*? If so, I will gladly change my strategy," I said.

"Honestly, I don't know and it doesn't matter. We are trying to find a murderer, and if something we say here today leads the *Dover Daily* to break the case wide open, as the television reporters like to say, and win all sorts of awards, well, justice will have been served. Now let's go see what we can learn." Dan opened his door and slid out of the car before I could answer.

As we walked into the newspaper office, I smiled to myself, once again rejoicing in the fact that Dan lacked any resemblance to Evelyn when it came to the best way to proceed.

A pert young woman dressed in jeans and a bright green

sweatshirt that declared *DOVER established 1623* was sorting papers atop an open filing cabinet drawer. She smiled at us. "Can I help you?"

"I hope so," Dan said. "My name is Dan Andrews, editor of the *Cabot Cove Gazette* up in Maine. We were wondering if Mr. Bélanger could spare us a few minutes of his time."

"Just let me check." She gathered the papers she had been sorting, shut the file drawer with a bang, and disappeared through a nearby door.

Within minutes the door opened and a burly man with curly gray hair and a mustache to match came through with his arms outstretched in greeting.

"Dan Andrews. Welcome to New Hampshire. I'm Michel Bélanger, but you can call me Mike. Everyone does. I heard you came from New York City to take over the *Gazette* from Evelyn Phillips. I know I've been remiss in making a 'welcome to the world of small-town newspapers' telephone call to you, but we can make up for that right now." He shook Dan's hand with great energy through that entire speech, and then he turned to me.

"And this is . . . ? Oh my goodness. Jessica Fletcher, my favorite mystery author. I reread *Murder Comes to Maine* quite often, although I have to admit that for sheer mystery nothing can compare to *A Faded Rose Beside Her.*" He shook my hand as vigorously as he'd shaken Dan's. I was afraid that before the day was over we were both going to have to do shoulder stretches to relieve our overworked arm and shoulder muscles.

"Please, come inside. I'll have Delia make us some tea." Mike opened the door he'd just come through and ushered us into a hallway and through another door at the far end. "Don't mind the mess." He indicated the piles of papers and folders scattered on literally every piece of furniture. He lifted piles off two chairs on the visitors' side of his desk and motioned for us to sit.

Then Mike bounced into the oversized captain's chair on the boss's side of the desk, leaned back, linked his fingers behind his head, and asked, "Okay, now, straight up: Why are you here and what can I do for you?"

Here we go, I thought.

Chapter Twenty-Five

Although I expected Dan to start the conversation, he gave me a slight nod and an encouraging smile. Perhaps he thought that since Mike was a fan of my books, he might find the story of Terranova's murder to be more intriguing coming from me.

I took out my cell phone, scrolled to the picture of Joseph Terranova's license, showed it to Mike Bélanger, and began my tale, starting with Evelyn's concerns about Bertha Mae and ending with the discovery of Martin Terranova's murdered body.

"Sheriff Metzger has been gathering evidence that indicates Martin Terranova is Joseph M. Terranova, as shown on this license. Dan and I are here, informally, to find out whatever we can about Terranova." I stopped there to give Mike time to digest everything I'd said.

Apparently he didn't need time. He turned to Dan. "And what

is the news angle here? I grant you have a murder, but where is the guts of the story?"

Dan didn't hesitate. "That's where you come in, Mike. We were hoping to look through your files for any mention of Terranova or his gym. We will also check for any signs of elderly women who appear to be victims of what Jessica calls his 'emotional predator' behavior. We're hunting for a pattern, a connection between Cabot Cove and Dover."

"And what's in it for me?" Mike sat straight in his chair and folded his hands on the desktop.

"Any info we find in your records, the *Dover Daily* gets full credit," Dan said.

"And?" Mike clearly wanted more.

"And you get a complete copy of our story an hour before it goes public, with full permission to take what you need for a story of your own," Dan said.

Mike leaned across the desk, hand outstretched to give Dan another of his energetic handshakes. "Done."

Then he stood up and I could see we were about to be dismissed. "I can lend you Delia for an hour or so. She knows more about how we store information around here than I do. But I'm going to need her back later today. Staff meeting—you know how that goes."

With such a short and specific timeline I was anxious to get started, but Dan, ever the gentleman, showered Mike with praise and admiration wrapped in gratitude. I had to admit it was a smart move. Before this murder was solved, it was possible we would have to come back to Mike for additional access or help. Besides, I have always believed it never hurts to be kind.

Mike opened his office door and Delia was sitting at the

nearest desk. She looked up from her computer screen and came toward us in answer to Mike's wave.

"Delia, our friends from Maine need to spend some time looking through our back issues. They'll give you the specifics. Please help them find anything they need. Nothing is off-limits." Mike clapped Dan on the back. "Anything for my new friends."

I got the feeling that down the road this might cost Dan, me, or both of us something in return, but if we could find any useful information right now, the price would probably be worth it.

Delia walked us into a large room filled with floor-to-ceiling file drawers. A rolling ladder similar to the ones some libraries use was leaning against the cabinets on the far wall. In the center of the room two long tables, scarred from years of use, held computers and printers. There was a copy machine at one end of one table and a scanner on the other.

I took a guess and said to Dan, "The morgue?"

Dan nodded. "And I have to confess, it is a lot neater than mine at the *Gazette*."

"You should have seen it when I got here," Delia said. "I was a junior in college and Mike advertised for part-time help: 'Must be tidy and good with a computer.' I was hoping to start as his ace reporter, but instead he hired me and a girl named Lily to get his back issues computerized. When we graduated last spring, Lily moved on to teach high school in Newmarket. I stayed here and moved up to full-time, still bucking for that ace reporter job."

"And how many years have you managed to computerize?" Impatient as I was to get started with my research, curiosity got the best of me.

"In the weeks before graduation Lily and I really pushed. We had a goal and we made it." Delia beamed with pride.

Then she waited for one of us to ask the obvious question, so I did. "And what was your goal?"

"July 20, 1969. It was the day of the moon landing, and the *Daily* put out a special edition the next day. We wanted to make sure both days were in the computers for eternity." Delia was visibly delighted with all that she and Lily had accomplished.

"What a laudable goal. And you and Lily met it. Kudos," I said.

"You are very kind." Delia thanked me. "I hope you won't want to check out any years earlier than 'sixty-nine, because then we'd have to search the file drawers, hoping the back issues aren't misfiled. Believe me—Lily and I ran into more issues that were misfiled than issues that were filed correctly. And it is no fun climbing up and down the ladder. When I am on it I feel nervous, like it's dangerous."

I glanced at the ladder. "I agree—it probably is dangerous. That ladder looks old and rickety, but the good news is we'll have no need of it today. Dan and I are looking back only a few years."

"Great. Let me boot these computers, and, well, I guess you are both computer literate and can find your way around. The issues are filed by date: year, dash; month, dash; day. Even though it is called the *Daily*, the paper only comes out on Thursdays, so we have this calendar book, which lists the Thursdays for every issue that we've computerized. That was Lily's idea. She made it, and we have extra copies should we lose this one, which is getting a little dog-eared."

"Efficient," Dan said, and I could see he was taking mental notes. I suspected the *Gazette*'s old and dusty morgue of back issues would soon be getting a makeover.

"And when I thought of a super helpful hint we made these instruction sheets for everyone to use." Delia handed us each a laminated piece of cardboard. "It goes from the simple—how to find and open any file—to the brilliant." Delia pointed to instruction number six. "When you are looking for a specific story or person, go to the front page of an issue, punch in this code, and you can search the entire newspaper at once instead of article by article or page by page."

Dan looked at his instruction sheet and said, "That will be a huge time-saver. Thanks so much. And if you are ever considering a location switch, think about Cabot Cove."

Delia laughed. "Thank you, but I am quite happy here. I live with my parents and my grandma. My married sister lives across the street with her husband and two children. My boyfriend is only three blocks away. Life is good right here in Dover. I will be at my desk if you need me." And she bounced out the door.

As soon as the door closed behind Delia, Dan rubbed his hands together and said, "How do you want to split this?"

"Well, I was thinking we should look at the two years immediately before Terranova's arrival in Cabot Cove. That should give us an idea about his life here in Dover. Shall we each take a year? That would be fifty-two issues."

I thought it was a lot to go through but Dan was quite cheerful. He held up Delia's instructions. "Thanks to Delia's cheat sheet, we can search each issue in a minute or two. Put in 'Terranova.' Search. Put in the gym's name. Search. Quick and easy."

"Put in 'obituaries' and search," I added.

"'Obituaries'?"

"Yes, I am looking specifically for single or widowed local

women with some financial means who were over the age of seventy-five and who died while Terranova lived here or even shortly after he left for Cabot Cove."

Dan snapped his fingers. "You are looking for the woman in the picture that Evelyn found. Ollie did say that Terranova's clients began dying off."

"Yes. We may also find her if there are pictures of members of Terranova's gym. It would be nicer if she were alive. I wish I had thought to snap that picture with my phone. Still, if I see her I think I will recognize her," I answered. "Shall we get started?"

"Yes indeed. I'll take year one and you can search year two. How's that?" Dan said.

"Fair enough. Let's do it."

I hadn't thought of it as a contest, but I will admit to being disappointed when Dan came across an article before I did. And since he had the earlier year, the first article was about certified instructor Joseph M. Terranova opening the Ladies Gym and Yoga Studio. In the accompanying picture the man we knew as Martin Terranova was accepting a certificate from the president of the local Rotary Club and the two men were flanked by a half dozen—ah, shall I call them mature women? The lady in the picture Evelyn found in Terranova's garage was not among them. Dan printed the article and we continued searching.

We searched quickly but efficiently and came across a number of advertisements for Joseph Terranova's business, as well as articles about and pictures of him participating in the usual business-owner events with groups like the chamber of commerce.

I skimmed the obits in every issue and finally found the first death notice that struck me as having possibilities. A woman named Elise Gagnon, aged seventy-eight, died within a few days of having a stroke. She was survived by two distant cousins and had left numerous bequests to charities and three local religious institutions. As someone who appeared not to have close relatives, she would have been a perfect target for an emotional predator like Terranova. My one disappointment was that her posed studio picture, which was obviously taken decades before her death, looked nothing like the picture that Evelyn had found.

Dan found an illustrated article touting the renewed fitness the women of Dover were experiencing as members of the Ladies Gym and Yoga Studio. I studied a number of pictures of women in various classes, all taught by Terranova, but in every picture the women were actively using machines, lifting hand weights, or holding yoga poses, so their faces were hard to discern.

Between us Dan and I found and printed a lot of information about Terranova's gym, but nothing of substance about the man himself. We were very close to the end of our search when Dan and I each found an obituary notice. His was of a widow who appeared to have few family ties and died of heart failure. The one I found struck me as haunting—it was extremely brief and had an extra tone of sadness I couldn't quite fathom.

We were arranging our printouts and hoping to borrow file folders when the door opened and, although I expected Delia, Mike Bélanger came into the room.

"Just thought I would see how you folks are doing. Can I have Delia bring you a coffee or something?" he offered.

"You are very kind. Actually, we are nearly done here, but we could use some file folders," I said.

Mike walked over to the far wall and opened a middle drawer, extracted about a dozen manila folders, and handed them to me.

Since he didn't seem to be hurrying us along, I took the opportunity to seek his help.

"I found this obituary, and it struck me as odd because it was the only one I saw that didn't include a picture of the deceased or a cause of death." I passed the printout to him. "Would you happen to remember her? She didn't die that long ago."

He barely glanced at the page, so I thought his answer would be "Sorry," but he surprised me by saying, "Oh, Lottie Miller. Now, that was a very sad story."

And he handed the paper back to me.

Chapter Twenty-Six

S ad in what way?" I wondered if Lottie was the woman I hoped we would find.

"Well, if you must know, she committed suicide. The whole town was aghast. Here she was, a kind, church-going woman living a nice, financially comfortable life, and then one night she up and mixed some rat poison in her tea and drank it down. Tragic. Inexplicable." Mike shook his head slowly, as if still trying to figure out why Lottie Miller had taken her own life.

"It was my decision not to print the cause of death in the obit. If there were folks in town who hadn't heard about the suicide by the time we went to print, I couldn't think of any reason for them to learn about it from me." Mike reached for the doorknob. "Be sure and stop to say good-bye before you leave."

As soon as the door closed behind Mike, Dan said, "Now, that is my idea of how the editor should run a small-town paper."

"Which is why we are so glad to have you editing the *Gazette*." I said.

Dan's cheeks reddened and he nodded his thanks.

We finished our inspections of the morgue records at nearly the same time. I went to the main office and waved at Delia, who jumped from her chair and came right to me. "All set to go, Mrs. Fletcher?"

"Nearly so. If you have a few minutes, could you take a look to be sure that we leave the room exactly as we found it?"

Delia laughed. "It would be my pleasure."

In under ten minutes the *Dover Daily* morgue looked as though we'd never touched a thing. Both Dan and I thanked Delia repeatedly for all her help, and then we stuck our heads into Mike's office. He was on the telephone but took a quick second to mouth *See you again* and give us a brief wave.

I was getting used to how quiet Dan was while driving, so I wasn't surprised when he didn't say a word until we crossed the Maine border from Dover and had driven halfway through South Berwick.

"I hope you aren't too disappointed, Jessica. When we get a chance to review the information we culled from the *Daily*, I don't think much of what we gathered will help us. There doesn't appear to be anything other than exercise and yoga classes that connects any of the women who live in Dover to Terranova."

"Ah, but, Dan, appearances can be deceiving. All those pictures and articles show us that Terranova had the opportunity to meet a variety of women. We need to dig a bit deeper to see if his relationship progressed with any of them," I said.

"How do you propose to do that?"

"Well, if it is all right with you, I am going to take these folders home, look at the articles, and match up the ones you found with the ones I found. Then I am going to revisit all the articles and pictures to see if any women show up around Terranova repeatedly."

"You mean, like groupies?" Dan chortled.

"That's exactly what I mean. If I am right, Terranova searched for and found women who responded to his attention by lavishing him with gifts and money. I'd certainly like to speak to some of them, find out about their experiences."

I asked Dan to drop me near the Fruit and Veg. I suspected if he knew my true destination, he would insist on coming with me, and that would surely foil my plan.

I waved good-bye to Dan and waited until he was out of sight before I began to walk down the street toward the Cove Tavern. I'd gone only a few steps when I heard someone call my name.

I turned and saw that Peter Whitlock was just behind me. "Please, if you have a minute, I'd like you to meet my sister, Penny. She's an enthusiastic reader and a big fan of your books."

The girl at his side was a petite brunette whose cheery smile emphasized the dimples in her cheeks.

"When Peter pointed you out, I told him not to bother you, but I am so glad he did." She giggled. "I started reading your mysteries in high school and continued all through nursing school, right up until today."

I was always surprised when I met an avid fan anywhere other than at a book signing or some other literary event. After Mike Bélanger was kind enough to praise my writing, I assumed I'd met my quota for the week, if not for the month, and yet here I was, shaking hands with still another reader.

"Why, thank you, Penny. It is always a pleasure to meet a

fellow mystery lover. I am so glad you enjoy my books." I changed the topic. "Are you here for a visit or are you thinking of joining Peter as a full-fledged resident of Cabot Cove?"

"I am just visiting, but I have taken a nursing position in a neonatal unit in a hospital in Portland, so I will be quite nearby. Our parents died in a boating accident when we were youngsters, so we lean heavily on each other to be sure neither of us ever feels alone in the world, especially now, with Granny gone." Penny smiled at her brother, who seemed a tad uncomfortable at having their family business be the topic of conversation on a busy street corner.

"It was great to see you, Mrs. Fletcher, and I am so happy that Penny got a chance to meet you. Sorry we have to rush away like this, but the clock is ticking and my meal break is wasting away." Peter took his sister's arm and guided her across the street.

I walked to the corner and walked up the two steps to the entrance of the Cove Tavern. It was known to attract a younger crowd with its nighttime entertainment and weekend pool and darts tournaments, so I expected it to be quiet at this time of day, and it was. Two middle-aged men still in their fishing garb were sitting at the bar sipping beers, and, as I hoped, Jasper Boxley was sitting at a table near the side door.

When I approached, he stood up and pulled out a chair. "Please have a seat, Mrs. Fletcher. I have to say you are the last person I expected to seek my services, but I take my business as I can get it. How can I help you today?" When he spoke, I noticed that several of his teeth were missing. I had to wonder if that was due to dental misfortune or a consequence of his line of work.

We both sat down and I folded my hands primly on the table and began. "Mr. Boxley—"

"No need to be formal. Please call me Jazzy." He gave me a crooked smile and patted my hands with one of his rough, calloused ones.

I immediately removed my hands from the tabletop and settled them in my lap, which caused him to raise an eyebrow, saying, "And here I thought we were going to become friends. Well, if it is only business that you want, tell me what you need. Maybe I can accommodate."

I was pleased to note that his smile had less of a leer to it now.

"Jazzy, I am in search of information. I understand that you are a businessman and I am quite willing to pay for your time." I believed that sounded better than saying I was willing to pay for the information, which was, of course, my intent.

"Hmm, you are every bit as feisty as the heroines in some of those stories you write. What information could I possibly have that would interest you? If this is research for a book—you'll have to find another source." Jazzy started to stand up. In his mind our conversation was finished.

"No, please don't misunderstand. This is about the recent murder here in Cabot Cove. You know, Martin Terranova." I must have rekindled his attention, because he settled back in his chair.

"The gym guy. Sure, I heard. What about him?"

"I need to know if he, at any time, borrowed a large sum of money from you," I said as softly as I could and still be sure he heard me.

Jazzy banged his hand on the table and hooted so loudly that the bartender and the two fishermen looked our way. Jazzy scowled and flicked a hand in the direction of the bar, and all three immediately turned their backs on us.

"I got to give it to you, lady. The sass of you, coming in here asking me questions like that. My business ain't any of your business. Now get out of here."

He pointed to the door but I was not ready to leave.

"Mr. Boxley, a friend of mine is under suspicion of murder. Another friend of mine has been falsely accused of being a thief. I believe Mr. Terranova had a secret life that led to his misfortune and also led to my friends being looked at suspiciously. Since we do know that Terranova moved here not too long ago and never seemed to hurt for money, I am merely trying to ascertain his financial sources." And I huffed a guttural "so there" sound at the end of what I was sure everyone in the room thought was an imprudent speech.

"The friend accused of being a thief—that would be Oscar Cisneros, correct?"

"Yes." I had the slightest glimmer of hope.

"I don't see how it will help Oscar, but on the off chance that you are right and this will help clear him, I can tell you I have never met this Terranova guy. From what I hear, he was too busy with the older ladies to bother hanging out in a place like this. So no, he and I never did business," Jazzy said.

"Thank you very much for your time."

I stood, and as I turned to the door Jazzy said, "It was nice to meet you, Mrs. Fletcher, but I don't think we will ever have a reason to meet again."

I took that as his version of *Here's your hat. What's your hurry?*

I hadn't realized how dark the inside of the tavern was until I stepped out into the sunlight. I stood still for a moment waiting for my eyes to adjust. It had been such a long day and I was in a hurry to go through the papers that Dan and I collected, so I pulled out my phone to call Demetri for a ride home, but fate intervened in the person of Eve Simpson, who *yoo-hoo*ed and waved as she was getting into her car, which was parked a few yards in front of me.

"Hi, Jessica. Can I give you a ride?" As always, Eve was perfectly groomed, with not a hair out of place or the smallest misapplication of makeup. She was dressed in a well-cut navy blue suit and a high-necked cream-colored blouse.

"Eve, you are a lifesaver. I have been on the go all day and I want nothing more than a nice cup of tea in my own kitchen," I said, and I climbed into the passenger seat of her late-model sedan.

"Actually, I am so glad I ran into you," Eve said. "I know I can tell you in the strictest confidence that I have a buyer from Boston, very rich, very handsome, and very eligible. He is looking for a weekend retreat with all the amenities for when he is able to enjoy *temps de détente*, or—shall I say?—time to relax."

I knew better than to comment. Whenever Eve was excited about a new client, everyone else's job was to listen to her talk elatedly about her plans for making the best sale ever and perhaps snagging a new beau in the bargain.

I was prepared to listen and nod as needed for the few minutes it would take to arrive at my front door. I was surprised when she said, "This is terribly important to me, and when I saw you on the street I realized that you are the one person who can help me make this all happen."

I was stunned. "Me? I don't know the first thing about real estate."

"But I'm sure you know more about the Terranova murder than anyone else in town," Eve said as she parked near my front gate and turned off the ignition. "Now, why don't we go into your kitchen for that cup of tea you crave and we can swap information?"

Chapter Twenty-Seven

I put the kettle on the stove and offered her a choice of apples, oranges, or bananas from the fruit bowl on my table.

"No, thank you. I am following a nothing-between-meals diet to get rid of those pesky extra pounds that seem to creep up in the winter, no matter what I do. I suppose I should have taken exercise classes at Perfection but, oh well, it is too late now."

I busied myself with setting cups on the table and readying the tea, but Eve must have expected me to reply, because after a minute she said, "Just between us, does Mort Metzger have any serious leads? How can I be expected to show the property when there is crime-scene tape all over the place shouting 'Danger! Danger!'?"

I poured the boiling water from the kettle into the teapot, put the pot on the table, and sat down. Then I took a shot in the dark. "Eve, have you been in touch with the property owner?"

"How can I when he is dead?" Eve shook her head as if I were an errant student who was not paying attention in class.

"Are you sure that Mr. Terranova owned rather than rented the property?"

"Quite sure," Eve answered. "I checked the county records. Joseph Martin Terranova is the sole owner of the property. I guess he didn't like his first name. Martin is certainly less common than Joe. And—get this—he had no mortgage. It was a cash purchase. Someone is going to inherit that gorgeous piece of property and I am hoping the beneficiary will want to cash in quickly. The property is perfect for my Boston buyer, but I need the murder solved and the property cleared. Oh, Jessica, how much longer will that take?"

I assured Eve that I had no answers about the murder, but while she chattered, I was musing that Joseph Martin Terranova may have had an entirely different reason for dropping his first name. I wondered what he was hiding or whom he was hiding from.

Eve took a genteel sip of tea, looked at her watch, and pushed away from the table. "Oh goodness, I have to run. I'm meeting a prospective buyer at the old Archer place. Hard to believe that anyone has an interest. The place is in shambles. Still, hope springs eternal in every Realtor's heart. *Au revoir.*"

Once Eve was out the door, I savored the silence in my kitchen as much as I savored my cup of tea. Then I spread out the pages Dan had printed from year one, as we were calling it, and I underlined any women's names that seemed familiar from my own research of the newspaper issues from year two. I hoped to find that some of the ladies in the obituaries had a definite connection with Terranova or his gym. Barring that, I was looking for a few repeat participants who might have developed a personal connection with him.

After an hour, my eyes were bleary and I decided to get back to my own work and my own life, which I was sure would include an earlier bedtime than usual this evening.

The next morning, as I rolled my bicycle from my yard to the curb, the sun was forcing its way between and around the leftover clouds from a middle-of-the-night rainstorm. I pedaled through town, waving to friends and neighbors, until I arrived at the bicycle rack near the wharf. I'd parked my bike and was walking to Mara's Luncheonette when I saw Seth coming from the opposite direction.

"Good morning, Jess. Are you ready for some blueberry pancakes?" Seth said as he pulled open the door to Mara's and the smells of fresh-brewed coffee and bacon sizzling on the grill washed over us.

"I believe I am." I was looking forward to a nice, relaxing breakfast with Seth before I began to tackle my chores of the day. Number one on my list was a visit to Joe Turco, the lawyer who was someone I considered to be a friend. He had led me in the right direction in the past and I hoped he could help me find information on Joseph Martin Terranova.

Mara poured our coffee and took our orders, but not before she said, "So, Jessica, I heard you and Dan Andrews were out and about for quite a while yesterday. Any news you'd like to share?"

I did some quick thinking and told what I thought was a plausible story. "Well, you know I am writing a book set in San Diego, California. Dan happened to mention it to a friend of his, another news editor, who worked in San Diego a few years ago, and the gentleman was kind enough to agree to lunch and conversation. We drove down to New Hampshire to meet him."

Mara said, "That's too bad. The gossip crowd—which is just about everyone who eats here—will be disappointed. Hilly Davis saw you two driving toward the interstate and he spread the word that you had one of your hunches about Terranova's murder and Dan was your wingman. Not sure why anyone would listen to Hilly, but that's the nature of town gossip. Give me a minute and I will be back with two small stacks of blueberry pancakes."

Seth got as far as "Ayuh—"

Mara cut him off, saying, "I know, Doc—extra butter."

As soon as Mara stepped away, Seth leaned in and began speaking in a near whisper. "You may have fooled Mara but you know you can't fool me. What were you and Dan Andrews up to gallivanting out of town for the better part of the day? I was planning on stopping by your place to ask you myself but I had an emergency call and was out at Tilly Abbott's place 'til all hours. I decided asking you could wait until breakfast, so now, spill it, woman."

Trying to look as innocent as I possibly could, I replied by asking how Tilly was doing after her emergency.

"Oh no, you don't. I am not about to violate Tilly's doctor-patient confidentiality to help you avoid answering my direct question. Where did you and Dan go and why?" Seth was also not about to be distracted.

I signaled him to stop talking by shifting my eyes toward Mara, who was carrying two steaming plates of pancakes in our direction.

"Here you go, folks. And I didn't forget your extra butter."

Then Mara pointed to the two syrup pitchers sitting on the table. "I know you are a maple syrup purist, Doc, but we've been getting requests, especially from the weekenders, for cinnamon-flavored maple syrup. Turns out the farmer up near Bangor who provides our maple syrup does something that adds subtle flavors to the syrup. He calls it suffusion—a word I think he made up 'cause it sounds fancy. I ordered the cinnamon, and it is popular. The pitchers are labeled—one says 'maple'; the other says 'maple-cinnamon.'"

"What is the world coming to when people have to fiddle with a food like maple syrup, which is perfect just the way it comes? No additives necessary," Seth grumbled.

Mara picked up the syrup pitcher marked *MAPLE*, handed it to Seth, and walked away. I supposed an argument over cinnamon-flavored syrup was not a fight she was prepared to have.

The pancakes kept Seth busy for a few minutes, and then he said, "Jess, it's not like you to keep secrets from me. You know I can be trusted."

"Seth, it's not you I don't trust. By any chance do you recall the old saying 'The walls have ears and the windows have eyes'?"

"Of course I do. Oh." Seth put down his fork and looked around. Hilly Davis was sitting at the counter talking and laughing with several fishermen. Charlie Evans was sitting two tables away from us with a very uncomfortable Tim Purdy. "I've seen enough. You win, Jess."

"We'll talk later, I promise. Let's just enjoy breakfast," I said.

Hilly Davis picked that exact moment to walk over to our table. "Morning, Doc, Jessica. Try the new syrup, did you? I didn't think it was half bad."

"Hilly, don't get me started," Seth said, as I casually placed my hand on his arm to remind him that it was never worth the energy to argue with Hilly. Seth took the hint and wedged a large slice of pancake into his mouth and began resolutely chewing.

Having failed to rile up Seth, Hilly turned to me; I was sure he thought I had a neon sign flashing *NEXT VICTIM* over my head. Not today.

"Hilly, we would ask you to join us but Seth is advising me on some very personal matters, and he will have to leave to begin his patient hours in a few minutes, so please excuse us." While I waited to see what he would do, I lifted my coffee cup slowly, ready to take a long sip if necessary to avoid responding to any of Hilly's nonsense.

However, he surprised me and probably the entire room by saying, "Doesn't matter. The whole town knows what you are up to. Don't need your word on it." And he walked away.

As soon as Hilly was out of earshot, Seth leaned in and whispered, "I love it when you go all schoolteacher-ish. Grown men tremble and beat a hasty retreat."

I whispered back, "You are assuming that, old as he is, Hilly is a grown-up. All I want is for us to be able to eat these delicious pancakes in peace."

And for the next few minutes while the town gossip hummed all around us, Seth and I enjoyed our pancakes and coffee and discussed the latest fundraiser for the hospital.

The front door opened and, out of habit more than curiosity, I looked up. There was Pierce Collymore, standing in the doorway, his eyes searching until he spotted me, and his look of relief told me that he wasn't coming in for breakfast or a take-out coffee and roll.

When he was sure he'd caught my eye, he gave a slight nod and stepped back outside, closing the door behind him.

I got the message. I opened my purse, took out some bills, and thrust them at Seth. "I know I promised to treat you to a leisurely breakfast, but something has come up and I have to run. Please use this to take care of the bill."

"Now, Jessica, just a minute . . ."

"Seth, I don't have the time to explain. I promise I will call you as soon as I can." I headed for the exit before he could object any further.

I waved good-bye to Mara and slipped out the door. Pierce was pacing back and forth. "Dan called your house and your cell—no answer. So he sent me to look for you on your usual bike ride routes. I was so relieved when I finally saw your bike and figured out you must be in Mara's."

I pulled my cell phone from my purse, and sure enough, I had forgotten to turn it on that morning, which often happened since I tended to think of it as something I used to reach out to others, and I forgot how often someone might be looking for me.

Pierce was still talking. "Angus got a check. He and Dan are waiting for us in the *Gazette* office. Dan says it is time to put the plan into action."

Chapter Twenty-Eight

Pierce offered to load my bicycle into the back of his Jeep and take it with us, but I knew it would be safe enough in the bike rack. In any event, after I met with Dan and Angus, I still had to attend to chores of my own at this end of Cabot Cove.

When Pierce started to park in front of the *Gazette* office, I suggested we'd be less visible if we parked around the corner. The last thing I wanted was for Evelyn to see Pierce's car and wonder once again what we were "up to," especially since I had no definite idea myself—at least I wouldn't until I saw the check Angus received and we could decide how to implement our vague plan to trap Olivia in a confession.

Pierce parked in an inconspicuous spot between a sedan and a delivery truck; then he asked, only half joking, "Do you want to go in first or shall I?"

"Let's be daring and walk around the block together," I answered in the same lighthearted tone.

Once inside the *Gazette* office, I could see that doom and gloom would be the order of the day. Dan came out of his private office and softly closed the door. "Angus is coming apart at the seams. He is ready to go to Mort, confess that he stole money, and spend the rest of his life in jail, which, of course, he won't, but right now he is so laden with guilt that he thinks he wants to be punished. I keep trying to reinforce to him that what he really wants—what we all want—is for the real criminal to be exposed for all the town to see."

"Jessica, he's known you the longest. He probably trusts you more than he trusts Dan or me," Pierce said. "Will you talk some sense into him?"

"I'll do my best. Dan, do you have any more of the water bottles you served us the other day?"

"I sure do, and as it happens, we have mini muffins compliments of Charlene Sassi, who dropped off a half dozen along with the ad she wants to run next week. Do you think that might help you calm Angus down a bit?" Dan sounded hopeful.

"Sassi's muffins certainly won't hurt," I said.

A few minutes later, Dan opened the door to let me into his office. Angus was sitting in a visitor's chair staring out the window. He looked up when I placed a water bottle and two muffins on the edge of the desk.

"Sent you to talk me into following their plan, did they?"

"Oh no. Not their plan. It's our plan, Angus. Don't you remember we all agreed to dedicate our energy to exposing the real crook, Olivia Quigley?" I tried to sound firm but not pushy.

"All of you keep saying that, but I went along with her, so, bad as she is, I carry a pile of guilt too, don't I?" Angus insisted.

"And now, Angus, if you go along with the idea we discussed the other day, you can make things right." I sat in the other visitor's chair and pushed the plate of muffins toward him. "Have a muffin and let's talk about this some more."

Half an hour later I came out of Dan's office with Angus by my side. Pierce and Dan looked keenly at us. Neither asked a question, and I didn't make them wait. "Angus has agreed that our strategy is a good one, and he will go along provided we do it today—the sooner, the better."

"I'm willing to give this a chance, but I can't carry the guilt no longer. We gotta do it now." Angus shuffled his feet like an errant schoolboy trying to provide an excuse for not doing his homework.

"I can go to the bank and withdraw the seven hundred dollars we'll need," I said.

"No need. I can cover it with money from the *Gazette* safe and we can replace it later," Dan offered. Clearly, he was afraid that anything that cost us time might heighten Angus's anxiety.

In a comforting gesture, Pierce put his arm around Angus and said, "Come on, Chief. I will drive you home."

Before I followed them out the door, I whispered to Dan, "Are you ready to round up our coconspirators?"

He gave me a thumbs-up bolstered by a confident smile.

Pierce dropped us at Angus's house and went to park the car a few blocks away. I offered to make Angus a cup of tea, hoping it would help to relax him, but he waved me off.

When Pierce arrived, we sat around the kitchen table until Angus reached for the wall phone saying, "Ready as I'll ever be."

Olivia Quigley answered her phone almost immediately, and Angus did not hem and haw. He sounded to me exactly as commanding as he was in the old days when he was in charge of the fire department. I didn't know what she said but Angus was stern.

"Your schedule ain't my problem. I got this check and cashed it like you want. But now I got to go to visit my brother in Thomaston. He's feeling poorly. So if you want your money, get it now, or I will send it back to the company that wrote the check and tell them it was all a big mistake." Angus winked at me as though he had come to realize that telling tales could be fun, even in this dire situation.

It took a few more minutes, but when Angus hung up the phone he said, "She's on her way." And there was the slightest hint of triumph in his voice.

Pierce picked up his cell and sent a text to Dan; then he and I walked with Angus into the room he liked to call his parlor. After he assured us that he was up to the coming task, we went into the dining room and securely closed the pocket doors behind us.

If she had soared through the skies on eagles' wings I wouldn't have understood how she could have gotten from town to Angus's house as quickly as she did, but in no time at all we could hear Olivia Quigley banging on Angus's front door.

Angus had barely opened the door a foot or two when Olivia started to squabble. "You listen to me, Angus Billingsworth. I can't jump whenever you snap your fingers. I have a very demanding job. Why would you think I can dash out of the office on your say-so?"

Listening with my ear to the door, I could barely stifle a giggle when Angus said, "And yet, here you be." And he led her into the parlor and began the conversation just as we had rehearsed.

"I might be staying with my brother for a long while. Like I said, he is doing poorly. So I think this is a good time for you to stop having your money sent to me."

Olivia heaved a sigh. "My money? Of course it's my money— I worked hard for it—but let me clarify that you have been the recipient of thousands of dollars in checks and cashed every one of them. Nothing traces to me and I see no reason to make alterations now. Why don't you see how your brother is doing and come home, say, sometime next week? I am expecting a 'refund' check for some water-rescue boats the fire department ordered and I need you to be here to cash it."

"Refund check. Ha. Why don't you call it what you used to— a kickback from the company for using them as our supplier? You order one more of whatever is needed, the town pays for it, the company never ships that item, and they throw half the cost back to you through me. It is a win-win. They give you back half the purchase price while they get fully paid by the town for an item they never sold."

"Angus, I am getting tired of going round and round about this with you. Now, give me my money from the purchase of those hoses." Impatient as Olivia was, in a very few minutes she would regret her words.

"Here you go," Angus said, and he counted aloud as he passed her each bill until he said, "Seven hundred. And today is the last time you will use me to steal from Cabot Cove. Find someone else."

"Oh, Angus, you have been part of this scheme for so many

years. If you stop now, I promise you I will 'uncover' your thievery. Tell me, who is going to believe your version of the story?"

I slid the pocket door open, stepped into the room, and said, "I certainly will."

Pierce Collymore came and stood next to me saying, "I will too."

Brazen as she was, Olivia waved her hand and tossed her hair over her shoulder. "I supervise the town's budget office. I'll just tell the mayor and the town council that you are all plotting against me because you have a political crony who wants my job. Rustics like you shouldn't ever count me out."

She hurried to the front door, grabbed the knob, flung the door open, and came face-to-face with Dan Andrews, Mort Metzger, and Cabot Cove mayor Jim Shevlin.

The mayor looked past her and said, "Angus, thanks for leaving the side window open. We could hear you and Olivia quite well." Then without missing a beat, he turned to Mort and said, "Sheriff, if you would escort Ms. Quigley to your office . . . I am sure you have some questions for her."

Evidently Olivia went into shock, because she stood perfectly still until Mort took her arm and began reciting her rights loudly and clearly as he walked her to his car.

Since I had already laid out this entire fiasco for Jim Shevlin and I was sure that Dan had reinforced to him that Angus's role was totally unwitting, we were not surprised when the mayor stepped forward and extended his hand to Angus. "Chief Billingsworth, I can't thank you enough for bringing this scandal to light before Ms. Quigley was able to do immeasurable harm to Cabot Cove's treasury."

Angus appeared to be at a loss for words. "But . . . Mayor Shevlin . . . I . . ."

Jim interrupted. "If you'll excuse me, I only stopped by so I could witness firsthand Olivia Quigley's arrest. I need to be able to tell the town council what I heard here today." He looked at his watch. "And now I have to rush. I'm on the verge of being late for a meeting."

And he hurried outside to his car and drove away, leaving Angus looking perplexed while Jim, Dan, and I were all standing around grinning.

Dan was the first to shake Angus by the hand. "You are a decent man who did a great service to your town today."

When Pierce and I chimed in, I think it was all too much for Angus. His eyes welled up. He pulled a wrinkled bandanna from his back pocket and wiped away any tears before they could fall; then he said, "And you needn't worry. I am ready for whatever is going to happen when Sheriff Metzger comes back for me."

After all the work we had to done to prepare Angus, I was astonished that he still believed that he was in trouble. "Angus, I assured you that I had received a guarantee that you would not be arrested or charged in any way. The mayor and the sheriff know that while you were the fire chief Olivia Quigley duped you, and once the checks continued to come after you retired, you confided in the new chief, as well as two members of the fire department, and we worked together to get the evidence Mort would need to arrest her."

"You are a hero," Dan said.

Angus was quiet and I thought he might be struggling to keep his composure, but he was quite calm when he said, "I appreciate all that you three have done for me, especially you, Jessica, but if you don't mind I need you to leave now so I can go to the church-yard and tell Sarah the good news."

As we walked to Pierce's car both he and Dan were elated that we had closed down a scam that cost the taxpayers of Cabot Cove a pretty penny or two, while my mind had already returned to my original plans for the morning.

So when Dan asked if I had time for a celebratory lunch, I declined. There were people I wanted to talk to about Joseph Martin Terranova, and although I'd lost the morning, I still had time to get to those conversations.

Chapter Twenty-Nine

Pierce and Dan parked near Mara's and headed inside for their lunch while I said my good-byes and pulled my bicycle out of the bike stand at the end of the block. It took me only a few minutes to ride to Joe Turco's office.

Since the evening Seth had explained to me why I shouldn't be surprised by Joe Turco's loyalty to Oscar Cisneros, I had hoped that when I explained to Joe why I wanted his help, we'd be able to connect a possible benefit to Oscar.

I dropped the kickstand and parked my bicycle to the left of the doorway. When I entered the tastefully decorated waiting room, Lena, Joe's assistant, was on the telephone and busily hitting computer keys at the same time.

"Yes, ma'am. I will see that Mr. Turco receives your message. Have a great afternoon." Lena hung up the phone, tapped a computer key, and smiled at me. "Hi, Mrs. Fletcher. Joe is on the phone, but if you can wait, I'm sure he will be done in a few minutes."

I sat in a comfortably padded blue chair, and I was about to pick up a magazine when Lena said, "I haven't told anyone yet, but now that the semester is almost over and I am sure I won't flunk out— Well, Joe knows, of course. He encouraged me."

Lena began twirling a cluster of her curly dark hair around her finger, and then she took a deep breath and blurted, "I am taking classes at the community college. I am studying to be a paralegal and Joe says I will make a fine one."

"Well, that is exciting news. Congratulations, Lena. And I think Joe is correct. Based on how you handle clients, including me, I think you will make a top-notch paralegal. Please, if you need any help with your studies, give me a call. I'd be happy to offer any assistance I can," I said.

"Jessica, I am always glad to see you. How nice of you to offer to help Lena should she need it." Joe Turco stood in the doorway of his private office. "Are you here to see me or to visit with your new protégé?"

"Excited as I am about Lena's news, I stopped by in the hope that I could have a few minutes of your time," I said.

Joe held his door open wide. "Come on in."

As soon as we sat down on either side of Joe's oversized maple desk, he surprised me by saying, "Before we start, on behalf of my client Oscar Cisneros I want to thank you for occasionally being nosier than Mort Metzger would like you to be."

Well, that certainly caught me unawares. "I'm sorry—I don't understand."

Joe laughed. "The way I hear it, you wandered into Martin

Terranova's house uninvited and unescorted. Then you managed to find a piece of evidence that Mort's deputies didn't find when they gave the place a cursory look-see after Terranova's body was found in the gym. Correct?"

I was dumbfounded. "Since you already know about what Seth Hazlitt likes to call my 'snooping,' I guess there is no harm in admitting it, but what has this to do with Oscar?"

Joe continued. "Mort sent his deputies back to the house to give it a thorough going-over and then make sure it was properly sealed. Several hours into the search, Floyd and Andy struck gold—at least from my perspective. In the guest bedroom there is an old what they may still call a hope chest—you know, like a storage chest for linens and things. Anyway, this one held a bunch of ancient quilts, and buried underneath them were some valuable antiques."

I leaned forward and held up my hand. "Stop right there. And the valuables belong to Bertha Mae!"

"Exactly. There is no doubt about it. One of the items is a picture of a much younger Bertha Mae and her parents. It is in a fourteen-karat-gold and crystal frame. Then there is a very fragile Union Army horse blanket from the Civil War . . ."

"Oh yes, Bertha Mae has always been extremely proud to have had several ancestors serve. I've seen the blanket myself. Bertha Mae allowed it to be displayed at a fundraiser we held for the library," I said.

"Then you get the idea. Finding these items, coupled with Tim Purdy's declaration that he saw Terranova going back and forth to Oscar's shed, should be enough to convince anyone that, for some unknown reason, Terranova stole the items and was planning on continuing to frame Oscar with them."

Joe was palpably excited to be able to save the future for the man who had once saved his father's life. But there was a catch, and I felt compelled to point it out immediately, before Joe got too elated. "As long as Terranova's murderer remains at large, although this information might obliterate the cloud of suspicion that Oscar is a thief, unfortunately it does raise him higher on the list of murder suspects."

"I did think of that," Joe said. "I am hoping that Mort's investigation will get some traction soon and the killer will be brought to justice so there won't be a doubt in anyone's mind that Oscar still is what he always was, a kind, quiet man who would never commit a crime of any sort."

I took three folded sheets of paper from my purse and said, "On that score, I hope that if you can help me find some information, we may eventually assist Mort in discovering what actually happened to Martin Terranova."

"Go on." Joe leaned forward, anxious to hear what I had to offer.

"We now know that Martin Terranova's real name was Joseph Martin Terranova, and that before coming to Cabot Cove, rather than living in South Berwick as he claimed, Terranova actually lived a few miles across Maine's southern border, in Dover, New Hampshire." I could tell by Joe's lack of reaction that so far, I hadn't surprised him at all, so I continued.

"I also recently learned from Eve Simpson that Terranova owned his house and the gym property free and clear. He purchased it for cash, according to the records Eve reviewed."

Joe nodded. "Eve is absolutely right. I checked the property records as well, and I have to wonder where he got the money required to buy such a prime piece of real estate mortgage free.

Maybe he was a trust-fund baby, or he invented a cell phone app and sold it for millions. I had no legal mechanism to search his bank records, but from what I could discern informally, Terranova had healthy bank accounts but the gym appears to be his only source of income."

"I have a theory as to how he gathered his income, and although it may sound far-fetched, please hear me out. I think that Terranova was an emotional predator who conned older women into believing he had a romantic interest in them. Then he would begin isolating them socially, until they were dependent on him and him alone. Finally, he would ask for and receive money from the women in ever-increasing amounts. From what Bertha Mae described, he also insinuated himself into their wills as chief beneficiary." I hoped I'd painted the picture graphically enough.

Joe moved into lawyer mode—lips pursed and eyes glued to the ceiling. Then, when he had mentally reviewed what I'd told him, he looked at me. "And exactly how do you know this? Or is it pure supposition? Have you any proof at all?"

I told him about Bertha Mae. First, I explained what Evelyn originally suspected; then I recounted what both she and I had observed in separate conversations with Bertha Mae.

"And, Joe, if you need to hear from an up-close-and-personal witness, speak to Greta Pacyna, who kept house for Bertha Mae. Greta told me that Terranova had the absolute run of Bertha Mae's house. He wandered in and out at all hours of the day and night. He even threatened Greta's job, and look how that turned out."

I ended with, "When I last spoke to Bertha Mae, she was devastated that Terranova had preceded her in death. She'd been planning their future life together and, more importantly, she had been planning to bequeath her entire estate to him so he could develop his Perfection gym into a worldwide health corporation or some such nonsense. Do you see what I mean?"

"You are right that the entire scenario sounds a bit far-fetched, but what is the old saying? There's no fool like an old fool," Joe said.

"That is exactly what Seth Hazlitt said, but I think you both are wrong and there is far more than foolishness going on here. I believe Terranova was deliberately leading Bertha Mae down the garden path, as it were. He intended to take her for every cent, but before he could, someone stopped him—and whoever it was stopped him for good," I emphasized.

I opened the papers I'd been holding in my hand and slid them across the desk so that Joe could see them. "These are the obituaries of three elderly women who appear to have developed close emotional relationships with Terranova during his time in Dover, New Hampshire."

Joe reached for the papers and said, "Jessica, please, don't tell me you think that he killed these women?"

I waved my hand from side to side to erase that impression immediately. "Oh no. Not at all. Two of them died from natural causes and the third—poor, tortured soul she must have been—committed suicide. Is there any way that we could find out if Joseph Martin Terranova inherited money or property from any or perhaps from all three?"

Joe glanced briefly at each page. "Well, off the top of my head I will say that in New Hampshire probate generally runs between a year and eighteen months, but since all of these deaths occurred more than two years ago, the estates should be settled and legally available to the public. I have a friend from law school who practices in Dover. I will give him a call and ask if he can send someone over to look at the probate papers and let me know what he finds. Might take a day or so, more if he is buried under a pile of work, but we should be able to satisfy your curiosity shortly."

I thanked Joe for his time, and on my way out I repeated my offer of study assistance to Lena, who smiled gratefully. I got on my bicycle feeling satisfied that I had set a major inquiry in motion, and I pedaled my way over to Charles Department Store.

I was pleased that the person I was looking for—one of my favorite sales associates, Sally Thompson—was sorting and folding a stack of T-shirts that had our state name, *MAINE*, embroidered on the front in large letters. She held up a light pink shirt with bright red embroidery. "What do you think, Jessica? These are designed specifically for women. No more boxy-shaped tees for us. These have slightly shaped waistlines, and darts sewn in the appropriate places."

"I think the female tourists will love them," I replied.

"That's the general idea." Sally laughed. "Now, how can I help you today?"

"Well, my basic black purse has seen better days. I really think it is past time for a replacement," I said.

"Right this way. We recently got a new shipment of purses, and several really smart-looking ones have those straps that convert from handheld to shoulder bag. You might find that convenient." Listening to Sally, I thought, as I often did, about how comforting it is to shop in a store where the staff knew me so well. It was also handy when I wanted to question them.

We stopped at a display of black purses and Sally asked me if cross-body bags were under consideration. "I know you have one in beige and I was wondering if you wanted to try one in a darker color."

"For now I think a handheld would be the best replacement for the one that is sadly on its way out. Do you remember it? Gold clasp, outside zipper pocket?"

Sally thought for a moment. "Oh yes, I do. That was years ago and we'd just started selling that particular brand. It has since become quite popular. Would you like to see the updated model?"

"I certainly would, and by the way, with all the misfortune going on nearby, I was wondering, since you live so nearby, if you'd seen Bertha Mae Cormier lately."

Chapter Thirty

F unny you should ask. I made some tea biscuits this morning. I like them fresh with my first cup of tea. Since I hadn't
seen her since the . . . the death, I decided to drop some off
for Bertha Mae. It took her a long time to open the door, and at
first I chalked that up to the fact that it was barely eight thirty. But
when I started to talk to her she seemed confused, definitely more
ditzy than usual. Once I stepped inside, she wouldn't let me past
the foyer."

Sally set two purses on the counter, both very similar to the
one I was replacing. "You'll notice that this one has quilted
leather and the strap is thinner and adjustable. That way it can be
either handheld or a shoulder strap." Then she held up the second
one. "This purse has a sleeker leather design and hand straps."

While I was examining the handbags, Sally switched back to
our neighborly conversation. "To tell you the truth, Jessica, I became more than a little concerned when I offered Bertha Mae the

tea biscuits and she told me that she would not eat anything that I brought into her house. What could I do? I set the plate of tea biscuits on that little mail table she keeps beside her door and I left. Honestly, I don't think she should be living alone."

"A lot of people in this town agree with you." I picked up the smooth bag with the hand straps and said, "I have one more question before I buy this stunning purse."

"Sure." Sally laughed. "Anything for a customer who is about to make a purchase."

When I asked who owned Martin Terranova's house before he did, Sally said, "It's no wonder you can't recall. They were week-enders, name of Mooney. Rarely ever showed up in Cabot Cove, and when they were here, they didn't mix much. I guess they decided having a weekend retreat they only used four or five times a year wasn't worth the cost. Now, is there anything else I can help you with today?"

Sally and I chatted while she wrapped my new purse, and then we said good-bye. As I was leaving, she called after me, "Jes-sica, if you hear anything about Bertha Mae . . . I mean, if there is anything you think I can do to help her, please let me know."

I promised I would.

I was constantly amazed that the bulkiest packages fit in my deep and wide rattan bicycle basket, and I was admiring how easily the securely wrapped box containing my new handbag slid into the basket when Penny Whitlock touched my arm and said hello.

"I have heard this is a well-stocked department store, and I am going to need a few things for my new job, so I thought I would browse," she said. "It is nice to see that one of the few people I know in Cabot Cove shops here as well."

"I recommend it highly. You'll probably be able to find everything you need, and the staff is extremely helpful," I said.

"I guess that shouldn't surprise me. Cabot Cove is a lovely town and everyone I have met has been so nice. My brother has really found a home here. He enjoys his job. He says meeting people is the best part, and he's even going back to school, which is something I have been hoping he would do." Penny smiled.

I was about to satisfy my own curiosity by asking why she and her brother were settling in different towns and where they had lived previously when Evelyn Phillips bellowed from the curbside, "Jessica! We've been looking all over for you."

Penny was clearly startled, and when she turned and saw Evelyn getting out of Dan Andrews's car, she said to me, "Nice to see you again. I'd better move along."

By the time Evelyn was standing in front of me, Penny had darted into the department store.

"Who was that? Never mind. We need to talk." She was so loud, heads were turning from every direction.

Knowing Evelyn was capable of saying anything and not caring in the least who might hear, I needed to get us off the public street, so I said the first thing that came into my head. "I'm on my way home. Why don't you meet me there?"

"Meet you? Can't you just leave the bike here? Or have Dan throw it in the trunk?" Evelyn demanded.

But it had been a long day and I was determined that I wanted a quiet, peaceful ride home, and once there I intended to have a sandwich and a cup of tea. After that I had planned to curl up on my recliner with the Sisters in Crime newsletter that came in yesterday's mail and catch up on the latest industry news. Evelyn might delay some of my plans but she was not going to ruin my ride home.

"Evelyn, I am going to ride home on this bicycle. You can meet me there or not—that is up to you—but one thing is certain. I will not get into Dan's car, with or without my bicycle."

She was momentarily taken aback, and then her surrender was swift and complete. "Okay, we'll meet you there."

I watched her walk back to the car and felt as victorious as if I'd slain the proverbial dragon. I climbed on my bike and, taking my time, I pedaled toward home.

I smiled and waved to Charlie Evans, who was puttering in his yard, close enough to his fence to stop any and all passersby. I pretended I didn't hear him ask for a minute of my time. In his case a minute often turned into twenty or more of boring, repetitious gossip. Besides, once I got home, I was going to have to face more conversation than I cared to, so I was determined to keep this ride peaceful.

As soon as my house came into view I could see Evelyn and Dan standing at my front gate. I stopped at Maeve O'Bannon's front door and rang the bell.

Maeve opened the door, grabbed me by the arm, and pulled me inside. "Jessica, I'm not sure you know this, but you have news reporters lying in wait at your front door. If you want to stop for a cuppa in my kitchen to avoid them, I am happy to oblige."

"You are such a good neighbor and I thank you for the offer, but I actually rang your bell in the hope that you would be available to join us," I said.

Maeve arched her brow. "Join you and the newsies? Whatever for?"

"Because I believe we are going to try to lay out a framework to help Bertha Mae Cormier get her life back to normal and I suspect you can help us. After all, you did mention that you were positive you could get Bertha Mae to offer Greta her old job back," I reminded her.

Maeve gave a hearty laugh. "I did indeed. Well, let's go join our collaborators and get Bertha Mae organized once and for all. As it happens, I have a freshly made apple cake. Shall I bring it along?"

Evelyn shot me a dubious look when I showed up with Maeve, and when I mentioned the apple cake as if that were reason enough for Maeve to join us, Evelyn merely nodded. We four converged on my kitchen and I put both the kettle and the coffeepot on the stove.

While I poured tea for Maeve and Dan and coffee for Evelyn and me, Maeve sliced the apple cake into generous servings for all four of us. Other than praising Maeve's apple cake, which was moist and delicious, we sat in silence.

I ate my piece of Maeve's apple cake in the tiniest of bites and sipped my coffee slowly so that this brief respite would be peaceful enough to prepare me for an onslaught of questions and orders from Evelyn—such as *What are we going to do about Bertha Mae?*, *Who is going to take charge of her?*, etc. etc.—so I was prepared when Evelyn pushed her empty cake plate toward the center of the table and said, "Okay, now to business."

When she had everyone's attention, she looked at me and said,

"Jessica, I can't get a word out of Mort Metzger, so where is he on the Terranova murder?"

Her question was not at all what I was expecting. I said, "I have no idea. Mort doesn't confide in me. I was under the impression you wanted to speak to me about helping Bertha Mae. That's been your thrust since you came back to Cabot Cove."

"Well, the one leads to the other," Evelyn said. "I believe that Terranova's overly friendly behavior toward Bertha Mae caused her to become a flibbertigibbet and now his death has completely rattled her brain."

"I don't disagree with anything you are saying, but since we can't solve a murder right here and now, let's work on what we can do. We can help Bertha Mae recover and get back to her customary life, the one she was living before Martin Terranova bought the property next door to her."

Although I was looking directly at Evelyn, out of the corner of my eye I could see Dan nodding in agreement. And I certainly knew where Maeve stood.

Evelyn began squirming in her chair. There was so much truth in what I had said that she would be hard-pressed to argue.

"Okay," she said, "what's the plan? I know you always have one."

"I can't call it a plan but I can outline a couple of problems. One is that Bertha Mae is all alone in that big house all day with no company to distract her from the 'what could have been' that has been her obsession since the murder," I said.

"I'm thinking that is a problem I can help you to solve," Maeve said.

The look on Evelyn's face was priceless. "What can you possibly contribute?"

Maeve said, "Well, as I told Jessica a while back, if you can guarantee that Greta Pacyna will take her old job back, I can guarantee that Bertha Mae will offer it to her. I just need to be sure that Greta will say yes."

I think we were all surprised when Dan was the first person to reply.

"I can speak to Greta. Shortly after she, ah, left Bertha Mae, Greta came to see me to ask if I needed a cleaner. Apparently, she had been asking around town, trying to find a few more hours of work. I hired her and her work is excellent. Since she left Bertha's employ, she has stepped up her search, but from what I understand she hasn't had much luck. Why don't I call her now?" Dan stood, picked up his cell phone, and walked out to the backyard, closing the door behind him.

I had another idea I was sure would work. "As far as socialization goes, Sally Thompson told me that she had stopped by to visit Bertha Mae but it didn't go well. She asked me to let her know if there was anything she could do to help. Perhaps we could put together a list of friends and acquaintances who would drop in on Bertha Mae now and again. We could organize it under the radar, and as Bertha Mae gets better adjusted it can become more informal."

"That sounds like it could work," Evelyn said. "But who is going to run it?"

I gave that a moment's thought. "How about Ideal Molloy? She knows Bertha Mae well, is very social, and loves to chat on the phone. If we give her a list of eight to ten volunteers to call, she can see that they stagger their visits and . . ."

Dan came in the back door and said, "Greta would be delighted. She thought about talking to Bertha Mae but didn't because they ended on such bad terms. Now all we have to do is get Bertha Mae to ask."

The three of us turned to Maeve, who said, "Not a problem. I will make sure that Hilly speaks to Bertha Mae first thing tomorrow."

"Hilly? Hilly Davis?" I was stunned.

"Oh yes, he and Bertha Mae were the greatest of friends—at least until that slippery Terranova came along. After the murder, Hilly went to see Bertha Mae and they made peace. He is the one who told me that Bertha Mae was sorry she let Greta go. She would have asked Greta to come back but didn't because they ended on such bad terms. Oh, I sound like I am echoing Dan." Maeve laughed and we all joined in.

Convinced that we had found a way to begin to steer Bertha Mae's life back toward normalcy, my guests settled in for more cake and conversation. I was not quite as sure as they were that polite social contact was all that Bertha Mae would need. After we all said good night and before I relaxed in my recliner with the Sisters in Crime newsletter, I picked up the phone and called Seth Hazlitt to ask for a favor.

Chapter Thirty-One

The next morning I took an extra-long bike ride. I avoided the ridge and my other usual haunts so if anyone decided to look for me, I would be difficult to find. I needed time to myself. It took more time than I expected, but eventually I was feeling refreshed and ready to wrangle the synopsis for *Murder at the Cabrillo Monument* into submission, so I headed for home.

Maeve O'Bannon hailed me as I reached her front gate. "Early morning to you, Jessica. Did you enjoy your ride?"

"It was invigorating and certainly got this day off to a fine start," I answered.

"I spoke to Hilly Davis at the crack of dawn, and he called me with an update not ten minutes ago. He went to Bertha Mae's house, and together they called Greta, and all is well on that score. I can report that Greta will be back to work certainly tomorrow if not this afternoon. Step one is complete."

"That is good news and it reminds me, I should call Ideal

Molloy and ask her to set up a 'Friends of Bertha Mae' group that we can keep active for the next little while." I put it on my mental to-do list.

"You can add my name if you like. Some years ago Bertha Mae and I both belonged to a knitting-and-sewing group that met at the library. I am sure I could get her interested in making some things for the children's hospital," Maeve said before she bent down over her garden. "But for now, well, these seedlings aren't going to tend to themselves."

After I put my bike away and went inside, I poured myself a large glass of water and sat down to call Ideal. Then I could cross that chore off my list and leave the rest of the day free for work. She answered on the second ring.

When I explained my thoughts on organizing Bertha Mae's visitors, Ideal quickly became enthusiastic.

"Of course Bertha Mae isn't feeling like herself. She was hanging around with that exercise freak, and look what happened to him. I'm surprised she didn't break her own neck doing all that yoga and such." As usual, Ideal had her own interpretation of the facts. "Tell me what I can do to help. Except on Thursday afternoons. I play cards on Thursday."

"I promise this will not interfere with your card playing for even a minute. I would like you to organize a group of women who know Bertha Mae and would be willing to stop in to spend a few minutes, certainly no more than half an hour, visiting with her once a week until she gets back to normal," I said. "And you can start with Sally Thompson, Maeve O'Bannon, and me. We'll all take turns."

"Well, Loretta Spiegel, Eve Simpson, and Charlene Sassi are probably too busy, what with working their jobs and all, so I'll skip them unless I get desperate. But I know for sure that since she retired from the bank, Margaret Jacobson is always looking for something to do. I will give her a call, and I have one or two others in mind. Leave it to me, Jessica. Bertha Mae will get her mojo back in no time. But before you go, I have to tell you about this recipe I found for buttermilk brownies . . ."

While I waited for Ideal to finish listing ingredients, I filled my kettle nearly to the brim, because I expected my work to require more than a few cups of tea, and put it on the back burner of the stove. Then I went into the dining room and pushed the button to boot my computer. At long last Ideal said, "You have to let them cool for at least fifteen minutes before you cut them into squares."

"That sounds delicious. I can't wait to try them." I bid her a hasty good-bye and dove into my work with a gusto I hadn't felt since before Martin Terranova's body was discovered.

As often happens when I am working, I nearly jumped out of my chair when the telephone rang, because my head was resolutely tracking a murderer in San Diego.

I looked at the clock as I snatched up the phone. I'd been working nonstop for hours and the day had moved well into the afternoon.

"How's the book coming along, Jess?" Seth Hazlitt always seemed to enjoy listening to me whine about the plot point I was stuck on or the character that simply refused to behave, so I gave him a good five minutes about what in the synopsis had me annoyed.

He listened patiently and then said, "Ayuh, well, that sounds like a tough nugget, but I'm sure you will get it all to rights. Listen, Jess. It occurred to me that there might still be a container or two of your lobster chowdah tucked away in your freezer."

I smiled because I knew where this was going. "As it happens, there is."

"Well, if you'd be willing to heat it up, I'd be willing to stop by Sassi's Bakery to pick up a loaf of Charlene's tasty sourdough bread and we could have dinner. Does five o'clock sound manageable?" Seth asked.

"It sounds absolutely perfect. I am walking to the freezer this very minute to begin defrosting the chowder. And by any chance will we have any tidbits of gossip to go with our chowder?"

"To find that out you will have to wait for the sourdough bread to arrive." Seth laughed and hung up the phone.

I took a quart of chowder out of the freezer, placed it, container and all, in a bowl of hot water, and glanced at the clock. I still had nearly two hours before I would have to start preparing dinner. As I sat down at my computer, it dawned on me that while I was complaining out loud to Seth about a clue I couldn't quite decipher, I'd actually answered my own question as to how to fix it.

By the time I'd stopped working for the day I was confident that my story line was moving in the right direction. I was sure that in another day or two, I would have a fully fleshed synopsis to send to my editor.

When I checked on my chowder, it had thawed around the edges but was still primarily a solid block of ice. I transferred it into a heavy saucepan and set it on medium-low heat. While I shredded kale, lettuce, and spinach for salad, I frequently stepped back to the stove to chip away at the ice and stir the chowder so that it didn't clump or burn.

When I added my last remaining cherry tomatoes and carrot slices to the salad, I made a mental note to order more from the Fruit and Veg.

I set the table and put a fresh stick of butter out so that it would soften just enough to be easily spread on Charlene Sassi's delicious sourdough bread.

The meal was coming together beautifully when Seth came through the back door.

"Woman, if I hadn't brought along my appetite, the smell of this kitchen would have found it for sure. And wait until you smell this bread. Charlene took it out of the oven not half an hour before I walked in and bought these two loaves." Seth dropped the bakery bag on the counter and the smell of fresh bread began to complement the fragrance of simmering chowder.

"Two loaves? Seth, we are having dinner by ourselves, not with half the town of Cabot Cove," I protested, even though I knew I was sure to eat more bread than was good for my waistline.

Seth hung his jacket on the hook by the door, rolled up his shirtsleeves, and stood at the sink soaping and scrubbing his hands well above his wrists in strict doctor mode. He took a towel off the rack and, while drying his hands, teased, "Aren't you going to nag me until I tell you that I did as you asked when you telephoned me yesterday?"

"Seth, I didn't think you could possibly have found anything out so quickly. Are you saying you did?" I stopped stirring the chowder and turned to see if he was serious.

"Wasn't much to it. I called Arnold Becker, who is Bertha Mae's current physician. Mind you, his office is way over in Wiscasset, so he isn't up on the Cabot Cove day-to-day gossip. When I described what's been going on here and how it has affected Bertha Mae, well, he checked her records and it seems she missed her most recent appointment." Seth pulled out a chair and sat at the table. "Could you pass me that sourdough while I wait for you to finish cooking the chowdah?"

"Not until you tell me what Dr. Becker said about Bertha Mae. Is she going to be all right?"

"Fit as a fiddle, I'm sure. Arnold was so alarmed by our conversation that he sent a nurse practitioner to visit Bertha Mae first thing this morning. Not to violate doctor–patient confidentiality, but I can tell you that Bertha Mae got some of her medicines confused and was taking too much of one and not enough of another." Seth pointed to the bread bags. "Now may I . . ."

I put half a loaf of bread on a small platter and placed it in front of him. "I suppose the fiasco when Bertha Mae's meds were disappearing and then turning up again all over her property added to her confusion. And I am quite sure that Martin Terranova, who by all accounts had free rein to wander in and out of her house whenever he pleased, was the culprit who hid the medicines, as part of his plan to get Greta fired and further isolate Bertha Mae."

"That would certainly give Greta a reason to want Terranova out of the way. Do you think it is possible that she . . ."

"Seth, if I thought Greta had murdered the man, I wouldn't have encouraged Maeve O'Bannon to help me to get Greta back into Bertha Mae's employ so that Bertha Mae wouldn't be rattling around alone in that house twenty-four hours a day." I gave the chowder a final stir and turned off the stove.

"Maeve O'Bannon? How on earth?" Seth was so wide-eyed that he actually stopped slathering butter on his sourdough.

I filled two salad bowls and put one in front of Seth, and I sat down with the other. "It's a long story but the point is that with her medicines straightened out and some company in the house, Bertha Mae should soon be back to her old self. Now, start in on your salad before you fill up on that bread," I said, sounding more schoolteacher-ish than I intended.

"Only if you assure me that there is a chess game or two in our immediate future."

"Definitely." I was delighted that Seth would have the time for us to relax and play. For my part, strategizing to take down Seth's king would be a welcome respite for my brain, which was becoming addled by murder and mayhem, both in my work and here in Cabot Cove.

Chapter Thirty-Two

Three days later, according to Ideal Molloy's newly devised "Ladies Who Visit Bertha Mae" schedule, it was my turn. The sky was gray and more than a little threatening, so I put on my yellow slicker in case the rains did in fact arrive. Then I rode my bicycle to Bertha Mae's house.

Greta Pacyna opened the door and greeted me with a huge smile. "Dan Andrews told me that you and Ms. O'Bannon and—although I can't quite believe it—Hilly Davis all had a hand in helping me get my job back. I can't thank you enough. Bertha Mae is in the kitchen."

I followed her to the kitchen, where Bertha Mae had spread cookbooks, scraps of paper, wrinkled manila folders, and an open loose-leaf binder all over the table.

She looked up from the folder she was sifting through. "Jessica, maybe you can help me. By any chance did I ever give you a copy of my mama's recipe for whoopie pies? You know the recipe

I mean—the one that uses shortening, not butter? Ideal Molloy called this morning. She promised she would make some for Eve Simpson's new client, and everyone knows Mama's recipe is the best, but I can't find it."

"Er, no. I'm sorry. The whoopie pie may be Maine's state treat, and for something that classic, I find it easier to let Charlene Sassi do the baking."

Bertha let out a holler and waved a piece of old and yellowed paper over her head. "I found it. Stuck right behind Mama's meat loaf recipe. Greta, be a dear and call Ideal and read her this. If I call, she'll have me on the phone forever, and I would much rather have a lovely chat with Jessica."

Swinging one arm from elbow to wrist, Bertha Mae pushed her recipe piles dangerously close to the far edge of the table and invited me to sit down.

I declined a cup of tea but was grateful when Greta put a pitcher of water and two glasses on the table. "Whenever I ride my bicycle, I try to remember how important it is to hydrate. Helps me feel my best," I segued. "How are you feeling these days, Bertha Mae?"

"To tell you the truth, I feel better than I have in a long time. It is kind of surprising, because I am very sad about dear Martin dying like that. For a while I was mad at the world, and especially angry at Hilly Davis because he seemed so happy when Martin died in that accident. But I guess it just goes to prove that healthy exercise isn't always for the best."

"Bertha Mae," I asked, "why would Hilly be glad that Martin Terranova died?"

Bertha Mae folded her hands on the tabletop. "That is a very long story, my dear. It's about the Mooney property. Hilly grew up on this ridge when it was nothing but fields and flowers. Even when the Mooneys bought that huge tract of land next door and built the house, the pool, and the pool house, they left about twenty acres to nature. Plus, Tyrone and Ethel Mooney were never here, so they hired Hilly as a sort of watchman. Even gave him a key. He could continue to roam the woods and act like it was all his own. You know, he has always claimed his family owned the entire ridge a hundred years ago. But then the day came when the Mooneys put the land up for sale." Bertha reached for the water pitcher.

I picked it up, filled her glass, and asked, "Then what happened?"

"Who knows? The land was for sale. Hilly made what offer he could. I heard Eve Simpson called it laughable. As these things happen, Martin swooped in and bought the property, and Hilly has wanted him gone ever since."

My cell phone rang. I looked and saw Joe Turco's number. "Excuse me, please."

I answered as I walked to the hallway.

"Mrs. Fletcher, hi. It's Lena from Joe Turco's office. He wanted me to tell you that he got the information you requested. He will be in the office all day today. He will be at a deposition tomorrow morning but should be back in the office in the late afternoon, if that is more convenient for you."

When she stopped for a breath, I thanked her for letting me know and told her I would be able to stop by the office within the hour.

I walked back into the kitchen and Bertha Mae said, "I suppose I should have asked Ideal, but maybe, if you wouldn't mind . . . do you think you could ask Loretta to come over here to give me a nice cut and curl? I am really not up to sitting in her shop listening to those old hens chattering, but I do need to do something with this." And she held up a hank of the hair that she had let grow so wild in recent months.

"Well, I will certainly speak to Loretta. If she can't come here, perhaps she could arrange for you to have an appointment at a quiet time of day. You might want to consider that."

Bertha Mae nodded but I could see she was far from convinced. On the other hand I was happy that she was considering doing something with her hair. Prior to meeting Martin Terranova she was a regular at Loretta's and prided herself on being neat and stylish.

Greta came into the kitchen to report that Ideal was thrilled with the whoopie pie recipe. "And as a bonus, she said to tell you she is going to put the recipe into her computer file and print you a dozen copies so you will never have to search for it again."

Greta's return to the kitchen was my opportunity to leave. I said my good-byes and promised to come back soon. Greta walked me to the door and whispered, "Can you believe it? The difference is like day and night."

"It does look like having the pieces of her old life fall back in place has helped Bertha Mae's fantasy life retreat into the world of imagination. Let's hope she continues to feel better each day," I said, and I waved good-bye as I went out the front door.

The clouds had cleared and the sunshine felt warm and welcoming. I was pedaling along Main Street only two blocks from Joe Turco's office when Penny Whitlock hailed me.

"Oh, Mrs. Fletcher, I am so glad to see you to get a chance to say good-bye. I got a call from the hospital asking if I could come to Portland sooner than I planned. A nurse broke her ankle and, well, how could I say no? It is a shame, though, as I really hoped to spend more time with Peter. We are all each other has." Penny's eyebrows knitted with worry.

"Yes. You mentioned that before. So I guess, now that you will be living right down the road in Portland, the proximity is some comfort to you both."

"When I got the offer from the hospital I tried to talk Peter into coming along to Portland, but he had already moved to Cabot Cove and said he felt a connection here he could not dismiss. I couldn't argue with that. It is such a lovely town."

"Hey! Whose car is blocking mine?" A man standing at the curb with his hand on his hips was scowling at passersby.

"Oh dear. I was so excited when I saw you that I double-parked, and look at the trouble I've caused. So long, Mrs. Fletcher." Penny hurried to her car, apologizing profusely to the man, who managed a smile for the pretty young girl.

In the back of my mind something struck me as odd as I watched her drive away, but I had too much going on to be able to process anything new at the moment.

I dropped my kickstand and left my bicycle parked at the side of Joe Turco's wide doorway. Then I put my phone on silent. I didn't want to be disturbed when Joe and I were going over the news from his friend in Dover. When I entered, Lena greeted me with her usual friendly smile. "Joe will be eager to see you. He was excited, although not in a happy way, when your information came through." She picked up the intercom, and before she finished announcing me, the door to Joe's inner office opened and he ushered me inside.

"Please have a seat, Jessica. It seems your inquiry has stirred up some memories for my old classmate, Clancy Duggan. One of the deceased women you had me inquire about was a client of Clancy's. He emailed copies of the probate of all three, but in her case he sent me a heartfelt text, which I will forward to you, but first would you like me to review all three probate papers with you? You may have an interest in one beneficiary."

"Really? In what way?"

"Well, as you can see"—he handed me some papers—"an Elise Gagnon left five thousand dollars to a Joseph Martin Terranova. I suppose that is the kind of thing you were hoping to find."

"It is definitely some of what I hoped to find. Was that the only reference to Terranova?"

"It was, but as I said, Clancy had a really troubled client—"

I interrupted him. "By any chance was your friend's client named Lottie Miller?"

"I suppose she was." Joe seemed surprised that I'd come up with a name. "Carlotta Miller was the decedent's legal name."

"She is the one I am most curious about. What can you tell me about her?"

Joe opened a file folder and skimmed its contents for a minute or two. Then he handed it to me and said, "There isn't much to tell. Unfortunately, she had very little in the way of assets when she passed. Her debts absorbed every penny."

I looked at the probate papers and agreed there wasn't much to learn from them.

Joe picked up his phone. "I'm forwarding Clancy's text to you. It will give you a more personal view of the client. Obviously, Clancy liked her and was bothered by her death."

My phone pinged and I opened the text:

Carlotta Miller was a fine woman, a widow of comfortable means who was generous to her family and her church. I don't know when she met the scoundrel who took her for every cent. I am wracked with guilt to this day that I did not see it and could not prevent the result, which was her early and regrettable death. In this picture I take with each of my clients when they sign their wills, you can see what a vibrant person she was.

I looked at the attached picture and my mouth dropped open. Lottie Miller was the woman in the picture that Evelyn had found in Martin Terranova's garage.

"What is it, Jessica? You look as if you have seen a ghost."

Not exactly a ghost, I thought, but close enough to start the puzzle pieces to connect.

"Everything is just fine, Joe. You and your friend Clancy have been a huge help. I have to run, but, well, I will explain it all later. Why don't you come to dinner at my house? Seven o'clock." And I ran out the door without hearing his answer. I had very little time to take care of a few other things.

I raced to the sheriff's office hoping for a few moments to speak with Mort, but my timing could not have been worse. The parking lot was filled with media: television trucks from as far away as Brunswick and Augusta; half a dozen radio stations; and, surrounding Dan and Evelyn, a group of men and women holding recorders or smartphones, with one or two having pens poised over old-fashioned steno pads. I supposed they were print reporters.

"What on earth is going on?" I wondered.

Chapter Thirty-Three

Amazing, isn't it?" Pierce Collymore came up behind me. "When I saw this crowd, I parked down the block. You might want to put your bike over there, near the wall. You don't want it getting mowed down by one of these news trucks."

"I'm not sure I understand. I stopped by to see Mort, and found this crowd." I looked to Pierce for an explanation.

"I thought you knew. I assumed that was why you are here. When Mort arrested Olivia Quigley, he and Mayor Shevlin decided it would be prudent to notify the jurisdictions where she had previously worked in town budget offices. Those towns initiated investigations, and Olivia was found to have committed similar financial infractions in two previous jobs, one while a bookkeeper in Monks Square and the other when she was a financial analyst in Nicefield."

"My goodness. So our local outrage has become a statewide

scandal. I guess there was no chance of keeping it quiet. I wonder how Angus will react when he learns about all this hoopla."

"When Dan called me a while ago, I went right to Angus's house and told him that we would do everything we could to keep his name out of it but that there was a chance he would be mentioned on the hero side of things. He told me that since he spoke to Sarah, he is at peace with whatever comes his way."

I smiled, thinking of the conversations I still had occasionally with my late husband, Frank. "They were an extremely close couple. Angus was the one who got easily agitated while Sarah was the diplomatic one, who constantly reminded him that whatever will be, will be. I am sure that was what he heard her say when he visited her grave the other day. In any event, I imagine I wouldn't have a chance of talking to Mort right now."

"On the contrary. Check your phone. I'm sure he's been looking for you. He texted me not twenty minutes ago. Oh, and he suggested the rear entrance to the building. Let's go."

Pierce took my arm and we edged around the crowd, which had taken on a carnival-like atmosphere. We could hear snippets of jokes and laughter; the reporters were whiling away the time as they waited for the serious business of crime reporting to begin.

Deputy Floyd McCallum was standing by the rear door, and he pulled it open as soon as he saw us turn the corner of the building. "Glad to see you both. The sheriff is a bit antsy to introduce you. I'll be right here making sure no one gets inside who shouldn't."

He waved us through the doorway.

"Pierce, do you know . . ." I began, but stopped when Deputy Andy Bloom came along and hurried us into another room.

"The sheriff has been waiting for you. Now we can start. Truth be told, I think he is a bit nervous. You know how he feels about Stateys."

Mort came in with two members of the Maine State Police and looked visibly relieved when he saw Pierce and me.

"Major Leblanc, Lieutenant MacNeil, let me introduce you to our two witnesses, Fire Chief Pierce Collymore and Mrs. Jessica Fletcher, who has been on the Fire Department Developmental Committee from day one."

We all shook hands, which gave me just enough time to realize what was going on.

The major said, "On behalf of the Maine State Police I've come to thank you for your role in uncovering one woman's plot to consistently steal from the taxpayers of the great state of Maine."

I thought he sounded more like a politician than a policeman. And as he rambled on, I began to look for a way I could get Mort alone for a couple of minutes.

The lieutenant's phone rang. He excused himself, and came back within three minutes to pull the major aside for a confidential conversation. I took the opportunity to signal Mort. He got the message, and we went out into the hallway.

"I will make this quick," I said, and I told him concisely what I wanted to do.

By the time Andy Bloom came looking for us, Mort and I had reached an agreement. As I followed them back to where the major was waiting impatiently, I said, "Mort, and how about coming to dinner tonight? You and Maureen, my place about seven?"

He replied, "Mrs. F., if this day ever ends, dinner sounds like a definite plan."

The major asked both Pierce and me a few questions regarding Olivia Quigley. Angus Billingsworth's name never came up, and I am sure we had Mort to thank for that.

Andy Bloom leaned into Mort's shoulder and said, "The press is getting restless out there."

Major Leblanc reached out to shake hands with me, and then with Pierce. "It was terrific to meet you. Thanks again for all you have done." Then he turned to Mort and said, "Lead the way, Sheriff Metzger."

Before he did, Mort gave me a broad wink to let me know he would not forget our conversation.

Since I was having folks over for dinner in the evening, I had planned to stop by the Fruit and Veg to place an order, but when Pierce offered me a ride home I had so much to do that I couldn't resist. I decided I would trade him a dinner invitation for the ride.

Pierce went to get his snazzy red Jeep, and I walked my bicycle to the curb to wait for him. I could hear Mort begin to quiet down the crowd of reporters, and then he introduced Major Leblanc.

Pierce arrived, loaded my bicycle into the back, and helped me into the front seat of the Jeep. We drove away, leaving the droning voice of the major behind us.

"I wonder why he is here," I said, half to myself, half to Pierce.

"You mean Leblanc? He's not going to let Mort, who he thinks of as nothing more than a small-town sheriff, take the credit for ending a one-woman statewide crime wave. And Mort is smart enough to let the Statey have his moment with the press; then he will leave Cabot Cove and our lives will be back to ordinary days."

"Not quite ordinary," I said. "We still have a murderer on the loose."

I sat down at the kitchen table and made a list of all the things I would need from the Fruit and Veg. Then I called my order in. Jenny was her usual cheerful self and said the delivery would be in about an hour.

My next call was to Maureen Metzger, who was bubbling over with delight. "Jessica, I am so glad you called. Ideal Molloy invited me to join your group of ladies who visit Bertha Mae. Tomorrow is my day. I am going to bring a piece of needlepoint that is giving me a hard time. I'm sure Bertha Mae can guide me through the intricate stitching."

Although generally I loved Maureen's enthusiasm, I had a lot to get done before dinner, so I got right to the point. "I know it is last-minute, but I already spoke to Mort to say I would love you two to come to dinner tonight. We haven't gotten together in such a long while."

"Why, that sounds great. Mort could use a little social time. His hours lately have been slam dash. What time would you like us to be there?"

"Dinner is at seven."

"We'll see you then! Thank you, Jessica."

My next call was to Seth, who sounded skeptical. "Seems like lately I am getting more than my fair share of dinners at your place. And tonight we are having friends join us? Woman, are you up to something I should know about?"

"Seth, it's a simple dinner party. I have been so busy with my synopsis, and then there was all that fuss about Bertha Mae. I'm just trying to get life back to normal."

"Jessica, normal for you is not always the same as everyone else's idea of normal."

I told him not to be silly, and then I hung up. Although I knew that they would be super busy after the press conference, I texted Dan Andrews and Evelyn Phillips, inviting them both to dinner.

Dan texted back immediately: Will try.

Okay, so, that was a definite maybe. I knew better than to expect to hear from Evelyn, but I did hope she would come along.

In my head I counted my guests. Seth, Joe Turco, Mort and Maureen, Pierce Collymore, Dan Andrews, Evelyn Phillips, and me. Then I cleared away my computer and the research materials that were scattered around the dining room and I set the dining room table for eight.

I checked the time and saw it was growing late. I went to the kitchen, closing the dining room door behind me. I rinsed some potatoes at the sink, getting them ready to be peeled. I was running out of time for so many things.

Chapter Thirty-Four

I was still peeling potatoes when Peter Whitlock knocked on my kitchen door.

I hollered, "My hands are wet. Please come in."

"Company again, Mrs. Fletcher?" Peter said, his smile friendly as always. I could see carrot greens peeking over the top of the box he held. "Do you want me to put your groceries on the table?"

"If you would." I dried my hands on a dish towel as I walked toward him. "By the way, I saw your sister today and noticed her car has New Hampshire license plates."

"Oh, thanks for letting me know. I better remind her to register the car in Portland and get Maine plates before she gets a ticket."

I decided it was time to get the clarity I needed. "By any chance did you and Penny live near your grandmother in Dover, New Hampshire?"

Peter looked at me warily but admitted that they did.

And that allowed me to continue. "Your grandmother Lottie Miller was too ashamed to tell you and Penny that she'd lost all her money by lavishing it on Joseph Terranova. I suspect you had no idea until after she died. That's when you found out from her lawyers that she was destitute. As her heirs, you and Penny went through her bank accounts and could easily see where her money had gone. Every cent went to Joseph Martin Terranova or was spent on him."

Peter pulled out a chair, set his elbows on the kitchen table, and buried his head in his hands. Then he looked directly at me. "She paid his rent. She bought him a car. She even paid off the mortgage he took out on that little storefront gym. Penny and I didn't know about the money, but we did know she was spending time with him. Anyone could see how happy she was. I was worried that he'd break her heart, but Penny said at Granny's age it was harmless enough. Little did we know."

I filled a glass with water and set it in front of him. Peter nodded his thanks and took a sip. Then he continued. "It was all sunshine and roses until, well, I guess the money dried up. Terranova stopped coming around and Granny got more and more depressed. Penny and I thought she was upset because of the lack of attention. We even tried to get her to go on one of those—I guess you call them dating sites, for senior citizens. But she was inconsolable. We didn't realize until . . . until it was too late that it wasn't only about losing him; it was more likely about losing every cent she had, money that she always planned to leave to us."

"That must have been heartbreaking for you and Penny," I said.

"Yes. If we knew, we could have helped her, but I guess since she had spent her life taking care of us, she was too embarrassed . . ." He trailed off and took another drink of water.

"When it was all over, I was determined to track him down and make him pay."

I could understand how he felt but I couldn't comprehend how this nice young man could resort to such violence.

Peter continued. "I only intended to punch him out, but when I tracked him here and saw the beautiful piece of property he bought with the money he'd swindled from Granny, well, I knew he deserved much worse. I showed up at the gym when he was alone and asked for a private weight session. I waited until he was lying on the bench to show me how to press gradually, by increasing from starting weight to heavier. As soon as he was in position and did his first full lift, I told him I was Lottie Miller's grandson and I accused him of stealing Granny's money. He laughed and said, 'You can't steal what is given so willingly.' That was it. I pounced on the bar and pressed it into his neck. He tried to push me away but I guess my adrenaline overpowered his muscles."

At that point the dining room door opened. Mort and Deputy Floyd walked into the kitchen. Mort gently put his hand on Peter's shoulder. "Stand up, son. Floyd here will take you to my office."

Peter stood. "Can I give Mrs. Fletcher my sister's phone number? She is going to want to know . . ."

Mort nodded and Peter recited Penny's number, which I tapped into my cell phone.

After Floyd and Peter left, Mort sat at the table and I poured him a cup of coffee. "Back in my office, with all the chaos of the press and the Statey major prancing around, when you put this on my plate, well, I was hard-pressed to believe it. Such a nice kid. I gotta ask how you were so sure."

"There were so many little things. Peter was generally vague about his past, but his sister, Penny, mentioned several times that they were all alone in the world and stressed that they had only each other. And when she mentioned it in front of Peter he got extremely uncomfortable, as if he didn't want it generally known. Can I freshen your coffee?"

After I refilled Mort's cup, I said, "Penny told me their parents died in a boating accident when they were very young. And she mentioned losing their grandmother more recently. Well, when Frank's brother and his wife died we immediately became Grady's guardians. I had to wonder who took care of Peter and Penny. A grandmother would be a natural. And just as Terranova tried to hide his connection to Dover, Peter never mentioned his past. He spoke about only his present and his future. Thanks to Evelyn Phillips I was at Perfection when a women's class ended and a men's class was scheduled to begin. Evelyn admitted she'd sent Dan Andrews to enroll in the class in order to spy on Terranova because of Bertha Mae.

"I looked around at the men's class and I had to wonder if anyone else was there for the same reason. By Cabot Cove standards, Terranova, Dan, and Peter were town newbies, and since I knew why Dan had come to Cabot Cove, that left Peter and Terranova as unknowns who sort of wandered into town. Was that a coincidence? Finally, there was Penny's New Hampshire license plate. That moved me to speak to you, and here we are."

Mort stood up, hitched his gun belt, and said, "Well, I better get back. I hope the major doesn't hear about this arrest, or he'll be calling another press conference and taking credit for it. Tell you the truth, I feel kind of sorry for Peter Whitlock."

"I do too," I answered. "And when you leave, I'll have the unenviable job of calling his sister, Penny, to tell her the terrible news."

"Do you think you could get that lawyer Ms. Tremblay from Wiscasset, the one who helped Coreen, to take on Whitlock's case? He's going to need a good lawyer," Mort said.

That was my exact thought as I dialed Penny's number. When my heart-to-heart talk with Penny was winding down, I gave her Regina Tremblay's phone number. "She's smart and tough. I think it will do Peter a world of good to have her by his side."

"And he will always have me," Penny said through the gentle tears she was crying for her brother and, it seemed likely, for her beloved granny.

Chapter Thirty-Five

I thought it would be a respite for me to have my friends over for a nice, quiet dinner this evening after the frantic time we'd gone through with Martin Terranova's murder and Olivia Quigley's corruption. But after the stress of watching Olivia Quigley's thievery becoming statewide if not national news, and that being followed by the tension of Peter Whitlock confessing to murder in my kitchen, I was beginning to doubt my wisdom. A bowl of soup and early to bed seemed like the best possible choice, but it was too late. Invitations were issued and the table was set. I was scurrying around the kitchen to ensure that dinner was in the oven and on the stove top so that I would be ready and able to enjoy the company of my guests.

Seth was the first to arrive. Rather than his usual teasing, he told me to sit down while he made me a cup of tea. "The entire town is in shock over the arrest of that nice young man Peter Whitlock. I'm sure it was worse for you." He looked at the vegetables scattered on the counter. "Why don't you drink your tea while I throw this salad together?"

I watched him put far more sliced carrots than I would have into the salad bowl, but a friend who helped out was certainly entitled to overload his favorite vegetables.

My doorbell rang, and when I opened it Joe Turco handed me a bottle of red wine. "Regina Tremblay called me, and I went over to the sheriff's office immediately to make sure Peter was okay and to remind him of his rights. He is doing fairly well."

"Thank you, Joe, for letting me know. Now, come in. Seth is in the kitchen."

"Hold that door," I heard Mort Metzger say. He and Maureen came down the walkway, along with Pierce Collymore. Maureen was kind enough to bring a tray of canapés.

The conversation was lively considering the gloomy day most of us had endured. Dan Andrews joined us and apologized for Evelyn. "I have called and texted her, but she refuses to answer. I didn't want to hold up dinner any longer, so here I am."

At that moment Seth came through from the kitchen and said, "Jessica, the oven timer has beeped twice. I'm afraid your roast will be overdone if we don't eat soon."

I smiled at Dan and said, "It sounds like you are just in time."

We seven sat around the dining room table, and by unspoken agreement our chatter left out the recent difficulties our community faced, and focused on the good. Seth told us that he'd heard from Gregory Leung that the fundraiser for the children's wing of the hospital had topped out and was still going strong.

Pierce Collymore said that one of his young firemen had come up with a plan to develop a fire-cadets program for teenagers and they were putting together a proposal to present to the school board. Maureen Metzger immediately volunteered to help design the uniforms.

I was clearing the table and about to serve dessert and coffee when Evelyn Phillips flung open the kitchen door. "Here you go, everyone. Read it here first." And she brushed past me with copies of tomorrow's *Cabot Cove Gazette*.

"Well, will you lookee here?" Seth read the headline: "'*Cabot Cove Shuts Down Swindler*,' and the byline is our own Daniel Andrews."

Evelyn beamed like a proud parent. "Not only will Bertha Mae be looked after, but I am absolutely sure that the *Gazette* is in great hands. Now I can enjoy retirement and go back to traipsing around the country visiting my family."

Then she lifted her nose and gave the air a deep sniff. "But first, is that Jessica Fletcher's famous roast beef au jus I smell?"

Joe Turco stood and pulled out the vacant chair next to him, indicating that Evelyn should have a seat, while Seth and I both went into the kitchen to pile roast beef, potatoes, and vegetables onto a plate. As we did so, Seth gave me a wink and a smile. "Jess, don't you think you should add a few more carrots?"

"Oh, Seth, this plate is for Evelyn, not for you." And we went into the dining room, where our friends were laughing at something I didn't quite catch, but I was happy to hear the sound of their laughter.